I0782161

THE
ENCHANTMENTS

THE ENCHANTMENTS

A Novel

David Orsini

THE ENCHANTMENTS

Copyright © 2024 by David Orsini
First Edition Quaternity™ Books 2024
Quaternity™ Books
ISBN 978-1-943691-46-3
Cover Design by James Buchanan

Other Books by David Orsini

The Reappearing

The Weaver of Plots

Schemes, Disguises, & Traps

Vanishing by Degrees

The Ghost Lovers

The Woman Who Loved Too Well

The Subtleties of Seduction

Bitterness / Seven Stories

CONTENTS

"Physical things depend on spiritual things..."
—*The Cloud of Unknowing*

"Teach me, like you, to drink creation whole
And, casting out myself, become a soul."
—Richard Wilbur, "The Aspen and the Stream,"
Advice to a Prophet

CHAPTER ONE

THREE SPIRITS

"I'm calling on the two of you to set things right," Robert Steerforth says. "There's much to be done, back there on Earth. There's so much that both of you can *do.*"

"To make things better?" Melanie asks him.

She wants Robert to clarify more precisely the nature of this new assignment.

"To influence what happens," he answers her after a moment's reflection. "To bring justice into the lives of the five persons that you will be meeting. To teach them how to accept responsibility for their behavior."

Now Captain Randall Johnson, Melanie's husband, comes into it.

"There's so much we can do *here*," he says. "There are so many lived-out lives to review and so many judgments to make about the newly dead."

Clearly, the captain and Melanie are uneasy. Their doubts are understandable. So Robert perceives as he considers their present situation. It is a long time since they completed their previous missions on Earth, millions of miles away. It is an even longer time since they walked along the various paths of the Earth as human beings who participated in the happenings of the era into which they had been born. It has been many decades since Randall died and several years since Melanie also sprang free of ordinary time. Right after that, they entered the world not of the dead. They left their dead selves far behind them, back there, within Earth that is time-trapped and temporary.

Robert understands exactly what they are feeling and why. Despite his experience and his assurance as a Spirit, he too has sometimes had misgivings just before he embarked upon a new mission to Earth. As a reliable and undaunted Spirit, he now regards that territory as somewhat foreign. Time-trapped and fallible, Earth often disguises its dangers and masks its deviousness. Even the hardiest Spirits need to navigate its treacheries with steel-true courage and keen-eyed awareness.

Sojourn, the new world that he and Melanie and the captain now inhabit, is also time-bound. But it is tethered to a more quickened, supernatural time that precedes the journey into the Eternal. Spirits, Shadows, and Shades live here. Apparitions, Phantoms, and Specters—their ghostly relatives—also reside here, roomless and unhoused as they navigate the waves and ripples…whorls and coils and spirals of always-mystical space. For those who are allowed to become embodied once again, Sojourn is a vast world that never seems crowded. Capacious rooms and long, wide halls and corridors go on expanding with sinuous velocity. Space keeps winding and curving and meandering even as it spreads its voluminous dimensions into still wider rooms, corridors, fields, plains, avenues, and whole cities. There is an Art Deco look to many of the rooms, and modernist architectural designs bring stylized individuality to private homes, corporate buildings, and thriving streets. The beauty of the decor within homes, inside business centers and halls of justice, and along public thoroughfares here in Sojourn melds with their functionality. Every room, every building, and every street offer precise amenities and understated usefulness.

In Sojourn, there is no need for food. Even during those times when the Spirits here become once again fully embodied, they do not need food. Water from purified lakes and springs provides all the nourishment that Spirits need.

Sojourn is a natural satellite of Earth that is located within a transitional space between one's Earthly home and the First Heaven. It is a haven and a temporary place for the newly dead that are waiting to make the journey to The First Heaven. Sojourn is invisible to even the largest telescopes, the swiftest spacecraft, and the most advanced NASA instruments. The dead who have recently arrived here only to discover that they are not dead in Sojourn have not lost their memories of Earth or their yearning to return to the places that knew them well and the people that gave them their unconditional love. Perhaps, they will never lose that memory or that yearning. But they are millions of miles away from Earth, which is The Second Heaven and the one that most human beings never recognize as a treasure beyond price and as a world filled with miracle workers and beneficent Spirits.

While he observes Captain Johnson and Melanie, Robert reviews all these truths. It is his habit to assess the continually evolving scenario that he and the other Spirits around him are presently occupying. Realist that he is, Robert rightly interprets the advantages and the liabilities attaching themselves to unpredictable missions and to the sometimes-enigmatic Spirits assigned to them. For the most part, he knows all that he needs to know about Captain Johnson and Melanie. He knows about their past lives on Earth. He knows, too, about their commendable work here in Sojourn. He also knows that, in times of danger, they have always summoned unstinting courage.

During the first months of their training in the Afterlife, Melanie and the captain each acquired the appropriate powers of every kind of ghost, including those of a Shadow, an Apparition, and a Phantom. For the first months after their deaths and all through their training in ghostliness, they often appeared to be full-bodied, even though their bodies of flesh and blood, yoked as they always are to the

Spirit-Life informing them, were vanishing by nearly imperceptible degrees. Gradually, they became fully radiant Spirits.

Right now, because they are preparing for a mission that will return them to Earth, they appear as full-bodied human beings once again. Even though they are fully embodied, the prospect of returning to Earth has made them uneasy. It has been almost eighty years since the captain was killed in a World War Two aerial battle. Nearly a decade has passed since Melanie died, yearning always for the fiancé that she lost to the war. In those days, she was Melanie Dickinson. One month after her Earthly death seven years ago, the First Spirit allowed the captain and eternally young Melanie to marry. On that festive day, all of Sojourn and the First Heaven rejoiced that so ideal a couple were being conjoined, body and soul, because of their love for each other.

On this radiant morning, though, the captain and his wife are about to enter a different kind of adventure. Their Earth-bound mission will propel them into episodes fraught with surprises and tensions. Connecting to the persons of an altogether different era whose lives they will be influencing complicates their mission.

Captain Johnson's unease, harnessed as it is to his military bearing, persuades him to ask Robert another question.

"Why are you choosing Melanie and me for this assignment? There is so much to do here in Sojourn. Why are you sending us back to Earth?"

"The two of you are the best Spirits for this mission," Robert answers him. "Besides, both of you need a change. You, Randall, are becoming too severe in your judgments of the new arrivals. It's difficult enough to deal with the newly dead who have not yet accepted their Earthly deaths. But, as our most meticulous judge, you have become too caustic and too harsh in your decisions. You lack empathy. You've lost touch with compassion."

"In all our courtroom trials, I serve justice first of all," the captain replies, his clipped words pausing at the cusp of bluntness. "My experience as a pilot in that war of long ago taught me well. It showed me the savage nature of most human beings."

"You are a fine realist," Robert says. "No one denies that. But you need to learn more about being an eternal. You are too harsh toward the dead who arrive here from Earth bewildered by the newness of their existence as Spirits and beleaguered by the wrongs that they committed during those years when they were alive on Earth."

"I do what has to be done," the captain insists. "Some of the dead have led rotten and even criminal lives. They deserve to be condemned to eternal disappearance."

With wise and heartfelt words, Melanie now urges this stalwart young man whom she so profoundly loves toward a new way to see. There is nothing tremulous in her petition. Self-possessed and intuitive, she is a confident woman who believes in her capacities for changing existence for the better, even here in Sojourn, a natural satellite located halfway between the luminous First Heaven—the home of the First Spirit which is millions of miles beyond Sojourn—and the finite Earth, which is the Second Heaven that most of its inhabitants fail to recognize. She is well aware of the tremendous responsibility that Captain Johnson—her prodigious Randall, her loyal husband and soul-damaged hero—as judge of the spirit and the flesh fulfills with rigorous morality and with careful exactitude.

When the newly dead arrive in Sojourn, Randall—one of the many judges who serve in various locations within this natural satellite presides over a courtroom of twelve Secondary Spirits, including herself, who serve as conscience-bound jurors. These jurors review the lives of the defendants whose fallible lives on Earth unfold once more with irrevocable and sometimes lacerating energies. Those lives flash up as vivid realities on the wall videos that surround the celestial courtroom. The videos reveal the truth about the defendants, though not the whole truth. Not even the vivid images propelling the video narratives or the testimonies of Spirit witnesses who knew the defendants while they wended their way together through their temporal existence reveal the layers of truth that stay hidden behind those images and beneath the testimonies. Those layers never disclose their intricate nature to anyone except the First Spirit, who knows everything that happened in the past and that is happening now and that will happen in the future.

Though they often command laser-sharp perceptions of the past, present, and future of every human being, Secondary Spirits are not all knowing. The eternal truths about the behavior of people, with their complicated causes and ambivalent consequences, often elude them. Within the harsh glare of a probing courtroom here in Sojourn, the twelve Spirit-laden jurors struggle to discover the authentic identity of each defendant. Yet too often they decipher only the shadows of truth. Despite the extraordinary powers of seeing that the First Spirit has granted them, these jurors apprehend surface impressions, incriminating foibles, and controversial occasions when they are examining the tarnished or bruised or broken lives of the defendants. At times, the brutal accuracy of the wall videos and the subjective recollections of the witnesses yield merely spurious correspondences of the defendants' lives—bogus revelations and makeshift news about their characters. What the video images show and the testimonies disclose are merely the shapes and shadows of the defendants' lives, with the reality of truth often taken out of them.

All of these problems Melanie comprehends with quick-witted insight and with respectful awareness of the responsibility—indeed, the ordeal—placed upon her husband, the brave Captain Randall Johnson, whose embattled Earthbound experience in the Second World War tested and proved his heroism even as it destroyed his belief in the goodness of most human beings.

Because she wants to dispel her husband's tension, hovering as it is beside his military officer's arrogance, Melanie chooses sensible words that may guide him onto a more promising path. She also wants to recognize the validity of Robert's remark about her beloved Randall's hard-heartedness.

"Have pity, Randall," she counsels her husband. "Have pity on all those newly dead persons who arrive here with some goodness still flickering within themselves, like the embers of a fire that has not yet burnt itself out. You can do it. You are capable of mercy. You have that gift within you—that quickened inspiration, that quiet sensibility. I know you have it."

She watches Randall as he watches her. He studies the whole, embodied form of her with the gleaming brown eyes that always reveal new layers of the love for her that pulses within him, undying and eternal. Stalwart and honest, he finds softer words that tell her all over again exactly what kind of man he is.

"I can only be the man that I really am," he explains. "I *am* judgmental. I *am* demanding. I uphold all the rules that the First Spirit has set forth and all His commandments. Yet, because you ask it, and—yes—because Robert has also requested it, I will try to bring at least a little more mercy to my judgment of wrongdoers. I will even summon all the pity that I have stored away. Yet I will not allow pity or mercy to tarnish the justice that I intend to uphold."

His answer pleases Melanie. She is not surprised that Randall refuses to compromise the unblemished nature of justice or of his character. But his willingness to explore the more forgiving aspects of his nature pleases her.

"I know that you will do your best. You will do the things that need to be done," she tells him. "You always do."

Robert has more to say.

"Good to hear," he tells Captain Johnson. "Even a dram of your mercy may save a few people who are not behaving well on Earth. You may also guide a few wrongdoers to a better path."

"Of course he will," Melanie declares. "When we return to Earth, Randall will be a wonderful guardian Spirit for all those persons whose lives we will be influencing."

A smile touches Captain Johnson's lips for just a moment. He is grateful for Melanie's kind words.

But Robert has still more to say. This time, he directs his words to Melanie.

"Randall's being a successful guardian will be more likely if you are with him," he says. "That is why the First Spirit is sending you on this mission with him. Your right-minded mercy will temper the quality of his stern justice. This mission may also teach you a thing or two about those persons who are beyond the reach of your mercy, as creditable as your mercy has always been."

His words spark Melanie's attention. Already, this new assignment intrigues her.

"I am always willing to learn more about other people," she says. After a pause, she says more. "I also like to learn more about myself."

Another smile touches Captain Johnson's lips. He perceives the promise of adventure in Melanie's words. He also appreciates Robert's realistic appraisal of him and ponders over the favorable predictions. The possibility that mercy will temper his stern justice impresses him. Yet there lives within his soul, immortal and resilient, the soldierly promise that he has made to the First Spirit. He will never hesitate to wage battle against deceivers, thieves, murderers, and the many other betrayers of innocence.

In her heart and soul, Melanie accepts Randall for the man that he is. So does Robert. For different reasons, perhaps, they would like Randall to explore a different aspect of his identity. They want him to become someone who, though not altogether new, has attained a different level of understanding, has experienced unanticipated Earthly adventures, and has reached even more astonishing chapters in his Spirit life.

Melanie is eager to begin their mission. She is pleased that Randall may learn more about himself. She is already wondering what events will teach them new truths about themselves.

On this bright Monday morning in Sojourn, where Time still imposes its mandates and its penalties upon the varied episodes unfolding here, Robert—ever dutiful and watchful—is also eager for Melanie and Randall to return to Earth to begin their mission. He observes the two of them with careful and prudent awareness. In the stillness of this moment, he reflects upon the persons they represent here in Sojourn. He also considers the persons they were while they lived on Earth. He never knew them while the three of them were alive on Earth. But their behavior in Sojourn validates the information that he has gathered about their exemplary lives on Earth.

Melanie and Randall sometimes reside in the First Heaven, millions of miles away from Sojourn. There, they mingle with the Blessed Angels and become further enlightened by the Presence of the First Spirit, who has created all that exists. Melanie's and Randall's exemplary conduct on Earth purified their Spirits even before they reached Sojourn, the first stopover for everyone who has died and whose lives unfold in review upon a vast wall video that encircles the courtroom and flashes with telling images before the eyes of a Spirit Judge and twelve Spirit Jurors. On frequent occasions, Captain Johnson has served as the Spirit Judge at many trials of the newly dead. Those court sessions have often yielded fierce legal battles involving rebellious and unrepentant defendants, letter-of-the-law prosecutors, and the sternest of Spirit Judges Captain Randall Johnson.

While observing Randall and Melanie, Robert remembers all these things. He respects Captain Johnson. He believes that he knows him as well as he can know any other human being or fellow Spirit. He also respects Melanie, whom he regards as the emblem of truth and decorum.

Robert recalls how Captain Johnson appears in the panoramic courtroom within Sojourn. The captain always makes a formidable presence, anchored as it is to his brisk manner and his military bearing. Standing at six foot, six inches as he enters the room and joins his colleagues at the interviewers' table, he is a very tall man. He is also a young man. Despite all the years that have passed since his earthly death, he has remained twenty-two, the age he was when his plane was shot down during an aerial battle over Berlin in July 1943. His brown-haired handsomeness still wears traces of battle fatigue and wartime bitterness. He rarely smiles. Beneath his no-nonsense demeanor, there lives a harnessed rage against the criminality, potential or activated, of most human beings. He is a prosecuting attorney. He is an emblem of Stern Justice. He is the fully embodied Spirit who may prevent wrongdoers from returning to Earth for important missions or from moving forward to the First Heaven. He well may be their executioner, condemning them to eternal disappearance. Captain Johnson is, nevertheless, an honorable man. Melanie is the love of his life, the one bright spark that stirs his ardor for her and influences his hard-won forgiveness of some wrongdoers.

Here in Sojourn, Melanie appears as a blue-eyed blonde woman of twenty-two, even though she died in 2013 when she was ninety-two. The man that she loved saw her on Earth for the last time when she was twenty-two. That was the year when her fiancé, Captain Randall Johnson, was killed in the Second World War. On Earth, she was a self-assured woman. She owned a successful dress shop in Boston. She also designed an impressive line of dresses and gowns that became a national brand. Always, during the many years she lived on Earth without him, she worried that in the Afterlife her fiancé would not recognize her because she had grown old. Shortly after her arrival in Sojourn, though, she was elated to learn that she could choose to be the age she was when her fiancé, Captain Randall Johnson, last saw her on Earth. After she died on Earth, she was reunited with her fiancé in the First Heaven. Knowing of their goodness, the First Spirit regards them as the perfect couple whose love is a healthy blend of the sensual and the spiritual.

"These two were born to be married," the First Spirit told the Blessed Angels in the First Heaven, not long after Melanie arrived there to be reunited with the man who had been her fiancé many decades earlier. "My plans for them did not allow them to be married while they lived on Earth. But the First Heaven is the ideal place for them to marry each other. Their marriage will last through all eternity."

Whenever she returns to Sojourn, Melanie is a temperate and good-natured mediator.

In this new mission to Earth, Randall and Melanie will appear most of the time as their full-bodied selves. They will be wearing contemporary clothes and modern haircuts. As he muses upon their unease, Robert in the secret chambers of his heart accords them his empathy. He, too, has sometimes returned to Earth for difficult assignments. He, too, has experienced the trauma of visiting a homeland that is no longer a home or even familiar except in vague or nebulous ways. No memory of having lived, enthusiastic and contented, within a white clapboard colonial house on a wide, clean street shaded by rows of flourishing elm trees atones for the later disappearance of all those cherished mementos. On Earth, Time kills everything and everyone, eventually.

Time killed him, the man who on Earth was a human being named Robert Steerforth, when he was not expecting to die. His Earthly life ended when he died of a brain aneurysm at the age of forty-two. In that period, he was a vice-president of a steel corporation in Pennsylvania. He died when he was addressing a symposium of global business leaders in Brazil. He had been speaking to ninety-nine other corporate leaders about the importance of diversifying their products and their markets. He believed that what he was saying was meaningful and helpful. He felt that everyone who was in that room appreciated what he was saying. He remembered thinking that he was living through one of his happiest days. That was his last thought before he keeled over and fell away from the speaker's podium. That was the moment he died, without a warning and without a chance to say goodbye to his wife, their two sons, and their daughter.

Eventually, his wife Amelia joined him here in Sojourn. Always adaptable, she soon came to enjoy her assignments as a Spirit Juror in the court trials of the newly dead and as a Shape Shifter or as her fully embodied self during missions that temporarily returned her to Earth. When she first arrived in Sojourn, she was astonished by his appearance. Here, in this natural satellite so far away from Earth, his lanky body sometimes glows. Its amber sheen moves in and out of brightness that often leaves the dead who have just arrived in Sojourn completely amazed. They wonder whether he is a god or some holy messenger. Whenever the brightness covering him becomes dim, they see him as the man he was in the moment that he died. His oblong face, with its forehead, cheekbones, and jawline similar in size; his slightly tousled dark hair; and his well-groomed beard give him the look of a college professor who may be in his mid-thirties or even forty. Eventually, they perceive him as a Spirit who is honest, reliable, and fair-minded.

All his present thoughts about the captain and his Melanie influence Robert's keen-sighted awareness of them and his comprehension of the conflicts that await them in this new mission that they are about to begin. To fulfill their mission, they will at times become Shadows and at other times become equally mysterious Shape Shifters, Apparitions, and Specters. They will also share the ability to see into the future. Clairvoyant and well-trained, they are not strangers to the unpredictable and the dangerous. Their hesitation about this mission has nothing to do with hidden fear or with eroding confidence. It is their returning to a homeland that they can no longer claim as their own that goads their unease and their sorrow. Most of the places that knew them well have altered beyond recognition or have entirely disappeared. Relatives and friends who meant so much to Melanie and her captain have reunited with them in Sojourn and in the First Heaven. This ideal couple has no pressing need or even a latent desire to return to Earth. But the possibility that they will be able to rescue five persons from their self-defeating errors, devious plots, and sensual inclinations has inspired new layers of Melanie's compassion even as that possibility has roused Randall's lawyerly aptitudes.

So Robert perceives and, perceiving, draws them more deeply into the complicated chapters that await them.

"You must try to help these five people," he tells them. "You may even be able to rescue some of them."

"To change them for the better," Melanie says, eager to simulate the positive spin of his words.

"Or to bring them face to face with their selfishness and with their crimes," Randall says. He obviously anticipates more stringent consequences and darker aftermaths in the rescue of these five persons.

"Helping them to navigate their lives more intelligently will be a very good thing, indeed," Robert says. "The First

Spirit is counting on the two of you to do everything that you can to help these five individuals to be honest with themselves and with other human beings. Help these lost persons to discover their souls. Help them to see that they live first of all as Spirits. Their Earthly bodies are merely temporary shelters. Help them to know that physical things depend upon spiritual things."

"We'll do everything we can to help them," Melanie says. Her genteel voice sounds confident and determined.

"We'll guide them to the destinies that they deserve," Randall promises. His words sound no less determined than Melanie's. But their implicated complexities are cryptic, ambiguous, and even mysterious.

Robert sees through these complexities. Yet he is not offended. Randall's ingrained cynicism and his low estimate of most human beings will hold the mission to its realistic bearings. Melanie's compassion—her inveterate belief in the regeneration of errant persons and in the soul-enhancing power of forgiveness—will effectively balance the captain's hardheartedness. That these two blessed Spirits may learn more about the limits of their judgments will make the mission even more significant.

"I'm certain that the two of you will work hard to save these persons from themselves," Robert says. "You will do everything that the First Spirit requires of you. Whether each of these five persons is willing to change is another matter. The First Spirit has given them free will. He, of course, already knows what is going to happen. But He is giving them the chance to choose their destinies. He is giving them the opportunity to save themselves. Since we sometimes think of life as a gamble, we might say that the First Spirit is loading the dice in their favor. He is sending the two of you to help these persons see things more clearly and less selfishly."

Robert wants Melanie and Randall to know more about these five people. For that reason, he hands them *résumés* that outline the essential facts about the five troubled people that they will soon be meeting on Earth. The instant that they see the names of these five individuals, the captain and Melanie recall their specific faces, as well as their achievements, failures, and aspirations. Their training as Spirits has granted Randall and Melanie a nearly omniscient awareness of everyone who is alive on Earth and everyone who has died there and reclaimed life here in Sojourn. They know the highlights of these lives, without the specific details that denote the hard-won moral victories and the soul-damaging compromises. The *résumés,* of course, are not enough to spark completely Melanie's and Randall's memories of the selfish motives and the bad deeds of the troubled individuals that they will soon be meeting. What prods their memories are the videos that, after a wave of Robert's right hand, flash across the giant walls encircling the capacious room and the long conference table where they are sitting. Instantly, scenarios filled with temporary happiness, long-lasting suffering, and bitter consequences cover the walls. Two young men, two equally young women, and one middle-aged man live and love—sometimes with hope, sometimes with despair, always striving for fulfillment that they rarely know how to earn. Some of them acquire wealth through honest or devious ways. Others learn to be faithful to their lovers and to their friends, and some learn how to betray them. Still others scheme so that they can ride roughshod over everyone who gets in their way. They disguise their malice, envy, and ambition. They devise ingenious plots, and they manipulate the rules when doing so is to their advantage. They dupe adversaries, they trap competitors, and they tarnish their souls.

These are the three men and the two women that the Captain and Melanie will try to rescue.

Right now, right after the video narratives have flashed before their seeing, the names and faces of these imperiled persons do not yet incite the captain's wrath or subdue Melanie's pity. What Melanie and her Randall draw from the tangled lives unfolding before them are the various plots that have already begun weaving their dangerous obsessions and betrayals.

There is, first of all, Brett Robinson—a popular young man who, although he is engaged to an emotionally repressed young woman, falls in love with her beautiful stepmother. This young man, a lawyer on his way to immense success, uses women for his carnal pleasure and bonds with powerful lawyers with whom he shares a predilection for wily courtroom maneuvering and other shady business practices.

There is Lisa Caulfield Calhern, the young stepmother and a former debutante, who has entered a loveless marriage to a wealthy man because he can enhance her social status and because his money can buy her privileged society's forgiveness for her previous scandals with wealthy, jaded playboys and with a charismatic movie actor.

There is Tate Calhern, the arrogant husband of the faithless stepmother. He secretly hates the daughter whose birth killed his first wife, the only woman he was capable of loving. This autocrat—this ruthless tyrant and lost soul— has made a mockery of his second marriage. He withholds his love from his second wife even though he pretends to be an ideal husband. Ironies further stymie his happiness. The two young men that he regards as substitute sons betray his trust when they become his dissatisfied wife's secret lovers.

There is Naomi Calhern, the emotionally repressed young woman who has allowed herself to become the victim of her father's hatred. She has brought similar insecurities to her relationship with two men who want to marry her for her money.

There is Jake Boldwood, the young man whose troubled past has made him a dangerous partner for the emotionally repressed daughter and a volatile adversary for the young lawyer who is using the repressed woman for his own gain.

"Some of these people may not be worth saving," Randall says, right after he and Melanie have reviewed the quickened flashes of the five troubled lives unraveling their fury and anger before him. "Only miracles could save them."

Robert quickly agrees.

"You are so right, Randall," he says. "Your no-nonsense approach to people provides you with special insight. To save these people, miracles are needed. You and Melanie are the right Spirits to make those miracles happen."

"What do you want us to do?" Melanie asks him. "Only because of the most grievous circumstances have we been asked to make miracles."

"That is true," Robert agrees. "This is one of the grievous times. The First Spirit wants you to you draw upon your previous training. Surely, you remember that, when you were first connecting to your ghostliness, you dabbled in the making of enchantments. You learned how to cast a spell over a person to compel a necessary response. To inspire troubled and even criminal individuals to change for the better, you invoked magical visions in their everyday surroundings and inside their nighttime dreams. Your enchantments challenged their willpower and subverted their evil plots. Those same enchantments brought these wrongdoers face to face with their betrayals and with their obsessions."

"Will that be enough to save them?" Melanie asks. "Will their coming face to face with their wrongdoing persuade them to make amends for their mistakes? Will our enchantments guide them to a better path?"

"In most cases, you would know the answer to those questions. Usually, you and Randall know what will happen to the persons you are sent to rescue. Your clairvoyance shows you their future long before it happens to them. But for this mission the First Spirit is preventing you from foreseeing the climactic episodes that will determine whether these five people discover the paths that will lead them to redemption or to eternal disappearance. This mission will be a test for you as well. It will test your judgment, your compassion, and your courage."

After hearing Robert's description of the challenges awaiting them, Randall and his Melanie have compassed their proper bearings. They are more certain than ever of the direction in which they must proceed.

They have two more questions. Melanie asks the first one.

"Who are the persons that Randall and I will become for this mission?"

With no hesitation, Robert tells her.

"You will be a clinical psychologist. You are also a married woman. Randall, your husband, will be a top-notch lawyer in Tate Calhern's law firm. Each of you will be twenty-nine years old."

Randall, speaking for himself as well as for Melanie, chooses the words that form the second question.

"When does our mission begin?"

"Right now," Robert answers him. "The two of you know all there is to know about teleporting. Concentrate. Focus upon Blue Ridge, a town in Fairfield County, Connecticut. Its vivid imagery will impress itself upon your awareness. It is, you will recall, an upscale community located fifty miles from New York City. The privileged human beings who live in Blue Ridge enjoy the luxuries of homes bordering Long Island Sound. Many of these persons are affluent careerists. Among them, there are uptight citizens with unforgiving hearts, uncaring immoralists, peddlers of deception, and potential murderers. Save them if you can. Do what you must do to bring them face to face with themselves."

"I'm eager to start," Melanie tells Randall. "Let's begin with Naomi Calhern and Brett Robinson. Naomi is the troubled young woman that Brett—a young lawyer on his way to the top—is courting, even though he has fallen in love with her beautiful stepmother."

"I'm all for that," Randall says. "Let's begin. Let's do the things that need to be done."

CHAPTER TWO
UNCERTAINTY

"Of course, I am pleased that Brett Robinson has asked me to marry him," Naomi Calhern says.

She brings a smile to her pale face. But her smile merely makes her voice sound tremulous. The words carry no conviction, and the smile merely subverts her intentions. She wants to tell the truth about her feelings. That has always been her way. She owes that to herself and to the woman to whom she is addressing her remark.

That woman is none other than Melanie, who has become her trusted friend. In this year that has as if by magic swiftly passed, Naomi has begun to regard Melanie as the sister and confidante that she always wanted, especially in those uneasy days when, as a lonely child, she yearned for a special friend to whom she could share her joys and her apprehension. But the Three Fates—or some other unseen Mysterious Powers that grant or deny a motherless, little girl's supplications—did not take note of her prayers. Or, perhaps, they did hear her petitions and believed that they carried little merit, so frightened and uncertain did they sound. Only when Melanie came into her life did she, Naomi Calhern—the privileged daughter of one of the wealthiest men in Blue Ridge, Connecticut—find a friend who really listened to the words that made her most private thoughts palpable and real. Sometimes, those thoughts were cries of sorrow that rose out of a forlorn soul. Sometimes, they were cries of elation that were filled with her tenuous discovery that happiness might, after all, be within her reach.

In this first year of knowing Melanie as her long-awaited friend, she has been discovering so much more about almost everything. Melanie has begun teaching her how to *see* with keen-eyed realism not only herself as effective and enterprising Naomi Calhern, but also the world in which with understated ingenuity she has been making a creditable name as a writer of children's books. Her literary success has brought a new radiance into her life. Interviews on television talk shows, in up-to-the minute news magazines and newspapers, on social media sites, and on podcasts and promotional videos have given her a global presence. Her pretty face on billboards and on the covers of fashion magazines has enhanced and intensified the public's awareness of her as a more-than-ordinary young woman whom The Fates have granted a life of privilege and influence. Yet despite this immense success and the fairy tale life her father's wealth has accorded her, she has never known genuine happiness. She has never freed herself from her habit of distrusting her feelings and her possibilities. Only now, when Brett Robinson has come into her life, has she permitted herself to believe that happiness is within her reach. Only on days like this one that is unfolding around her with promising intimations of soulful rebirth and longed-for bliss—only on such a splendid and one-of-a-kind day does she allow herself to imagine that a new door is opening for her. That door is drawing her, fragile human though she may be, into a magical-seeming world that has always been *here*—right *here*, in Blue Ridge—waiting for her to step forward and claim it.

In Naomi's eyes, Melanie is the new friend whom she regards as an emblem of decorum and wisdom, as an honorable counselor and prudent observer of the wider world, and as a decorous blonde woman who has partnered with an exemplary husband. She is also a woman whose sense of fashion impresses her. Today, Melanie is wearing a beige knit suit that is up-to-the-minute stylish with its spread collar long-sleeve jacket, gold-buttoned double-breasted front, loose belt at the back, and below-the-knees skirt. The lapel of the jacket holds a gold, heart-shaped Eternal Love brooch clustered with five-carat diamonds—a gift from her husband.

That Naomi regards her appearance as authentic pleases Melanie. When she was a young woman alive on Earth in the nineteen-fifties, she was Melanie Dickinson, a famous designer of women's dresses and gowns. She was the youngest of three daughters in an affluent Connecticut family. Her father and her two brothers were eminent architects, her two sisters were lawyers, and her mother was a renowned psychiatrist. Each of them thrived in their busy careers. In fact, her career saved Melanie from despair. She had lost Randall, the love of her life, to the Second World War. Her heart never yearned for any other man. She made her mark as a businesswoman.

Naomi is unaware of Melanie's earlier biography. She will ask no questions. Melanie has cast a spell upon Naomi. Never will she connect her to the Melanie Dickinson who was born in 1921. This troubled young woman will regard her as a life-loving psychologist who was born in 1991. In this year of 2020, Melanie's father is an eminent Philadelphia oncologist, and her mother is a pediatrician. Her two brothers are research scientists for a pharmaceutical corporation, and her two sisters are United States senators, representing New York and Connecticut.

Once again, though in a different century, Melanie is a fashionable young woman. She is also a new, respected friend to Naomi Calhern, a troubled woman who is twenty-seven years old. Melanie is the special individual who has guided Naomi to the magical door that is waiting for her to open it and to pass across its threshold. That she also happens to be Dr. Melanie Johnson, her equally trustworthy psychologist, makes the friendship even more extraordinary.

Keen-minded and helpful, Melanie continues to observe Naomi. In this hour, because the First Spirit has consented, she sees not merely the outward form of this young woman, not merely the willowy figure that moves and sits with feminine grace. She sees into her mind and her soul. She sees that Naomi has never trusted the promise of happiness. Nor has she felt comfortable during those rare times when she has been in the presence of happiness.

On this sun-filled April afternoon, Melanie is seated behind a handcrafted desk that is impressive because of its rectangular shape, solid cherry wood, intricate hand carvings, and ebony and gold-leaf accents. She is sitting in an executive swivel chair that is upholstered in an elegant indigo blue with a tufted back, a poly-fiber seat cushion, and a knee-tilt mechanism. An Impressionist canvas fills the wall behind and above her desk. Within that canvas, a young woman who uncannily resembles Naomi sits alone in a small, hardy boat, working its oars so that she can safely navigate the storm-fused ocean on which she is making her way. Like Naomi in this very moment, the woman has titian hair, an upturned nose, and teal-blue eyes. Her tense face reveals a tight-lipped determination, and she wears a gold-gleaming oilskin hat and coat. Storm clouds hover nearby, and turbulent waves are hastening toward her. Whether this young woman will rescue herself from the gathering storm, the painting offers no clue except the woman's determined expression and her proficient working of the oars against the windswept, leaping ocean.

In the privacy of this office on the twelfth floor of a modern skyscraper that dominates a prime location within affluent Blue Ridge, the sun-glanced surround of a panoramic window brightens the atmosphere. Gleaming cedar wood floors, oriental rugs, and richly upholstered chairs give this spacious room a look that is both fashionable and comforting.

If Naomi notices any one of these things, her pensive face gives no evidence. The capacious and well-appointed room, the handcrafted desk, the gleaming cedar floors and oriental rugs, and the luminous blue of the sun-filled sky that peers through the panoramic window—all these solacing images do not influence her steadfast gaze or even an oblique awareness. Nor do her eyes with studious glance attend her mirror image in that Impressionist canvas or the dark gray storm clouds there or the belligerent ocean waters.

With alert and pensive gaze Melanie continues to observe her—Tate Calhern's only daughter and only offspring—and notices once more the traceries of melancholy and tension that to her knowing and doctor-trained eyes not even the gleam of a twenty-seven-year-old woman's smile can conceal. Naomi is aware of her notice. The psychologist part of Melanie is trying to connect the enigmatic nature of her patient's personality to that hint of uneasiness and to her attractive appearance. On the surface, Naomi looks stylish and assured. Her cropped fringe titian hair, her oval face, her teal blue eyes and upturned nose, and her bee-stung lips make her beauty distinctive and appealing. Her azure blue tank top, cropped black pants, and black ballet flats accentuate her slim figure. She wears her clothes with authority. There is nothing reticent about her presentation of herself. Yet churning inside her is her steadfast conviction that she is not good enough for the world and especially not for so charismatic a young man as Brett Robinson.

So Melanie perceives, harboring within her silence an awareness of Naomi's surprise and apprehension.

"Of course, I am pleased that Brett has asked me to marry him," Naomi says once again, as though these words are part of a mystical chant that, when repeated, will keep misfortune at bay. She wants to persuade Melanie as well as herself that her recent engagement to Brett has brought her the happiness that she has always been seeking.

"But his asking you to marry him is not enough," Melanie tells her, reading her mind and soul with Spirit-driven clarity. "It can't be enough, because you wouldn't be trying to convince yourself and me that his proposal of marriage is going to make your life infinitely better. You wouldn't be doubting that his asking you to marry him is the game-changer for which you have been waiting."

"Is it so wrong to have doubts? Is it so terrible to hesitate before leaping into the unknown?"

"Not always," Melanie answers her. "Marriage, after all, does require us to take that leap. But the unknown should not seem dangerous. The leap should not feel like a free fall into misery, sorrow, and self-destruction."

"Do you think that is what I'm feeling?"

"I know you are," Melanie says, with the quiet conviction that recognizes hidden sadness and suppressed fear. "After all our sessions together, I understand you as well as I can understand any one of my patients. I understand you even when you try to hide your feelings from me."

Her remarks make Naomi pause. A frown touches her brow. She presses her lips tightly together, as though she is making a prisoner of whatever words might hurry forward to reveal the heartache she still prefers to conceal. For just a moment, she touches with the fingers of her right hand the engagement ring that adorns the fourth finger of her left hand. The ring is exquisite, with its three carat, round diamond and its platinum side stones. It is a ring meant for a fairy tale princess. It is a ring designed for a hand as perfect as Naomi's, with its long, delicate fingers that are enhanced by the nude gloss of her fingernails. It is a ring that a corporate prince or one aspiring to that status might confer upon his bride-to-be.

Melanie notices all these things. As she notices, she recalls what she had learned about the Ancient Roman tradition of a young woman's wearing an engagement ring on the fourth finger of her left hand. In that long-ago time, the Romans believed that the fourth finger of the left hand had a vein that ran directly to the heart—the *Vena Amoris*, the vein of love. Because they believed that the heart was the center of emotions, the Romans chose the fourth finger of a girl's or a woman's hand for the wearing of a ring of betrothal. The ring showed to everyone who noticed it the symbol of a love that was going to last forever. It showed, too, that a prospective groom had claimed the heart of the wearer.

This ring-wearer—this stylish yet uneasy Naomi, this complicated young woman entangled by hesitation and second guessing—leans into her stillness. The honest words that she wants to speak remain hidden, at least for the moment.

Melanie does not push. She waits for Naomi to choose the honest words.

When she does speak, Naomi connects with her through a steady gaze and through the quickened fluency of spontaneous words.

"I don't trust my happiness," she says. "I don't deserve it. I can't really understand why, suddenly, so completely and strangely suddenly—when I wasn't in any way anticipating it—happiness has come so easily to me. Too easily, I feel. Something must be wrong with it. Maybe it's not happiness at all. Maybe I'm like the forlorn girl in a fairy tale that some marvel-making wizard has enchanted. Maybe, while caught inside this enchantment, this magic-seeming spell, I am being primed for disappointment and disillusionment."

"Who is this wizard that has enchanted you? Not all wizards are diabolical. Not all sorcerers and conjurers and enchanters do harm. Sometimes, in the stories that we once read during our childhood and that we remember for years afterward, wizards and enchanters are benevolent. They bring us gifts. They use their magic to counsel us. Sometimes they show us the future. Sometimes, they even save our lives."

"I don't know that a wizard or an enchanter is really involved with what has been happening to me," Naomi says. "I only feel that somebody like a wizard—some enchanter—has been working to change my life."

"That may not be a bad thing."

"I wish I could be certain of that."

"I'm surprised that you say so," Melanie says. "Not so long ago, you told me that certainties did not exist."

"That was before I met Brett. That was before I fell in love with him. That was before he told me that he loved me."

"You don't really believe him," Melanie says. "That's it, isn't it? That's your problem. That's the root of your uncertainty."

"I want to believe him," Naomi declares. "I want to believe that I deserve his love. I want to believe that I'm pretty enough and carefree and sophisticated and confident in every way that he thinks I am. I want to believe that all the words he tells me, and all his looks, and all his gestures are true."

"Apparently they are," Melanie says. "After all, he made the first move. At the February ball, he danced only with you. I was there. I saw everything that was happening. He made you feel that you were the only young woman in that grand room."

"Yes," Naomi agrees. "He did all of those things. Yet..."

She pauses once again, assailed by familiar doubts.

Melanie nudges her forward.

"Yet you are not really convinced."

"No."

"Is it Brett that you are doubting? Or is it yourself?"

"It must be myself. It has to be. Brett is so good. He is such a fine man. The fault is my own. I don't believe in me. I don't believe that I'm good enough for Brett."

"At that February ball, before he asked you to dance, you had already heard about him."

"Of course, I did. I couldn't help hearing. All my friends were talking about him. He was the most charismatic young lawyer they'd ever met. Because he was working in my father's law office, they thought that I knew everything there was to know about him. But I hadn't even met him. Nor did I learn anything about him from my father, who rarely mentions the men and women who are on his staff."

"But a few weeks before the night of the February ball, you found out some of the important details of his life."

"Yes."

"Did some of your girlfriends tell you those details?"

"They told me everything that they'd heard. But none of it was really important."

"You said that, on the night of the ball, you felt that you already knew him. What made you feel that way? Who prepared you for him?"

"It was Lisa, my stepmother. A few months before the ball, we'd been riding our Appaloosas on Ben Wilder's horse farm a few miles from my father's home. You remember the place. You and I have sometimes gone riding there, though never alone together. Usually, you and your husband are part of our country club's riding competitions. All for charity, of course."

"Yes," Melanie says. "Randall and I have such great fun whenever we go riding there."

"Then you remember that the Wilders' farm is located at the foot of those wonderful, green rolling hills."

"I do remember. I'm always intrigued by the way that the farm fans outward to hundreds of acres of land that on clear days seems to be hurrying forward to the sunglow of a quiet lake."

"Yes, the Wilder farmland is a beautiful place. It was especially beautiful on the day that Lisa and I went horse riding. The day was unusually warm for December. There was very little wind to disturb our cantering across the wide expanse of the trail. In our riding jackets and jodhpurs, Lisa and I looked like sisters. You know what I mean. You've met my stepmother. She's only two years older than I am."

"Yes, I know her," Melanie says, held now to ambivalence and discretion. "She is a very glamorous woman."

"Indeed, she is. Well, it was Lisa who told me so much about Brett. She and my father sometimes dined with Brett and any number of his temporary girlfriends."

"Your father thinks well of Brett. That's not surprising. Brett is a lawyer on his way to the top. Everybody who meets him knows that. My husband regards him as an ambitious colleague who makes all the right moves. Brett Robinson will do everything he can to win a case. His friends and his adversaries agree that he is one tough attorney."

"My father has begun mentioning him only lately, now that Brett and I have become engaged. My father never dispenses praise indiscriminately. He says that Brett and your husband are two of the finest attorneys on his staff."

"Yes, your father does respect Randall. He has given him a great deal of responsibility. He counts on his always being precision-plus. He also respects Brett. He thinks that he has an extraordinary mind and a winner-take-all manner in and out of court."

Hearing these words, Naomi falls silent.

Melanie continues to observe her. She reads her mind. She understands that, despite her keen intelligence, Naomi has not yet learned to fathom the moral ambiguities of most human beings. She is too willing to temporize or excuse other people's failings. She is reluctant to condemn or even criticize anyone but herself. From her emotionally deprived childhood, she learned to value friendships, even when they included spiritually damaged contemporaries and self-defeating rebels.

Like Melanie, Naomi has noticed her father's special regard of Brett. But she does not recognize their similar natures. She does not yet perceive that they are like-minded. They are *simpatico* for all the wrong reasons. She has never allowed herself to imagine that they share similar characteristics and interests. She knows her father too well to connect his moral failings with her idealized perception of Brett as self-effacing and altruistic. Nevertheless, they are mirror images of each other. There is a furious energy in her father's and Brett's ambitions. That fury—that driving intensity, that willingness to ride roughshod over comrades and adversaries—has made her father and Brett cragged souls, chipped fragments of fallible humanity.

Naomi sees Brett as the lover she wishes him to be, not as the fallible man he really is. Never, not even in a million years—so Naomi believes—could Brett become an *alter ego* of her father, a cynical avatar, a speckled counterpart. He is an altogether different kind of man. Yet she is willing to admit that her father's liking Brett has forged a bond between them. Her father's liking Brett goes beyond respect.

"His attitude is fatherly," she tells Melanie after emerging from her musing. "I know. I have observed them when they are at a dinner party or at a Philharmonic concert or playing golf or sailing. My father regards Brett as a loyal son—a replacement for the son that my mother did not give him. Brett is the kind of son my father has always wanted."

"Is that what Lisa told you?"

"She didn't have to," Naomi says. "I've watched them when they are together. My father gives Brett all the attention that he denied me. I am his daughter, but he does not love me. He does not even like me. I am the human being who killed his wife by being born. He has never forgiven me for that."

"Is Lisa aware of your father's dislike of you?"

"Yes, she is aware, even though my father keeps his dislike of me subtle and private. At any rate, Lisa and I rarely mention it."

"Yet she has drawn you to Brett."

"She believes that we make a good fit. 'You are the one woman who can tame Brett,' she keeps telling me. 'All his other women are his playthings. They are superficial. They are temporary. They are spoiled debutantes and self-centered heiresses and promiscuous playgirls. They aren't worth much, even with their fortunes. They might make his life adventurous. But they could never make it a worthwhile life. They could never help him to become the more-than-ordinary man he is meant to be.'"

"Lisa told you all those things?"

"Yes. She really wants me to marry Brett. She believes that the marriage will strengthen my bond with my father.

She says that it's possible my father will always favor Brett over me. But, because I will be Brett's wife, the one woman who can help him to be a great man, my father will look at me with new eyes."

"Lisa knows a great deal about Brett."

"Yes, I suppose she does," Naomi says. "She is often in Brett's company, because my father enjoys his being at our weekly dinner parties, at the business conferences that take place in his home office, and during horse riding and sailing weekends."

"You have been there, too—at the dinner parties and during the horse riding and sailing weekends."

"I have been," Naomi replies. "It has all been so exhilarating because Brett has been there with me. Everything about these days with him keeps surprising me."

"There's nothing wrong with your being surprised, as long as you are getting to know more about Brett."

"I'll never know enough," Naomi says, while elation sparks her voice. "That is such a wonderful thing! There will always be more to find out about Brett."

"Yes," Melanie answers her. "Keep finding out more about him. That is the thing you must do."

"With pleasure," Naomi says. "Always with pleasure."

"Let's hope so. At any rate, you will find out more about him at the dinner that your father and your stepmother are hosting tomorrow evening at the country club. Randall and I will be joining the party. All of us will have another chance to learn more about Brett."

"I can hardly wait. I'm already excited."

Naomi pauses. A new thought prods a doubt of a different kind.

"My friend Kayla Ericson and her husband, Hayden, will also be there."

"Wonderful," Melanie exclaims. "We'll have a very special evening together."

"I don't know," Naomi says. "There may be trouble."

"Why do you say that?"

"My father frowns on my friendship with Kayla. She is Black, and she is married to a white man."

Naomi's remark does not surprise Melanie. She and Randall know the many prejudices that are tarnishing the soul of Tate Calhern. What will finally happen to Tate, Randall and Melanie do not know. The First Spirit has limited their knowledge of outcomes, consequences, and resolutions. But they do know that Tate will figure importantly in the scenarios that have already begun to unfold. They also know that tonight Tate will, for the most, part suppress his anger. Its whiplash fury will flare up in later, intense confrontations.

In this present moment, when she is completing her counseling session with Naomi, Melanie finds appropriate words in defense of Kayla and Hayden.

"Kayla and Hayden make a very fine couple," she says. "They are using their law skills to assist underprivileged people. They are also combating racism. Randall and I look forward to seeing them."

"I'm pleased that you and Randall like them," Naomi says. "I'm glad that they will be joining us at the dinner dance. They will make the evening spin with excitement. They always do."

"They make evenings spin in an acceptable way. That is their stock in trade. That is what makes them exciting."

"Of course, Brett will provide the most intense excitement. He's one of the most exciting persons in the world. You and Randall already know that. He's become your friend."

"Yes, Randall and I know Brett—at least a little. At the dinner dance, we may get to know him a little more. You will, most certainly."

Once again, elation sparks Naomi's voice. Familiar words spill out of her, echoing her previous anticipation.

"I can hardly wait," she says. "I know that Brett will surprise me. He always does."

Melanie is not yet ready to cast a spell over Naomi so that she can more accurately perceive the hidden intricacies of her situation. Nor is she ready to invoke a magical vision in Naomi's everyday surroundings or inside her uneasy dreams. All that will come later. Instead, while offering her prudent words and a lighthearted manner as she responds to her eagerness to be with Brett, she begins to prepare her for the unexpected.

"I understand exactly what you are feeling," Melanie says. "After all, you will be learning more about Brett. You may even find out something that you were not anticipating."

CHAPTER THREE
AMBIVALENCE

On the following Saturday, Randall and Melanie arrive at Blue Ridge Country Club in a timely manner. They make an impressive arrival in Randall's Mercedes Benz. The valet, a young and confident man with a mane of thick blond hair and a face that wears his handsome features with ingrained assurance, courteously greets them. His blue eyes light up with muted recognition, but he carefully abstains from any words that might reveal his pleasure in their arriving here on this crisp and unusually cool evening in the third week of April. Rather, it is Melanie who crosses that invisible and sometimes uncomfortable barrier called protocol and, with quietly calibrated decorum, offers him a greeting that is both friendly and natural.

"It's good to see you, Kevin," she tells him. "I hope the evening finds you well."

He beams with appreciation and quietly answers her.

"It does, indeed, Doctor Johnson. It does, indeed. Thank you for asking."

They make their way into the club with a nearly tense anticipation of the troubled scenes that the evening may dispense to them. Two women not yet twenty and pretty with red hair, blue eyes, and reed-thin figures, welcome them with light-hearted courtesy and help them to remove their coats—Randall's beige cashmere topcoat with its oversized notched collar and double-breasted button front and Melanie's azure blue sheath coat, with its shirt collar, long sleeves, and cobalt blue piping.

Right after that, a white-haired *maître d'* warmly receives them and guides them up the long, wine-colored carpeted staircase to a dining room on the second floor, where the preferred placement enhances the privacy and the pleasures of the evening. Once inside its guarded serenity, Randall and Melanie move with familiar ease through the capacious room, noticing without acknowledging them his business acquaintances chatting with their wives or girlfriends, the editor of Naomi's most recent novel dining with her professorial husband and six other couples, and many friends that have remained their steadfast advocates—Melanie's and Randall's—during storm-laden times as well as on days filled with praise and other public rewards. Though they returned to Earth only a year ago, Randall and Melanie cast a spell upon the entire Blue Ridge community and upon all those visitors to this affluent city whose lives are connecting with their own. Spellbound and credulous, all the persons who interrelate with them believe that they have shared friendships with Randall and Melanie for many years.

In the southwest corner of the room, a young, sandy-haired pianist, sitting with relaxed poise at a satin walnut Steinway, plays the romantic melodies of Andrew Lloyd Webber, Richard Rodgers, Lorenz Hart, Stephen Sondheim, and John Lennon. As they have done in so many previous visits here, Randall and Melanie scan the room's well-ordered design with attentive admiration and with a tinge of nostalgia, recalling as they do the other evenings when they have dined here. With its crystal chandeliers, beautiful antiques, burnished mahogany, rich fabrics, and dignified atmosphere, as well as original canvases by Winslow Homer, John Singer Sargent, Mary Cassatt, Grandma Moses, and Andrew Wyeth, the room creates a setting that is both elegant and stately.

As this dining room and all its amenities unfold their influences around them, Melanie and Randall guess with genuine appreciation and well-honed awareness that Lisa Calhern has chosen so sumptuous a setting for this dinner party because the refined atmosphere, the upright conduct of guests young and older at neighboring tables, and the disciplined cordiality of the servers might hold her senses still. The Calherns are eager to celebrate Naomi's engagement to Brett. But dark clouds hover over Lisa and over Brett and Naomi as well. Lisa has fallen in love with Brett. He is the man she would have married if they had met five years earlier and if he were as wealthy as Tate Calhern. He is the only man that she will ever love—passionately and completely and even dangerously. He is the man with whom Lisa has been having a secret affair for more than a year. He is the man whose marriage to Naomi she has arranged. She wants always to have Brett in her life. Willful and determined, she will tolerate Naomi's being Brett's wife. She—Lisa—will fill a role in his life that is far more important than that of a conventional wife. She will continue to be the only woman that he loves.

Brett is *here* in this grand dining room. But, to Lisa's regret, he is not *there*, keen-minded and alert, in that lakeside hideaway house that Tate owns and that has become the primary meeting place for their lovemaking.

The charismatic Brett Robinson, who thinks and feels and moves with well-honed agility and is an ambitious man making his way to the top, arrived here with punctual ease twenty minutes ago. He arrived here, rugged and palpable and princely, with Naomi by his side. Tate and Lisa, his future in-laws, noticed the romantic glow that surrounded them. Randall and Melanie know. Their supernatural eyes caught sight of that moment, flashing its vitality inside their quickened minds and by means of their magical perceiving as they were driving through the private roads that have brought them to this prestigious country club.

In those moments that unfolded a half hour earlier, their supernatural eyes also caught sight of eerie, horrific scenes that, they realized, might well take place in the future hurrying toward them. As they continue to observe Tate and his wife, Lisa, and Naomi with her Brett, the violent scenes flash once again before Randall's and Melanie's private seeing. There, with foreboding and terror, right *there* in the fearful scenes suddenly rising like ominous flares before their eyes, Tate Calhern is firing his Beretta pistol into Brett's forehead and heart. Blood and brain cells are spilling out of Brett's head, and his right eye with gleaming brownness is popping out of its socket and resting uneasily upon his cheek. A third bullet smashes through the bridge of his nose and a fourth bullet is tearing through his mouth. More blood gushes out of his collapsing features. Brett's body, jolted and pushed back by the exploding bullets, begins dropping very slowly in paranormal slow motion. The surprise and horror of his death transfixes themselves upon his ruined face. He is Brett and yet no longer Brett. The physical images that reveal who he is at least on the surface cave in, fold into themselves, buckle, crumple, and implode. But the left eye retains its glazed stare, steady and unremitting, unrelieved of its witnessing astonishment.

Deep inside the clouded space behind Brett, another scene is fanning outward and apart from the episode of Tate murdering Brett. Nevertheless, this new scene is connected with ghostly implications to that murder. This new apparition that is enfolding their senses—Randall's and Melanie's—challenges their hope and their belief that they can rescue the five persons who are becoming the instruments of their own destruction. Vivid and phantasmagorical within a summer rose garden, the inert body of Naomi is dangling from an ornamental tree. A thick rope entwines itself with tautened powers about a protruding branch and entwines itself just as tautly about her slender neck. Her oxygen-deprived face has turned blue, and the macabre appearance of her tongue, protruding between her lips, instantly robs her of the delicate beauty that had always adorned her.

This sight of violent endings that might not be endings at all, but only the beginnings of more violence set loose inside the conflicted lives of the Calherns and their ambitious friends—this gruesome imagery that tarnishes the beauty of Naomi, the handsomeness of Brett, and the flowering life of this summerlike, enchanted April gives Randall and Melanie pause. In days to come, they might be confronting scenes just as grisly as these that are flaring their horrors now, the spawn of nightmare messages sent them by Robert Steerforth and by the First Spirit. The messages carry not only a prediction, but also a warning. They must do everything that is humanly possible and a few things that are supernatural to save the Calherns and their ambitious friends from the violent endings that are waiting to overtake them.

Pushing these ominous thoughts way back inside the hidden corners of their minds—way, way back so that they cannot disturb the precise calibrations of their affability, Randall and Melanie arrive at a large, round table that appears to be waiting for them by the floor-to-ceiling window. The gold-hued velvet drapes are drawn so that the light of the moon that gleams upon the wide expanse of green lawn fanning out to the even more expansive greenery of a golf course also caresses the more private area where they will be seated. Moonlight touches, as well, the gold tablecloth with its delicately woven jacquard poinsettia design and the yellow, red, and white roses that are tucked into a crystal vase with ivy and ferns. They notice at once Tate and Lisa, patrician and sociable as they converse with Brett and Naomi, who are sharing the table with them. Randall and Melanie know the young couple well. During their tenure in Sojourn and even during their residence in the First Heaven, they saw the complicated future that would bring them into the lives of Naomi and Brett, intertwined as those lives are with the anguished soul of Lisa and the hardened heart of Tate Calhern. With as much compassion as they are capable of summoning and with the right-minded actions their mission compels them to take, they recall once again, as though they are remembering the words of a prayer, the compelling reasons why the First Spirit has sent them on this mission. They have come here to Blue Ridge to rescue Brett from his wily and destructive ways, to prevent Lisa from causing a tragedy that will ruin her life and the lives of others, to influence Naomi to become self-believing and courageous, and to persuade Tate to see his daughter—as well as Lisa and Brett—with discerning eyes.

Now, after a waiter with precision-plus aptitudes guides them to their places at the table, Randall and Melanie exchange cordial greetings with Tate and Lisa and with Brett and Naomi. Hayden and Kayla have not yet arrived. With his brusque manner, Tate quickly mentions that Kayla, who is a well-meaning idealist, will eventually be arriving with her husband, who is also a cockeyed do-gooder. He does not at first mention the reason why they are late. But Randall and Melanie know. Altruistic and strong-minded, Hayden and Kayla have spent a long day in court defending innocent Blacks who have been accused of inciting a riot during a peaceful protest against white supremacists and neo-Nazis.

"They are busy with their charity work for their latest gaggle of impoverished and troublemaking clients," Tate says after Naomi asks why Hayden and Kayla have not yet arrived.

"I've heard such good things about their charity work," Randall says, smoothly deflecting Tate's sarcasm. "I'm looking forward to seeing them."

Naomi also speaks up, her voice nearly tremulous. She is, after all, countering her father's unhappy remark about Hayden and Kayla. Perhaps it is the comforting presence of Brett beside her that encourages her to defend her friends.

"They are a delightful couple," she says. "They never disappoint me."

Melanie joins in this exchange of words, her ingrained poise and her gentle voice a solacing influence upon the tension that has been hovering like a brooding intruder come here to listen to all of their words and to observe their faces.

"I'm certain that they will make the evening even more memorable."

Attentive though she is to the conversation that with bright energies and ambiguous subtexts is already quickening the dinner dance atmosphere, Melanie focuses, at the same time, upon what everyone is wearing. It is a way to hold her senses still, so keen is her anticipation of the persons that Naomi and Brett and Lisa and Tate will prove to be and the influence that Randall and she may have upon their lives.

The six people here make up a well-groomed party.

Randall looks casually impressive in his gray suit, its slim, masculine lines made perfect because of the symmetry of its notch lapels, waist flap pockets, and dual back vents. His necktie in blue silk twill, complementing an azure shirt, is printed with a red polka dot pattern and a background of blue, red, and gray swirls.

Tate's well-guarded dignity enhances a double-breasted black suit, with its notch collar, double-breasted button front, and chest welt and front welt pockets. His gray shirt and his tie, a paisley print with gold, gray, cream white, and rose colors on a black wool base, lend vibrancy to his suit.

Brett, brown-haired and wind-burned, brings a tall, rangy physique and a stylized vitality to a navy-blue suit in a check pattern with a peak lapel, a two-button front with horn buttons, front flap pockets, and a double vented back. His white shirt and his tie, navy with light blue rhombi designs, nicely bond with the suit.

The well-groomed appearance of these men intensifies Melanie's appreciation of fabrics and colors and their designers. She knows very well the works of Ralph Lauren, Christian Dior, Hugo Bass, Calvin Klein, Giorgio Armani, and Salvatore Ferragamo. Their careers were flourishing long before she died in 2013.

The women look equally impressive.

With her tall, slender figure and honey blonde hair pulled back to make a neat coil at the nape of her neck, Lisa looks especially lovely in her boat-neck, dark blue A-line party dress that has long sleeves and a floral embroidered skirt.

Naomi brings beauty and elegance to a sleeveless black A-line evening dress that has a crew neck and blue, green, and gold floral embellishments.

Melanie is wearing a cobalt blue sweater dress that has a turtleneck collar, long sleeves, and gold abstract designs on its front and back, as well as on its shoulders. She tells herself that she is in her glamour mode.

She wants this evening to work for everyone. She wants Brett to love Naomi, though why she imagines that he will do so she cannot say, so uneasy and disarranged are her feelings on this strange-seeming evening when she is anticipating a new turn on the dark path that all of them are traveling. She wants Lisa to withdraw from her illicit relationship with Brett. She wants Tate to rediscover the humanity he so carelessly squandered when he anchored his career as an attorney to a take-no-prisoners philosophy. Secretly tense and excited, she is waiting for a clue—a Divine inspiration, perhaps, or an Earth-bound intimation—that will help Randall and her to keep these four people from falling into an oblivion from which there will be no return.

As soon as the *maître d'* has brought them to their table, a young, red-haired waiter—tall, lean, and immaculately groomed in a black tuxedo—brings everyone their drinks. Tate, Brett, and Randall enjoy scotch on the rocks. Lisa, Naomi, and Melanie find pleasure in delicate stem glasses of *Veuve Clicquot.*

Convivial within the boundaries of decorum, they talk about many things. They are playing a serious game, sharing stories that will subdue their unease about the ways that this evening unfolding around them might reveal a fault line in their plans for a happy future. Their complicated feelings toward one another make ambivalence—their simultaneous attraction and repulsion—an invisible presence alive and influential here with them at the dinner table.

Tate and Lisa reminisce about their river rafting adventure on the Sjoa River in Norway. During those daredevil hours two years earlier, they as well as Naomi and a professional skipper paddled along an eleven-mile route beside a cluster of big mountains. On that morning, they funneled their way into numerous gorges, canyons, and waterfalls, and they raced through the heave and swirl of rushing rapids.

"What an adrenalin rush that day was!" Tate says.

His face beams with the happy memory.

Naomi has a different kind of recollection. She remembers the adventure with a mixture of elation and sentimentality.

"I was there with two of the most important persons in my life," she says. "That's what made the river rafting special."

Tate acknowledges his daughter's respect with the hint of a smile. On this evening, he does not offer a blunt review of her rafting skills or compare her performance to that of the beautiful mother who died giving birth to her. His first wife was a first-rate sailor and a proficient athlete. He is learning to tolerate this daughter that he has always resented and has always regarded as mediocre and inept in almost everything that she does. For once, she is doing the right thing. She has managed to get herself engaged to a young man on his way to the top. This Brett—this enigmatic and wily arrogance—is a younger version of himself, the Tate Calhern who existed two decades earlier. No, he will not critique his daughter's rafting performance, as he has often done on all the occasions when she was not engaged. He merely offers her a smile, the emblem of their new accord and his willingness to tolerate with diplomatic acceptance the lacerating punishment that her presence in his life has always represented—this problematic daughter whose very birth killed the only woman he could ever really love.

Instead, it is Lisa who dispenses praise.

"That journey along the Sjoa River *was* special," she says. "Tate and Naomi made it special. Navigating those white waters, they were agile, skillful, fearless, and adventurous. In my book, they are A-Plus!"

Naomi smiles when she hears Lisa's remarks. She admires Lisa and believes that, ever since her marriage to Tate four years ago, she has been a reliable stepmother. She regards her affection as genuine. Sensitive to other people's feelings and helpful whenever she can be helpful, Lisa inspires her trust and her respect. She is one of the most beautiful women in Blue Ridge. Her honey blonde hair, fair skin, oval face, and straight nose, as well as her tapered jaw, round chin, and full lips intensify her beauty. A top-notch lawyer in Tate's premier Blue Ridge law firm, Lisa is making impressive achievements in her career. She is also making her marriage to the always ambitious and sometimes cold-hearted Tate Calhern a happy one.

So Naomi believes.

As she observes Lisa, who is seated next to Tate across the round table, Naomi is pleased to recognize her as a most reliable friend. Even when, despite her success as a novelist, she seemed to be doing everything wrong in her life more than a year ago—even then, when her life had fallen apart, smashed up and apparently beyond repair because of her disappointing friendships with eligible men and because of her self-hatred and her loneliness, Lisa stood by her. She guided her to Melanie and, after that, to Brett. It was Lisa first of all who made her believe that, already, she was doing wonderful things with her life.

With her soft voice and precise diction, Melanie shares with the group the elation that she felt when she and Randall, as well as Brett and Naomi and Tate and Lisa, went scuba diving at Barracuda Point on Sipadan Island in Malaysia. During that exhilarating vacation nearly six months ago, Brett and Naomi were beginning their romance. Tate was pleased to see his daughter partnered with a successful man who was making all the smart moves. Lisa was playing the role of the dutiful and very young stepmother who delighted in observing Naomi's newfound happiness with Brett. In that season, Randall and Melanie were pleased to share the diving adventures with both couples. They were especially pleased to offer Naomi and Brett friendly remarks about the thrills and the challenges of married life.

"I never imagined that scuba diving could be so astonishing," Melanie tells the five persons who are listening to her. Her blue eyes sparkle with elation as she calls back to her conscious awareness the lift and surprise of that time. "Under water, I saw schools of barracuda moving like a hurricane, and walls of coral that sparkled like indigo jewels. I saw grey reef sharks patrolling the edge of the reefs and buffalo fish leaving their caves. I saw colorful batfishes, giant turtles, and bullet-fast parrot fish. I saw each of us—Brett and Naomi, Tate and Lisa, and Randall and me—with masks, snorkels, and fins and head-mounted dive lights flashing red, yellow, and green. We looked otherworldly. I saw Randall next to me and, farther away, Brett with Naomi and Tate with Lisa swimming as though we were magical creatures of the sea. I felt that I'd been allowed to enter an underwater kingdom and that I had become supernatural."

The group enjoys Melanie's reminiscence without understanding that for several years and long before scuba diving in Malaysia she has been supernatural. Her words take on a shared meaning because everyone listening to her had been part of the scuba diving adventure. Only Lisa experiences some uneasiness, not because of Melanie's fluent telling of that time they shared in Malaysia. Instead, it is Brett who is disturbing Lisa's composure.

As a way of deflecting the tension that she is feeling because Brett—with a few shots of scotch whiskey inside him—is allowing his gaze upon her to linger too long and too sensually, Lisa makes a lighthearted remark. She draws Randall into its orbit.

"If that underwater kingdom made Melanie feel otherworldly, did it make you feel supernatural, too?"

Randall is amused by her question and by the irony of Melanie's remark about feeling supernatural. He laughs a hearty laugh and smoothly lobs a quick-witted retort to Lisa.

"Melanie gives that underwater kingdom too much credit," he says. "In the private chambers of her soul, she has always been supernatural. The coral reef understood that. It simply spruced itself up and invited her into its color and glitter."

Lisa decides to tease Randall, good-naturedly. It is her way of keeping the mood in this group carefree and freewheeling.

"You haven't answered my question. Did diving into that kingdom make you feel supernatural?"

For just a moment, Randall ponders her question. Then, with a husky energy that anchors itself to the lightheartedness, he carries the banter forward.

"Well, in that reef, batfish, lionfish, and leopard sharks were swimming around us. They didn't look supernatural to me."

"You still haven't answered my question. Did diving in Malaysia make *you* feel supernatural?"

Randall pauses once again. Then, when he is ready to answer, his voice becomes low-key and serious.

"Melanie made me feel supernatural," he says. "She made me feel supernatural the first time she kissed me."

"What a wonderful thing to say," Lisa exclaims. "And how brave of you. You *are* a romantic. These days, that makes you a very special man."

Everyone laughs. Everyone is having a good time—everyone except Tate.

He frowns. He finds no pleasure in his wife's remark. He is definitely old guard. He believes that a married woman should refrain from public remarks about romance and from gracious presentations of herself that invite the inordinate attention of men who are not her husband.

Has he noticed Brett's sensual gaze upon Lisa?

He *has* noticed, though only Lisa and the Johnsons—Randall and Melanie—recognize the full meaning of that gaze. Bonded with Brett in a fatherly way that nearly deflects the enmity that lives, suppressed and resentful, between him and his daughter, Tate makes excuses for Brett's lingering gaze upon Lisa. Tonight, Brett is not himself. He has had a few drinks too many.

Heedless of Tate's frown, Brett goes on gazing, though with more subtle increments of his attention. His wiliness compels him to gaze as well upon Naomi, with contrived emphases that even Tate grudgingly accepts as genuine.

Tate finds words that dispel his ambivalence toward the scuba diving episode and this talk of the supernatural. He is not yet ready to admit that in his wife's eyes it is Brett, not Randall, who has the looks of a supernatural hero, though in almost everyone else's eyes Randall's handsome authority grants him assured and authentic charisma. Tate also harnesses his ambivalence toward his lovely wife who is two decades younger than he is.

"I'll admit that in some ways scuba diving in Malaysia was exciting," he says. "But I'm a full-fledged American lawyer. Exotic places do not impress me. Nor does the sight of sharks especially intrigue me. I meet enough of that sort in the day-to-day encounters of a courtroom."

Hearing his remark, Lisa chooses clever words that further dissuade him from his anger and, possibly, from his suspicion.

"Well, bully for you!" she exclaims. "I'll remember not to invite anyone exotic to our dinners."

Before new tensions can hurry back to this table, hovering with insidious powers around Tate's doubts, Naomi's lack of confidence while in her father's presence, and Lisa and Brett's duplicity, Randall and Melanie take charge of the moment. They change the subject from this talk of favorite travels. As though they are testing their ability to rescue these four persons who have not yet claimed their souls, Melanie and Randall draw them more deeply into this game that they are adroitly playing—this verbal stratagem, this juggle of words they are performing, this series of narrative ploys that keep at bay latent hostilities, subtle betrayals, and bitter recriminations. They throw forth words that, like magnets, draw everybody toward different topics. Randall prods the group, especially Brett and Tate, with his mention of the excitement of hockey and with talk of great players such as Bobby Orr, Gordie Howe, Wayne Gretzky, and Maurice Richard. Melanie speaks of her favorite blue-chip stocks—including Berkshire Hathaway, Lockheed Martin, and Duke Energy— and elicits probing questions and knowing remarks from everyone at the table.

Randall fields inquiries and comments about the political turbulence in Washington. He understands why his remarks rouse Tate's interest especially. Blue Ridge's wealthiest and most ambitious attorney is aiming for a place in the cabinet of the next President, possibly as Secretary of State or more likely as Attorney General. Right after these discussions of great hockey players, prudent investing, and Washington turmoil, Melanie reminds Lisa and Brett about the value of community service, especially in the less affluent districts that border Blue Ridge. Discreet and knowledgeable, the Johnsons—Randall and Melanie— manage to defuse the tensions that had threatened to overturn the festive atmosphere. Even Tate, who believes that people should help themselves and not depend upon charitable handouts, collaborates with this steadying influence that Randall and Melanie have brought to the table. He admires their upright presentation of themselves and their assurance. He respects them. He listens to their forthright statements. He manages a smile. He is not aware of the transformative episodes that Randall and Melanie are going to initiate.

Again and again Randall and Melanie tell themselves, as though they are reciting a prayerful refrain, all the miraculous and enchanting deeds they need to accomplish if they are to save these four, conflicted souls. They want to help Brett to change his life for the better by turning away from his illicit relationship with Lisa. They want to persuade Lisa to free herself from deception and betrayal. They want to teach Naomi to summon the courage she often suppresses. They want to influence Tate to become a wise and just man. They tell themselves that they will do everything they can to save these persons from their speckled selves. They want them to recharge their dormant souls. They will use enchantments and spells and magic of every kind to help them to *see*—to *see* profoundly and exuberantly as if for the first time—the heft and substance and potency and beauty of being completely alive in the tremendous world. They will teach them to embrace the Spirit-driven Earth and, by so embracing the thrill of living with new and prodigious awareness, to become authentic and Spirit-fused souls.

So Randall and Melanie tell themselves, in the privacies of their minds reciting the sacred pledge that they have made not only to themselves, but also to Robert Steerforth and especially and predominantly to the First Spirit.

But way back in the hidden corners of their awareness—way, way back within a darkness that even they cannot always fathom—a thought lives, furtive and dangerous. If they cannot teach these fallible individuals how to recover their lost virtues and, by so recovering, become newborn souls, if they cannot show arrogant Brett, devious Lisa, repressed Naomi, and bitter Tate how to rescue themselves, if in the crucial days that will determine their destinies these four people resist the lessons set forth by enchantments and miracles, the First Spirit will condemn them—Tate and Lisa and Naomi and Brett—to eternal disappearance. There is a fifth person that they need to rescue. His name is Jake Boldwood, and his conflicted past is linked to that of Lisa. Jake is not here tonight. He will come back to Lisa's life in the swift-moving days that are imminent and inevitable.

Now, in this very instant—as though their arrival were sudden and unanticipated—Hayden Ericson and his wife Kayla appear. The *maître d'*, silver-haired and rangy, has guided them with meticulous proficiency through the glamorous expanse of the music-filled dining room with its profusion of elegant tables and prestigious couples to this ample, round table that appears to be waiting for them not far from the floor-to-ceiling window. The gold-hued velvet drapes are still drawn so that the light of the moon that gleams upon the green lawn keeps fanning out to the even more expansive greenery of a golf course. Moonlight continues to caress the more private area where they will be seated with the six persons who have been waiting for them. That same light, magic-seeming because of its night-time dazzle, goes on touching the gold tablecloth with its delicately woven jacquard poinsettia design and the yellow, red, and white roses that are tucked into a crystal vase with ivy and ferns. The light also touches the Royal Copenhagen blue-fluted porcelain dinner plates, cups, and saucers, as well as the Waterford crystal goblets and the sterling silver knives, forks, and spoons that are decorated with crowns of curling leaves, center rosettes with tapering tendrils, and scrolls and flutes along the violin-shaped handles.

The scene seems to be a replay of Tate and Lisa's arrival with Naomi and Brett. Yet something special enhances this new arriving—something beneficent and transcendental. In this flash of an instant, light—effulgent and shimmering— radiates from the tall, muscular body of Hayden and from the willowy body of Kayla. This wondrous light glistens and shimmers only for a moment, enhancing though not overtaking their humanness. Nevertheless, this light belongs to them, not to the moon. They have earned its otherworldly glow. They have been doing all the right things with their lives. Randall and Melanie know them well, even though they have met them only a few times.

When they were in the First Heaven, Captain Johnson and his Melanie saw Hayden's and Kayla's lives unfolding upon a celestial wall. They saw their past, and they saw their present. But the First Spirit did not permit them to see their future. Nevertheless, they recognized the merit of these morally centered human beings.

"They are ideal and nearly infallible," the First Spirit explained. "I have tested them in rigorous ways, and they have never failed themselves or the individuals who have been a part of their lives. They are like you, Randall and Melanie. They are nearly perfect."

"It will be a joy to meet them," Melanie said.

"Keep in mind," the First Spirit counseled them, "that Kayla and Hayden are not the reasons that I am sending you back to Earth. Their lives are exemplary. They do not require your help. But Tate and Lisa need your help, though they may never admit it. Naomi, Brett, and Jake also need your help. They need you to save them from a bad end."

"We promise to help them, if we can."

"That you must do," the First Spirit answered her. "It is imperative that you help them."

Randall wanted to know more.

"What can we do to help them?"

"You must make them understand the wrongness of their ways. You must do everything you can to persuade them to follow the path of goodness. You must give them the opportunity to redeem themselves."

Randall asked one more question.

"What will happen if they do not listen to us? What is in store for them if they do not change their ways?"

"Eternal disappearance," the First Spirit said. "That is the fate of all wrongdoers who refuse to redeem themselves."

Melanie's concern for Tate Calhern and his family and for Brett Robinson prods her to ask other questions.

"What about Naomi? What about her relationship to her father, the man who pretends to love her? How can we persuade Lisa to turn away from her adulterous relationship with Brett?"

"You and Randall must find a way to change things for the better. You must try to rescue them. You must try to keep them from doing harm to themselves and to one another. Spells and enchantments may assist you. Robert Steerforth will keep advising you. But, in all the important ways, you will be on your own. You have to be ready to meet the challenge."

"And the danger?" Randall asked.

"That depends on you," the First Spirit said. "Your own courage will be tested."

The memory of that conference with the First Spirit has never left Randall and Melanie, though it occurred a year ago. Nor have they forgotten their most recent meeting with Robert Steerforth in Sojourn. They understand their assignment. They know their obligations. Already, they are working to bring into the lives of the individuals whom they have met or will be meeting some clarifying behavior, some profound meaning, and some necessary transformations. The sight of Hayden and Kayla, suffused with a halcyon glow, has engendered these memories of their meetings with the First Spirit and with Robert Steerforth. That same sight has brought forth their awareness of Hayden's and Kayla's virtuous lives and the imminent peril confronting Tate and Lisa, as well as Brett, Naomi, and Jake.

With these thoughts in mind, Melanie and Randall take hold of the scene that is now unfolding its joys and its complications. In this very instant, right after Naomi and Brett and Lisa and Tate have greeted the newcomers to the table, Tate draws Hayden and Kayla into the quickened conversation.

So this telling hour begins.

Tate, mean-spirited and willful, pushes it forward. After drinking a double scotch or two, he accommodates with savage ease his need to hurt other people. The sight of Hayden paired with a Black wife continues to rankle him. Hayden is a privileged white man, the son of an eminent and wealthy architect. It does not matter that Kayla's father,

Dr. Edward Lancaster, is an esteemed oncologist and that her mother, Janelle, is an equally respected pediatrician. They are Black, and they have usurped financial and social powers that should belong exclusively to the whites.

Spurred forward by his hatred of Blacks and his disdain of interracial marriages, Tate spews out bitter and hate-filled remarks.

"Here is Hayden," he announces. "He is Kayla's always extraordinary and sometimes brilliant husband. They make their living as lawyers, but they might as well call themselves old-fashioned idealists. When you get to know them, you will find that they are defenders of the indigent, the oppressed, and every other specimen of the downtrodden. They rescue orphans, foster children, juvenile delinquents, victimized widows, and alcoholic wrecks. But they can't seem to rescue themselves from their noble intentions."

"I hope that we never do," Hayden says, speaking for Kayla as well as for himself. "Rescuing people is our reason for being here. It's what we do. It makes us who we are."

He and Kayla smile affectionately as he speaks to Naomi's father. His deep, confident voice carries no anger because this wretched man—this lonely and bitter man who has become a prisoner of his grief at the loss of his first and forever beloved wife, this hardhearted attorney whose damaged soul compels him to hate and to hurt so many people—has anchored his ingrained arrogance to his displeasure with Naomi, the daughter whom he has deprived of fatherly acceptance. Hayden—this different kind of man, this unyielding idealist—and Kayla, who matches his courage and uprightness, bear no ill will toward this bitter man. Nor do they feel contempt for his moral failings. They pity him. They perceive that, beneath his abrasive exterior, Tate Calhern is an unhappy and hollow man.

Not only morally, but also physically, Hayden is a giant of a man. He stands at six foot, five inches. His well-honed muscularity and assured gait intensify his self-possession. He has an oblong face with rounded corners. His broad forehead is similar in size to his cheekbones and his jawline. His black-haired crew cut, blue eyes, straight-edged nose, and gleaming smile suggest an affable personality that has made wise negotiations with his meticulous, serious-minded character. On this special evening, when he is joining his and Kayla's friends, he is wearing a classic, tailored suit. The iridescent color effect of its navy blue enhances the herringbone pattern. The jacket is tapered through the chest and has slightly pronounced shoulders to highlight his physique. An azure blue shirt and a silk tie with navy, red, and gray diagonal stripes intensify the quality and coherence of his appearance. With Hayden, what you see is what you get. The formality of his appearance is nicely undercut by an unpretentious manner and a good-natured disposition.

This brief exchange between Hayden and Tate, burdened as it is with Tate's jaundiced words and blatant resentment, does not deter Lisa from directing the group's attention to Hayden's wife, Kayla. She is a light-skinned Black and a great beauty. Her diamond-shaped face with its narrow forehead and jawline and its wide cheekbones grants her extraordinary loveliness. She stands at five foot, nine inches, and her body is as supple as it is slim. Tonight, she looks especially radiant in a knee-length, polyester beige cocktail dress that has a bateau neckline, half sleeves, and an A-line silhouette. Her beige-and-black leather-and-satin-ribbon pumps, with their three-inch stiletto heels and slip-on style, suggest a subdued glamour even as they accentuate her height. She wears no jewelry except her marriage ring, but her brown eyes gleam with the sheer joy of being here with her husband and with the intriguing personalities who represent Naomi's family and the friends of her family.

"What a pleasure to be here!" she exclaims. "We've met only a few times, yet each time is more pleasant than ever before. Even before I met you, Hayden told me so many wonderful things about all of you. Yet I want to know so much more. I want us to become close friends."

"Well, there is no better time than right now," Lisa says, relieved that Kayla has drawn Tate's attention away from the ardency of Brett's glances at her and away as well—if only for this fleeting moment—from his antipathy toward Kayla because she is Black and not a white girl from exclusive Blue Ridge circles. "Let's all become close friends. Let's make this evening a time for coming to know more about each other."

Randall has something to say, though only Melanie understands the significance of his words.

"Getting to know more about one another tonight is inevitable," he says. "I have a feeling that we will remember this night for a long time."

"Of course we will," Naomi agrees. "That's why we are here. We are celebrating each other. That's the easiest way to become better friends."

"Let's begin by dancing," Melanie says. "Other guests are doing so. Let's be merry. Let's have a good time."

"I can have a good time without dancing," Tate says, addressing Lisa more than the group while he makes a grudging concession. "However, if you feel like dancing, let's do it."

Now they move into the southeast area of the capacious room, with its polished dance floor and a gifted orchestra. A glamorous brunette is singing ballads that tell of love that promises or inspires or betrays. She is singing of romantic love that is fulfilled or unrequited as well as carnal or soulful or earthbound or eternal. Fervent lyrics and sumptuous melodies are filling the room. Couples young and older are allowing themselves to be caught up inside the happy or wistful or melancholic messages. Songs familiar or sensual or world-weary or nostalgic are filling the room and persuading the dancers to connect to the music and the lyrics and, through their swaying motions, to enter the stories within the ballads. Still the glamorous brunette goes on singing of new loves and lost loves. Still the orchestra sends its melodious riffs across the wide expanse of the sumptuous room. Some dancing couples move together and toward each other, their choreographic gestures intensifying their union. Other couples move away from each other, as though they are resisting the sweep and swirl of profound attachment. Then, in the next instant, as if they have come to terms with their ambivalence, they move toward one another.

The singer draws these dancing couples to ballads that tell about the truth of love and about its ambiguities. Over and over, whether lamenting her fate or singing out her joy, she presents herself as a woman who has known the bliss and the sorrow of love. The lyrics reveal her biography: "Secret Love," "What I Did for Love," "All I Ask of You," "Through the Eyes of Love," "Yesterdays," "Don't Cry Out Loud," and "Come in from the Rain."

The singer's stories are in her songs.

The dancing couples carry their stories within themselves.

Brett keeps dancing with Naomi, though he yearns to hold Lisa in his arms. His brisk movements and his agreeable smile lend conviction to his impersonation of an honest lover. For her part, Naomi is willing—at least for tonight—to accept his gestures as authentic. Hayden and Kayla are dancing together and bringing sparks of happiness to their synchronous rhythms. There is no hesitation as their bodies sway to and fro. There is no ambivalence in their timing or in the touch of their hands or in the glow of their eyes. Tate holds Lisa close to his body as he sways and dips to the soaring energies and pulsating motions of a samba, a foxtrot, and a waltz. He holds her not as though she were the love of his life. He holds her as a possession that he claimed when he married her. On that day, he offered her the prestige of his name and the fortune that he had built. But he could not offer her passion or love of any kind. His capacity for loving had begun to dry up when his first wife died. That capacity has burned its way to its socket.

When they return to their table, seven of these eight persons allow their senses to soar upon new waves of exhilaration. Only Tate holds back. Only he, burdened by his adamant hatreds and his sadistic tyrannies, views the merry scene with envious detachment, as though he is an outsider looking in a window at a scene in which he has earned no valid place. Because he manages a makeshift smile, nobody notices his bitterness or his unease. Everyone else is raising glasses or tumblers and toasting each other. Stem glasses sparkle with Champagne. Tumblers of scotch beam with caramel color. Everyone except Tate begins singing the friendly Rodgers and Hammerstein tune "It's a Grand Night for Singing." They talk of future vacations in the Bahamas, on the French Riviera, and along South Island in New Zealand. Everyone, even Tate, mentions the thrill of flying in the Gulfstream G550, a high-powered business jet with a spacious cabin that accommodates eighteen passengers. The Gulfstream G550 has the thrusting power of two Rolls-Royce engines that can fly seven thousand nautical miles nonstop. The group talks of many other things, including good wines, good books, and good iPhones. Quickened words excite the atmosphere. Astute remarks and casual comments intensify the festive proceedings.

Dinner has the aura of a banquet. Young, cadet-like waiters serve the delicious meal. It includes a red-and-green cabbage salad arranged around a mound of apples and heavy cream; *filets mignons* with artichoke bottoms and *béarnaise* sauce with its spicy mixture of shallots, white wine, pepper, and tarragon; *Pont Neuf* potatoes; and a

Basque cake filled with almond pastry cream. The men eat heartily, but the women—enthralled by the glamour of the evening—merely nibble at their food.

Right after dinner, Tate joins corporate executives, investment brokers, and an attorney specializing in divorce cases in the billiards room that is located on the third floor of this fashionable country club. There, he activates his competitive nature in a well-calibrated game of eight ball. Tonight, the game is a men-only sport that involves five players on each of the two teams. Like Tate, most of the players are heavy drinkers who handle their liquor well. All of them are past forty. All of them are married. All of them except Tate are sharing three mistresses—a nightclub hostess, a fashion model, and a legal secretary—that they have set up in Manhattan apartments. Tate's unwillingness to join his friends in their promiscuous escapades has nothing to do with moral integrity or ingrained ethical codes. It has everything to do with his hatred of loose women and his haunted regard of his first wife as an emblem of propriety and every other virtue.

At this same time, Hayden and Kayla saunter into the lush, enchanted garden that surrounds the country club. Path lights, floodlights, and outdoor wall lights illuminate and intensify the beauty of blue and pink hydrangeas; purple, pink, and yellow lilacs; red and white roses; red, white, and pink rhododendrons; and velvet red and soft rose camellias. The main garden path leads them to a moonlit lake and to the distant sight of a sailboat making its way through the breeze-tossed chill of the evening. As they saunter toward the lake, Hayden and Kayla are clasping each other's hand. They move in unison. They move in silence. The solacing touch of fingers upon fingers, the immense pleasure they find in walking together beneath a star-filled sky, the tremendous joy of being here as a married couple, *right here* near the marble perfection of a water fountain, the pristine whiteness of lawn chairs, the undulating greenness of the always-expanding lawn, and the red brick steps that hurry them down to the waiting jetty and the adjacent boathouse—all these emblems of the night fuse with their keen-minded awareness of the gifts that the night has granted them and of the gift that each of them is to the other.

Meanwhile, on the second-floor terrace of this glamorous country club, Brett is standing alone, peering in brooding silence at the immensity of the night sky and perceiving that the light of the moon with sinuous tentacles disguises the ominous darkness. White, puffy clouds appear to float, just for an instant, and with wily aptitudes cover the radiance of a few stars. Other stars work with the moon to reveal for his seeing the sailboat on the lake that Hayden and Kayla are noticing in this same moment. He notices them and feels for an instant the envy and the melancholy that have lately influenced his moods. He envies them their apparently uncomplicated happiness. He feels the sorrow of dissatisfaction with his too-complicated life. Nearer than the moon and the stars or the lake or the sailboat or Hayden and Kayla, below and beyond the second-story terrace where he is standing, that light also reveals the gurgling marble fountain, the quickening progression of the red brick steps, and the expansive sweep of the undulating lawn.

Brett takes a drag on his cigarette. Though he has been drinking heavily, he has his wits about him. He remains in full control of his senses. He has hurried away from the dinner dance, away from the exhilarating music, the arrogant chatter, and the careless laughter. He needs to be alone. He needs to breathe fresh air. He needs to find his proper bearings. He needs to chart the hard-edged realism that has always guided him through storm-threatening journeys. That a storm is on its way, his gut instinct has warned him. His contrived exploitation of the father-son relationship that Tate has devised for them has nearly run its course. He will have to marry a girl that he does not love if he is to prevail in his combat against the Fates, in his collaboration with Blind Chance, and in his negotiations with ambition, avarice, and duplicity.

His obsession for Lisa is a dangerous liability. His sexual need of her, the astonishing influence of her discreet sensuality upon his desire, puzzles and angers him. He has never before felt so profound a need with any of the other women who have slept with him. Nor has he ever before entangled himself with a married woman. But entangled he most certainly is. That is the raw truth of things, without the honesty or honor that usually attends truth. Being ensnared by his feelings for a woman keeps surprising him. The poets of old who wrote about becoming prisoners of love often romanticized their experiences. They reveled in the velocity of their passion. They found joy in their hearts' anguish. They felt exalted by the imprisoning effects of their love. Perhaps they told the truth about their experiences. Perhaps they lied. What does it matter? Brett knows only what he feels. There is nothing mystical in his love for Lisa. His love for her is carnal, a corporeal and earthbound sensation. It is a love of every inch of her body, every pore within her skin. It is a craving to be deep inside her, stroking her faster and faster and reveling in their mutual ecstasy.

As though his thoughts of her have drawn her to this terrace, Lisa suddenly appears to him. She is standing on the threshold of the terrace, warily looking about her and debating whether she should go or stay. She has not yet completely disengaged herself from the festive dinner dance behind her. Nor has she stepped forward to join him in the exhilarated privacy of standing with him, together and apart from all the other guests who have come to celebrate the sheer joy of being alive, ambitious, and privileged. Yet quite suddenly and with no expectation on his part that she would join him, Lisa is standing on the threshold of this terrace, a poised tension overtaking her while she looks back at the dining room and forward to face him directly. His eyes do not deceive him. It is she, Lisa Caulfield Calhern—the love of his life, the self-possessed career woman who keeps enchanting him, the usually discreet mistress who has abandoned the party so that she can be with him. It is *that* extraordinary Lisa who so suddenly and marvelously has arrived to join him. He watches her watching him. He guesses at what she must see. She is observing his pensive face and his tall, rugged physique, right here beneath the cloud-covered stars and the mysterious, moonlit darkness of the sky. She looks lovely and desirable. She also looks apprehensive.

Now she steps forward. Now she hurries to the assured virility that is he, himself, Brett Robinson—the ambitious young man who is climbing up and up to the top even if it means scheming his way there. She caresses his right shoulder and lightly touches his lips with her lips. Her blue eyes glow with desire, but that same desire cannot conceal the traceries of fear in her eyes and the tremulousness of her voice.

"You can't stay here," she says, while imploring him with a loving glance and with the soft touch of her hand upon his cheek. "Everyone will notice that you have gone missing. Naomi will notice, too, and so will Tate."

"I know. I know," he answers her. "But I need this fresh air. I need to breathe as though I am a free man. I need to retreat even for a few minutes. I need to rest before I go back to my battle."

Lisa moves nearer and he, understanding her need, encloses her inside his embrace. He presses his lips upon her lips, accepting the thrill that rushes through his body, as essential to him now as the blood that flows though his veins. Her body trembles because of the pleasure of his kiss. After this exquisite moment of togetherness, after this marriage of desire and lips, right after the rapture of this prolonged kiss, he breaks away and caresses her now not with hands or a kiss but with a glance, yearning and erotic.

She offers him an equivalent glance, her eyes revealing *her* yearning and *her* desire. But only for a moment longer does she permit desire to overtake her reason for having hurried here, within the surround of the white marble columns and flooring, the wall-pack lighting, the azure blue chairs and umbrella tables made of moisture-resistant solid mahogany and solid eucalyptus wood, and magical, spellbound potted planters profuse with scarlet red and lavender New Guinea impatiens, blue and white lobelia, dark pink hibiscus, and the cascading whiteness of sweet alyssum. Only for this moment does she allow her glance to linger upon his handsome face. Then, satisfied that she has calmed him, she says all the words that need to be spoken.

"We can have everything we want," she tells him. "Everything. But you have to follow our plan."

"I want you," he says. "I want everything else, too. I wish there were an easier way to get it."

"We'll have all of it," she says, her soft words sinuous and tempting. "Some day. That's a promise."

Once more the sight of her rouses his desire. He takes hold of her again and kisses her even more passionately. He fondles her breast and is about to place his big hand beneath her dress when, suddenly and with an abruptness that startles him, she pushes him away. Never before had she resisted the touch of his hand beneath her dress and inside her lingerie. Always, his touch had thrilled her and brought her to the pitch of ecstasy.

He studies her face and instantly he understands that someone is watching them. He turns to observe this watcher. He sees. He comprehends. He knows. Naomi is the watcher. How long she has been watching them, he does not yet know.

Standing on the threshold to the terrace, she is very still. For the first time this evening, he notices what every other guest has observed with admiration. She brings beauty and elegance to a sleeveless black A-line evening dress that has a crew neck and blue, green, and gold floral embellishments. Her cropped fringe titian hair, her oval face, her teal blue eyes and upturned nose, and her bee-stung lips make her beauty distinctive and appealing. Her patrician features, with their light-skinned delicacy, enhance her genteel manner. She is every privileged man's idea of the qualities that a fiancée from the upper class should possess. Yet no flame burns within his groin as he observes her. No breathlessness seizes him. Perhaps, a hint of pity and a pang of conscience influence his response to her suddenly being there, on the threshold of the terrace. But the pity and the self-recrimination quickly die away. Neither his brain, nor his soul gives lasting life to them. Instead, a wily and self-protective reaction to Naomi's being so suddenly there pushes him forward.

"Welcome!" he says, throwing out a greeting that carries well-calibrated portions of ardor and appreciation. "You are the delightful girl of the moment. You are the one-and-only girl that has made this night possible."

To this warmhearted greeting, Naomi says nothing. She does not move. Instead, she sends Lisa and him a beaming smile. She gives them her apparent assent. But she gives no sign that she is going to move forward to explore the privacy of being there with them.

It is Lisa who moves forward, her right arm and her bejeweled fingers stretched out as though she intends to take hold of Naomi's hand with caring, step-motherly poise and bring her into the center of the terrace.

"Brett has been telling me about all of the exciting adventures that are in store for the two of you. You really are the girl of the moment. In fact, you are going to be the girl of the year."

Naomi laughs a joyful laugh. Her eyes gleam with anticipation. She throws her head back and lifts her hands in a gesture of exhilaration. But no words accompany her glee. No remark with jubilant subtexts hurries out of her smiling mouth. She laughs without offering any words. Then quite suddenly, and with altogether unexpected and mysterious and fearful implications, she gradually disappears, as though her body were slowly evaporating or melting away. She vanishes, swallowed by a flash like lightning.

Now, just as suddenly and with a calm that seems extraordinary and even beatific, Randall and Melanie are standing on the threshold. It is as if they have replaced Naomi, displaced her, or with a magical wave of their hands sent her into some faraway realm that remains invisible to ordinary seeing. Only for a split second do Brett and Lisa permit themselves to think so. No sooner does Naomi's vanishing astonish them, no sooner does her disappearance leave them with the tension of surprise and with a tough-minded resolve to weather this unexpected incident—this temporary illusion, this will-o'-the-wisp sighting, this apparition upon their senses—no sooner has her mysterious leave-taking lived through its surprise and its enchantment than they hasten to greet Randall Johnson and his sweet-natured Melanie.

"It's you!" Lisa exclaims. "It's both of you. How wonderful to see you here! Come join us."

Randall notices their unease, almost completely concealed beneath the artifice of Lisa's greeting and Brett's casual-seeming self-possession.

"We've surprised you," he says, his words probing beneath their apparent equanimity. "Perhaps you were expecting someone else."

Neither Brett nor Lisa answers him at once. With the stillness of polite reflectiveness, they consider his remark without forfeiting their air of self-possession. After that, Lisa tells them what they want to know.

"For a moment, we thought we saw Naomi," she says. "The glow of the moon makes everything and everyone seem mysterious tonight, and wonderful."

"So it does," Randall agrees. "The full moon often does that. It has a talent for creating mystery."

Melanie has something to say after she and Randall accompany Lisa and Brett to the center of the terrace and look up at the gold disc that is the moon—the cynosure of night more splendid than the cluster of clouds surrounding it and the constellation of stars that serve its splendor.

"There is a legend that tells us the full moon creates all sorts of magic," Melanie tells them. "It sends us signs and portents. It sends us friends and sometimes adversaries who cast spells and enchantments upon us. Through them, through the spells and enchantments, the full moon shows us a better way to perceive the life that is unfolding around us."

Cynical in all ways of his knowing, Brett resists this legend about the powers of the full moon and its emissaries.

"Do you really believe that? Do you actually believe that spells and enchantments can influence our destiny?"

Now Randall speaks for Melanie as well as for himself.

"We do," he says.

"I wish that I could believe," Lisa says. "But experience has made me too realistic. I can never imagine that any enchantment could alter the person who I am or change the course of my life."

"With or without a full moon," Brett says, "I'll always make my way without any magic frills and without any talk of magic or enchantment."

Randall has more to say.

"If we didn't believe in enchantment, what would happen to possibility? What would happen to faith?"

Music is floating its way into the terrace. The orchestra has begun a new set. The glamorous singer is offering a new ballad about love unexpectedly found and just as unexpectedly squandered.

"It's time to go back," Lisa says, relieved that she and Brett can spring free of this talk about spells and enchantment. "The party will be missing all of us."

"So it will," Randall says. "So it will."

As they take their leave of the terrace, Brett asks Randall another question.

"You've been teasing us, haven't you? You don't really believe in enchantments."

Randall answers him directly.

"I've already told you that Melanie and I absolutely believe in the powers of enchantment. Our experiences have taught us to believe."

Brett smiles. He remains unconvinced. He is beginning to believe that Randall has had one drink too many and that Melanie has found his teasing a witty exercise.

The four of them pass through the threshold of the terrace without speaking any other words. Brett, politic and cautious once again, plans to search for Naomi. Lisa, equally cautious and just as duplicitous, intends to join Tate. This encounter with Randall and Melanie has left them uneasy and even puzzled. Did Randall and Melanie see Naomi arriving on the threshold of the terrace? Did they pretend that they had not seen her, because they rightly interpreted her flight from the scene and from the intimacy of her fiancé and her stepmother alone together on the terrace?

Brett and Lisa wonder.

Before they go in search of Naomi and Tate, they turn to accord Randall and Melanie a courteous nod and a promise to catch up with them later. But before they can find the lighthearted words that will serve as a capstone to their meeting on the terrace, surprise and astonishment overtake them once again. Randall's eyes and Melanie's eyes are glowing in some supernatural way. Light radiates from their bodies, efflorescent and magical. They look otherworldly. They glow like Spirits from some faraway Heaven or planet. Rendered speechless, Brett and Lisa cannot move. Something, someone or some power, has held them to their places. They can merely stare at this suddenly strange couple.

Lisa is mystified.

Brett is angry.

Something about Randall and Melanie is more than strange. Something is amiss.

Ambivalence replaces Brett's and Lisa's acceptance of them. Are Randall and Melanie well-trained spies from an adversarial country who have come here to foment disturbance? Are they two-of-a-kind intellectuals who enjoy assuming the roles of pranksters? Has Tate sent them as a warning about the steps he could take if they—Brett and Lisa—continue sleeping with each other?

These thoughts assail both Lisa and Brett and at the same time. Tough-minded and defensive nevertheless, they reach out to touch inside and beyond the radiance that has consumed both Randall and Melanie. They want to stop this charade. They want to discover the source behind this trickery. They want to expose the magic as mere fakery.

But as soon as they reach out to scatter the radiance and to dispel what they regard as trickery, Randall and Melanie suddenly emerge from the radiance and, just as quickly, disappear.

For an instant, Brett and Lisa are left not only mystified, but also despairing. These two strange beings, this exemplary lawyer who calls himself Randall Johnson and this gifted psychiatrist who is known as Melanie Dickinson Johnson, know everything there is to know about Lisa's dishonorable marriage and Brett's shameful betrothal to Naomi. Lisa regrets her carelessness in meeting Brett on the terrace, though the sensuality of that meeting still fires her wellbeing. Brett refuses to regret anything. What's done is done. He is prepared to lie, to cheat, and to confuse any adversary on his trail. Lying and cheating are his stock in trade. He tells himself that he will bear up. He will soldier through.

Now, something extraordinary happens. As soon as they return to Tate and Naomi, they forget everything that happened on the terrace. Randall has cast a spell of forgetfulness upon Brett and Lisa. Melanie has cast the same kind of spell upon Naomi. These enchantments work their powers in other ways. Although Brett, Lisa, and Naomi forget what happened on the terrace, they do not completely forget. In a secluded corner of their conscience, there lives a new awareness of their ambivalent natures. Brett's conscience holds the dark reality of his excessive ambition, his dishonest relationship with Naomi, and his self-centered use of Tate's fatherly regard of him. Lisa's conscience, wily and alert, will conceal for a brief while her betrayal of her marriage vows and her treachery against her stepdaughter. Naomi's conscience will one day reveal her lack of courage in her relationship with her father and the wrongness of regarding Brett as godlike and perfect.

"Time will deal with them soon enough," Randall says as he suddenly and with the most natural self-possession appears with Melanie on the dance floor. They give themselves completely to the rhythms of the waltz. Other couples are dancing around them. They sight Brett, affectionate and courtly, dancing with Naomi. They see Lisa, demure and attentive, dancing with Tate. They glance at Hayden, tall as a church steeple, dancing with lovely Kayla. Once again, the music of the orchestra floats across the spacious room. Once again and with the same fervent intensity, the dark-haired, glamorous singer is offering a dramatic rendition of a ballad that tells of the ecstasy of loving and that warns of its ambivalence.

CHAPTER FOUR
PROMISES

"This time, I'll really court Naomi," Brett promises himself upon awakening during a Saturday morning one week after the dinner dance. "I'll woo her. I'll do everything to convince her that she is the only woman that I could ever love."

He does not remember that Naomi may have witnessed him kissing Lisa on the country club terrace. Enchantment has erased that moment from his memory. But some other influence is working its subtleties upon his conscience. Some tincture of regret is activating newborn energies within his awareness. He has not been treating Naomi with even a modicum of fairness. His wily disposition has undermined an authentic relationship with her. His ingrained narcissism has often subverted her efforts toward genuine intimacy. Yet his deviousness, his casual self-assurance, and his talent for fabrication have thus far protected him. He has used these skills well. He has employed them with caution and with the guarded discipline that has ably served him. But awakening to this sun-filled morning, when the recollection of his relationship with Naomi is working in strange and surprising ways as a fuse to recrimination and guilt, he promises himself that he will chart a different course. He will navigate a new and creditable voyage to Naomi's heart. He will, with legitimate and earnest feelings, claim a place for himself inside her soul.

This sea change, this rip current within his Spirit nature, mystifies him. Yet he is eager to make this new beginning. Though the swell and heave and storm-driven fury of the voyage are occurring within the mind and heart and soul of his most private self, that same voyage will bring him to Naomi in a new way. If, as he believes, he is the captain of his destiny, Naomi will regard him as the ideal man in whom she has always believed, even when he was offering her mere flashes of that ideal.

All these thoughts reinforce his determination to create an honest relationship with Naomi. Why, when he had so eagerly involved himself with the intricacies of his secret affair with Lisa, he should consent to this sea change, this new and sudden re-charting of his voyage to Naomi, he cannot explain even to the most private self he closes to any eyes except his own. On this third Saturday morning in April, as he showers and shaves inside the sleek modernity of his townhouse in Blue Ridge, he has no need for profound inquiry into his motives or even for haphazard guesswork. He is determined to make amends for his indifferent treatment of Naomi. That is the action he must take. That, for the present moment at least, is all he needs to understand.

Randall and Melanie have cast a spell upon him. They have limited the powers inside its enchantment. They have not preempted the power of Brett's fallible will. They have merely constrained its waywardness. They are giving Brett a chance to redeem himself. At the same time, and with precise awareness of the complications that will attend his illicit relationship with Lisa, they have altered his perception of her and of himself with her. The spell will last for only a day. Yet the happenings within that day will influence what happens later. Randall and Melanie have set loose storm-fed repercussions. With their keen-eyed comprehension of cause and effect, of deed and consequence, they have created what they deem to be an appropriate scenario for the next meeting between Brett and Naomi.

The meeting will take place not on the sea. This particular voyage to Naomi, this sea change within himself, involves Brett when he is ostensibly alone and ostensibly the only emphasis upon the workings of his soul. But Randall and Melanie have imposed their own subtle emphases upon his soul. Spellbound, Brett goes forward to make an honest claim for the love of Naomi. The sea change that is influencing his soul voyage brings him now to his fiancée. They meet on land. They meet in springtime, the season of rebirth and restoration.

On this bright spring day that his fate allows him to experience as though it were the beginning of a new possibility, he and Naomi are riding their favorite roan-colored Arabian bays along the horse trail that stretches across the wide expanse of Ben Wilder's horse farm seven or eight miles from the Calherns' home and Brett's townhouse. The equestrian section of the Wilders' property covers only fifty acres of this eight-hundred-acre farmland that fans out to suddenly spellbound and magical green pastures where sheep and cows graze, to equally magical and flourishing fields of corn, rye, and potatoes, to ample and enchanted orchards of apple trees, and to greenhouses where mineral nutrient solutions in a water solvent feed rows upon rows of lettuce and tomatoes.

Today, Brett and Naomi do not see Mr. Wilder, who is busy with his wife and their three sons connecting irrigation lines in one of the greenhouses. He is an impressive man. Tall and muscular, he is not only a dedicated horse breeder. He is also a meticulous farmer. His shock of white hair and his slightly weathered, sculpted face make him appear older than his forty-eight years. Whenever they meet him, his level gaze and gravelly voice tell Brett and Naomi right away that Mr. Wilder has taken an accurate measure of the world and is still on friendly terms with it, despite its various depredations and malpractices. He is a morally centered man, committed to the creation of a more just and equitable Blue Ridge. With a team of socially conscious men and women, he has initiated and advanced community programs that promote racial justice, women's empowerment, fair housing, and violence prevention in homes and schools. Brett, especially, will miss seeing him today. He is an adult whom he trusts. Ben Wilder's keen-minded awareness of being part of an interrelated community of others, his ethical behavior, and his steadfast resilience radiate ingrained strength and the staunch power that has made him a survivor.

At the age of twenty-seven, Brett has found that kind of strength within his imperfect character. But he needs to find valid ways to use it. Lately and more frequently, he has been stumbling on to an errant path. Sometimes, he hurries toward it, willful and bitter. The bitterness derives in large measure, paradoxically, from his father's having died a hero's death as a Navy SEAL commando in Iraq. That valiant death left his mother without financial security and left him, an eight-year-old boy, to face a future without the loving bond that guides a son on his journey into manhood. Always an activist on his own behalf, he—Brett Robinson, the only son of a genuine patriot—overcame every obstacle that the Fates placed on his path. From an early age, he learned the wisdom of not pitying himself. He drove himself with an unsentimental and wily disposition. Pushed forward with merit scholarships and generous gifts from his grandfathers, he attended prestigious schools. He became an honor graduate at The Choate School in Connecticut and in the law program at the University of Pennsylvania. He also became an excellent boxer, a swift hockey wingman, an adept horseman, and a reliable pilot. He drew the respect of Wall Street men and circuit court judges who counted. He also won the trust of Tate Calhern, who regarded him as a son, and he quickly secured a place in that cynical man's law firm.

Now, on this warm, enchanted April morning when even the soft breezes collaborate with his wakened need of Naomi's love, he drives himself forward with new intensity and with a quickened intention of winning all of the love of which Naomi is capable.

One of the groomsmen, a wiry, twenty-year-old man named Antonio Lamas, who is good looking and has brown eyes, dark hair, and light brown skin, greets Brett and Naomi courteously and brings from the stables the Arabian bays that they are going to ride. These Arabian horses impress with their bay coloring; broad forehead; concave profile; large eyes and nostrils; graceful, curving neck; and apparently floating gait. On each horse, Antonio has already placed the seat of a Crosby close-contact saddle. Their forward-cut flaps allow riders to keep their legs close to the saddle, while making more secure their positions over the horse's center of balance. Brett and Naomi put hard hats on their heads and gloves over their hands, mount their horses, and are ready to ride.

For an hour or so, they will ride their bays across the April flare of the land that is caught inside the enchantment that also holds them—love-quickened Brett and his equally romantic Naomi—in its spell. Before they begin, it is clear at once to the groomsman and to four other riders who are observing the way that they sit on a horse, hold the reins, and signal him to move forward that Brett and Naomi are accomplished riders. When they enter the trail, they ride together for twenty minutes. Both have often visited this place before, though rarely together. To Brett, so much of its beauty seems familiar and yet strangely new. *He* feels new. He feels different. Once again, he hears the murmuring chant of the wind, and he sees the sunglow splendor of undulating fields of scented grasses and the ascending emphases of Blue Ridge hills.

He is riding side by side with Naomi, observing her ease and confidence as she rides her horse. She has been riding since she was five years old. He notices that she is sitting with the weight of her body in the center of the saddle. She is allowing her hip joints to be open and her legs positioned as close as possible around the horse's sides. At the same time, she is relaxing her arms at the shoulder and elbow so that she can move with the movement of the horse's head. She holds her hands correctly with palms facing each other and thumbs uppermost. Without using her arms, she clasps the reins by wrapping her fingers around them and almost closing her hands to make a fist. It is as though arms and reins belong to the horse, the better to follow its motion.

They have been riding at a leisurely pace while enjoying the late April warmth and the pleasure of being together on a day when they are both free of career obligations. But, after twenty minutes, Naomi wants her ride to be more exciting.

"Brett, I'll race you to the edge of the forest," she exclaims. "That way, we'll make this ride very special."

"All right," he calls out to her, caught up in the free-spirited lift of the moment. "We'll have a race. Let's go!"

Instantly, they ask their horses to go forward into a canter on the left rein. As he does, so does Naomi sit deep and press her left leg on the fine leather band contoured about the belly of the horse to keep the saddle in place. Then, once again they make the same moves. With a squeeze of the right leg back behind the leather band, they ask their Arabian bays more actively to go forward into a canter.

Naomi and her horse shoot ahead of him.

He sees, as a vivid image that will be printed forever upon his mind, how skillfully Naomi collaborates with the kinetic energies of her horse. As he comes cantering behind her, he can see the Arabian bay lengthening out its body and neck and fully extending its legs as his fiancée, this suddenly delightful Naomi, powers over the winding trail. Riding with the seat taken out of the saddle, she tucks her upper body in behind her horse's neck and extends her arms forward as with each stride the horse stretches his neck forward. She fuses the outline of their forms. On this afternoon, she is riding with shorter stirrups to make it easier for her weight to be lifted out of the saddle. Through the reins, she is always keeping contact with the horse's mouth in order to help balance him. Onward and more swiftly she goes galloping.

So, also, does he—proficient rider and lover of all outdoor activities—ride swiftly onward, cantering and galloping toward the forest that is looming up out of the April mist. Teeming apple orchards, colorful brush, and wildflower fields go flashing by him. Adolescent youths harvesting a passing field and a rugged man driving a tractor over a southerly hill leap into his vision and just as quickly scatter away. On and on he gallops, while trees and hills soar, waver aloft, and disappear. Even the radiant sun tilts, and the cloud-laden sky darts, lopes, and vaults. So it seems to his excited senses as he rides swiftly toward the forest, always keeping in his sight his fiancée's fast-moving race toward the edge of the woods.

Minutes later, when Naomi reaches the entrance to the woods, he is caught by surprise. She does not pause there to bring their horse race to a close. She does not push her lower leg forward while still squeezing both legs against her horse's sides. Nor does she brace herself against the stirrup, shorten up her reins, and push the hand that holds one of the reins into the horse's neck. She does not use her other hand to keep a strong hold on the second rein, as the horse starts to slow down. Naomi does none of these things. Instead, she races along the clearing into the woods.

He quickly follows her.

But only for an instant does he see her, riding her roan-colored bay even more swiftly toward the receding distance, before she disappears in the midst of a towering array of white ash trees, with the new, fluttering greenness of their canopies and their late April enchantment of summerlike efflorescence. Nor does he see her when he reaches a circuitous turn in the clearing and passes by ornamental cypresses, their early leaves already tinged with blue-gray and yellow-gold hues. Riding now in search of her, he hears as a faraway sound the strong, slurring notes of a tawny-colored ovenbird. He witnesses as blurring motions or animated flares upon his senses the sprint of a horseshoe hare and the scurrying motion of a red squirrel. He sees a whitetail deer leaping with athletic ease into the shaded, receding space that is the forest path beyond him. Still he rides briskly forward, his keen eyes looking for Naomi or for any sign that she and her Arabian bay have powered through the area.

But there is no sign. There is not the slightest evidence that she has ever arrived here. Even when he dismounts and, while leading his horse into the deep folds of the forest, he searches all the byways and the unexpected intricacies of the trail, he cannot find Naomi. Then cloud darkness comes upon him, covering the sky and the forest and the trail that twists its paths before and behind him. Suddenly, without his understanding why apprehension is so untypically seizing him, he believes that Naomi has vanished within the dark forest maze. Maddened by the thought that Naomi is lost to him forever, he cries out his rage and his sorrow.

"Naomi! Naomi! Where are you? Call out to me. Let me hear you, so that I can find you."

Only the wind answers his cry, though. The forest darkness that hides her inside its murky prison and covers everything else rises, nebulous and daunting, into a towering wall that he can neither fathom nor scale.

Then, once again, he cries out his rage and calls to his fiancée who never answers him.

"Naomi! Naomi!"

He goes on calling out her name. Taut sounds of alarm rip out of his throat, and beads of perspiration trickle down his weary face. His anguish, prevailing and deep-seated, pushes him forward. The enchantment is still bearing its influences upon him. He believes that he loves Naomi with a passionate, undying love. He longs for her presence. The fear that he has lost her forever keeps rising within him. He resists the fear. He summons the courage that has always existed, steadfast and impervious, inside his mind and soul and inside the vigorous body that has always been his trusted ally. Now, because he is rescuing himself from apprehension and misery, he decides to go back to the stables from which Naomi and he began their ride.

Caught inside the tension of his search, he rides with furious abandon. Because he alone is riding, there along the wide, tree-lined trail, he hurries forward to whatever resolution of Naomi's disappearance the fury of his speed will find for him.

For this brief time, he feels otherworldly. He is a man whom Blind Chance or some equally mysterious Spirit-Power has granted a temporary reprieve from the prison he has made of his life. He is racing out of his own body. He is leaving everything behind him—all the punishing hours and days and years that have bruised him, and all the rewarding hours, days, and years that he has exploited to his advantage. He is rushing away from even this hour, leaving in his wake the lost, flickering imagery of Naomi sitting tall in the saddle and leaving also, as a spun velocity upon his seeing, his adulterous coupling with Lisa.

His Arab Bay is galloping even faster now, at full stretch with body and neck lengthening and each leg fully extended as it powers along the winding trail. Behind his horse's neck, he tucks his upper torso precisely and fuses the outline of their forms. He lifts himself out of his saddle, so that he can drop his weight down into his heels and push it further back, allowing his upper body to tuck in behind the horse's neck. Onward and more swiftly he goes galloping, riding with shorter stirrups to make it easier to lift his weight out of the saddle. He keeps his lower legs on the girth and keeps his arms extended forward, as his horse stretches its neck within each stride.

Once again, teeming orchards, colorful brush, and wildflower fields go flashing by him. Women and men are tending a passing field, and a rugged man is driving a tractor over a northerly hill. Now five or six young, married couples canoeing on a distant lake leap into his vision and just as quickly scatter away. Flights of gray-backed gulls overtake fleecy clouds, enter their pockets, and then soar above the chalky cliff that rises out of the lake. He feels himself soaring, too—flying aloft—away from the reach of the self that he is shedding even as he chases the self that is unknown to him. Quite suddenly and without sufficient preparation, he feels enchanted, though he has neither the intuition nor the conviction to explain his feeling.

Only when he sees in the looming distance Naomi's horse grazing with three other horses in a paddock does he push his lower leg forward while still squeezing both legs against his horse's sides. He braces himself against the stirrup, shortens up his reins, and puts the hand that holds one of the reins tight into the horse's neck. He uses his other hand to keep a strong hold on the second rein, as the horse starts to listen and to slow down. The race that he has run for half an hour instantly yields the sight he has sought. Naomi is here, standing twenty feet in front of him and already greeting him with an affectionate smile.

A tremendous wave of relief rushes over him. He breathes more easily.

Now he dismounts and leads his horse into the paddock that is filled with perennial rye grass, creeping red fescue, wild white clover, and smooth-stalked meadow grass and is encircled by a cedar wood fence. He is not altogether surprised to find Naomi waiting by the fence. Only a few days ago, Melanie Johnson mentioned that Naomi was just as fine a rider as Lisa, Kayla, and Hayden. Naomi has outraced him and teased him at the same time by riding back to the paddock while he searched for her in the forest. Naomi's horse, frisky and playful, is cantering around the soft turf of the paddock. Good-humored and relaxed now, he tells himself that Naomi and her Arab Bay share the same personality. At this very moment, Naomi is watching him with a careful gaze that influences her affectionate smile. Though she stands there, with no words to greet him yet alert in her silence, Brett imagines that she has an appreciation of his riding skills. After she closes the fence, she finds words to praise him.

"You look great in the saddle," she says. "You and that Arab Bay are meant for each other. You are soul Spirits."

"That's good to hear," he says. "Your praise is special because you are a terrific rider."

"I always speak the truth when I praise my friends."

"Am I only your friend?"

"You are especially my friend. You are most importantly my friend. You couldn't be my fiancé with any credibility unless you were first of all my friend."

"I'm happy to be your friend." Brett tells her. "I'm even happier to be more than a friend."

Now she teases him once again. Yet there is a serious subtext inside her question.

"Do you think that you will be happy being my husband?"

Without hesitation, he answers her.

"I know I will. I know as certainly as if I were a seer looking into a crystal ball."

Naomi lightly laughs. Hers is a merry laugh. It is a laugh that is elated and grateful and playful.

"I'm glad that you will be happy. I'm very glad, indeed."

Her remark pleases him. It persuades him to say more. Yet not only her remark persuades him. Something—some beneficent force or spell, someone, some invisible Spirit who makes spells and enchantments—compels him to tell her the thoughts that are visiting his mind and his soul.

"When we are married, we will know more about each other," he says. "Maybe we will discover that we were meant to love each other. Maybe some Fate or Guardian Spirit has brought us together."

"That is a lovely thought," she says. "It's a thought that can carry a woman through a lifetime of grief and disappointment."

Her words, soft and heartfelt, ease his conscience. For a few minutes, they say no more. There is no need to call forth new words that might break the calm that holds them in its spell. There are no new words that can intensify Naomi's elation at being here with Brett. There are no new remarks that can rouse Brett's temporarily dormant cynicism or that can diminish the excitement and joy of being here together. Instead, they leave the paddock and walk side-by-side along the trail that is flanked by lavender fields and scented meadows. They are accepting the silence between them as a pact newly formed between them, an accord that will seal their bond, an alliance that validates the rightness of their being here together, *here* in this very moment that neither time nor chance will call back. Only when this trail leaves the fields behind and leads them to the top of a promontory does Naomi break the stillness between them.

Standing there with him, upon one of the highest hills in the area, she speaks words that reveal more than what his eyes perceive as her spontaneous elation.

"I love this place," she says, as she looks out upon a blue mist greenery of hills beyond hills, cloud laden implications of mountains, and the sun-spotted expanse of corridors of space wheeling freely around and below and above them. "Whenever I come here, I believe in the possibility of happiness more than ever. Maybe, that's because the place gives me a vision of peace and the illusion of safety. It gives me a promise of happiness. It persuades me that one day I will break free of all my troubles."

On this one day that is different from so many of the days and weeks and months that he has spent with Naomi, Brett responds to her remark. He keeps on speaking the truth. The enchantment that binds him to its ordinances requires him to tell the truth. He is not trying to fool Naomi with make-believe pledges of his love and with empty talk of easily acquired happy endings. He knows that their journey together will be a learning experience for both of them. Their road to happiness will require their belief in each other as well as their faith in the makers of spells and enchantments.

Swiftly now, while responding with gentler words to her remark about breaking free of her troubles, Brett reminds Naomi of the way things really are.

"Nobody is happy all of the time," he says. "Each of us has to learn how to soldier through the rough times. We often learn those lessons alone and, if we are lucky, sometimes when we are with a person we love."

Naomi gazes at him with unabated attention. Her blue eyes gleam, and her lips part in a smile, showing her perfect, white teeth and enhancing her demure consent to his words.

"You are so right," she tells him. "The matter-of-fact side of me knows that."

She pauses, and then she says more.

"You are a different Brett today," she says. "To me, you have always been perfect. But right now you absolutely amaze me. Before this hour, I knew that you have become a hard-driving lawyer. I knew that you have been making my father your mentor. I knew that you bring tremendous energy to everything that you do. I have always noticed your excellent work ethic. Today, though, you look like a man who has fallen in love with life, perhaps for the first time."

With his brown-eyed gaze, Brett gently caresses the whole, beautiful form of her. His hands do not touch her. Only his luminous gaze and his new, tender words suggest that he wants to be as one with her—heart, body, and soul.

"Maybe today I do look like a man who has fallen in love with life for the first time," he tells her. "If I do, it's because today I have fallen in love with you—really fallen in love—for the first time."

Naomi, hearing his words, is supremely happy. At first, she says nothing. He guesses that she is searching for the right words to say. His honest confession has stirred her soul. His authentic words have awed her.

When she does speak, she opens to him the secret places of her heart.

"What a wonderful thing to say to me," she tells him. "What an astonishing thing—to know that you love me as much as I love you."

He draws her to him now. He enfolds her within his embrace. He kisses her a long and sensual kiss that leaves both of them breathless. When he breaks away from her, his eyes gleam with vibrant light. He is overjoyed with the sight and the touch of her. Her eyes gleam, as well. They are misty because of the rare happiness that a happy Fate or her blessed Angel has granted her.

Without speaking another word, she allows her gaze to turn back to the colorful panorama that has always solaced her and that today subdues the surprise of her excitement. Brett, in turn, studying her every move, sees what with clarified awareness she is observing. Below them, a motorboat is speeding across a lake, leaving in its wake the spume and ripples of blue-green waters. In the faraway distance, at the edge of the sun-tinted forest that stands across from the lake, Chilean willow trees, Scotch elms, and blueberry ash trees are bringing flares of excited color to the summer-in-spring afternoon. Higher than that, though still within the opaque blue furling of distance, a stray herring gull is curving the dark flash of its wings against the tumescence of ponderous clouds. After an instant's pause, it plummets with wily skill to the consenting lips of lake waters, the better to pluck for its meal a raw, ample fish or a tiny, mackerel-tinted seabird.

Though the vision gives them back what they have not sought, a predatory image shown natural and insistent, they grasp comfortably its familiar message and find again their realistic measure for comprehending things. Turning once more, still toward the east, they are not surprised to sight the zinc-white hang of a wind-bleached cliff glaring like the bones of a devoured world. The limestone solidity of the gargantuan form impresses them, as does the cliff's having endured a wilderness of centuries. The imagery puts them in mind of their own resilience, as tested and time trapped as that is. In a world of uncertainty and aggression, their capacity to withstand brutal enemies and wrenching setbacks is, they feel, their most essential weapon. Their good fortune in loving each other is another stay against confusion and against the world's depredations. The stark messages they take from the wind-bleached cliff and from their new confession of love quicken their awareness of things more acutely than any of the colors of the earth that surround them.

They notice, too, across and above the disquieted lake and on the crest of sun glanced fertile hills—right *there*, at the wavering margins of the shadow-laden woods—a gray-blue immensity of swaying larches that apparently grow into the sky and, before their troubled eyes, join all of heaven's restless and eerie motion. The sudden wind is billowing now, like a flare of wings lifted by lower winds and pushing upward against moist, lake-scented air. This feeling of space actively stirring, this sense that here on a sun-hued promontory the wind has come sweeping through the day's intricate layers and, spinning always its rapid coils, has come to claim them—it is this feeling that stops their firm gait and holds them in taut surprise back upon their heels while cliff and clouds and festive colors go wheeling by them. The earth itself seems to revolve with visible motion. They notice once more the receding diagonals of the forest across the lake—a shadow flecked welling of foliage and trees, an instant's ambiguity of surface and space.

Naomi notices, too, Brett's scrutiny of that same sequestered place. She wonders whether, on this day that has been a romantic interlude for them, he is maintaining his realistic sense of things. He is even more knowing than she is about the world's equivocal promises and about its bruising, addictive textures.

He turns to her now, eyeing her steadily, as though he is coming back to her after a long absence. His brown hair and tan-skinned radiance, partially concealed by the light that shimmers around him, gives him the spectral look of a mirage or an apparition. Then, because the whorls of slanted light begin slowly to recede from him, she sees more clearly his satisfied face and offers, as a correspondent sign of satisfaction, her appraisal of these surroundings.

"I've taken from this wonderful place all that I need," she tells him. "It has served me well. Perhaps it has done the same for you."

"It has."

They laugh lightly, giving themselves completely to the pleasure of this moment.

"Oh, Brett, it is wonderful to be happy here with you. Let's promise always to be happy when we are together."

Her blue eyes are once again misty with tears as she touches his large, strong hands.

"That's an easy promise to keep," he answers her, his words as direct as they are love fused. "I'm all for that. I promise I will always remember that you and I belong to each other. I promise to do everything to make you happy."

He observes Naomi quietly, but only for an instant. He takes hold of her hand and walks briskly beside her. He is eager to extend this hour of happiness. His enchanted mind yearns to give her some here-and-now proof of his loyalty to her.

"We've had our ride," he says. "The Arab Bays have been terrific. Now it's time to make the day work for us in other ways."

"A lovely idea."

"First, let's ride back together," he says, apparently satisfied that during this hour he has shown Naomi a more favorable aspect of his character. "We'll go back to Blue Ridge for lunch. Afterwards, we can fly as high as we want in my Piper Cherokee."

"Wonderful," she says. "It will be absolutely wonderful to get lost in the clouds with you."

As they walk back to the paddock, something unexpected happens. Naomi trips and falls toward a large, cragged rock at the edge of the road and toward the razor-sharp edges that can cut across her face or slash her shoulders. With quick-as-a-flash agility, Brett catches hold of her and draws her back to him. He turns the long, slender form of her toward him. For one moment that thrills their senses, their bodies are intertwined. His rugged arms are pressing her to him. His sensual eyes reveal his concern and his need for her. His clean breathing merges with her sweet-scented breath. His lips are nearly touching her lips. For this one moment, his urgent sensuality compels him to hold her body tightly into the nearness of his rugged and dominating physique. For this one revealing moment, here within the privacy of the woods, he wants to kiss her. She feels the urgency in his touch. She sees it in his eyes. She sees the need in the fleshy folds of his lips. She has roused him. He needs to kiss her.

With an urgency that surprises her, he does kiss her. It is a long kiss that leaves her breathless. Even when he breaks away from her, he won't let her go.

"I need you," he says. "Stay at my place tonight. I want us to see the magic lights together. I want it to be the way it was on that first night when we made love."

"Oh, it will be," she answers him. "It will be just the way I dreamed that it will always be."

He guides her into the paddock, and they deftly mount their horses. They head back and canter along the trail in unison. Though they speak no words to each other, they impart through their gleaming smiles the lighter spirit that has attended them during all of this bright morning. They consent to a modulated variation of this lightheartedness even after they have dismounted their horses outside Mr. Wilder's stables and the groomsmen have unsaddled them and guided them to a nearby paddock.

All through the drive to Blue Ridge and even during their lunch at a fashionable lakeside restaurant often attended by well-groomed patrons in their riding outfits, they talk of their future travel plans that will sometimes include their Blue Ridge business friends, occasionally Randall and Melanie, and oftentimes Hayden and Kayla. Within the next year or two or perhaps three, there will be an exciting trip to Vera Cruz, a vacation in the Bahamas, a hiking expedition along the Larapinta Trail in Australia, a week of skiing in Lausanne, and deep-sea diving in Tahiti. Their lightheartedness, Brett's and Naomi's, is a subtle complicity, an unspoken agreement that they are entering a new and more thrilling location within romantic territory. But even their temperate language cannot dispel this new sensation, this sheer exhilaration they are feeling because they are together.

Because of the enchantment that Randall and Melanie have cast upon him, Brett will revel with Naomi in all the hours of this day and night that they are together. For a brief moment, he imagines that he will yearn for her on all the other days and nights when they are not together.

There is, of course, a complication that Brett cannot perceive. The love that he suddenly feels for Naomi will spark his soul only for today, unless the message that this day is sending to his conscience works as a fuse for his transformation. Randall and Melanie promised Robert Steerforth that they would intervene only in limited ways in the complicated lives of Brett and Naomi, as well as of Tate and Lisa. These troubled persons need to take full responsibility for what happens to them. Randall and Melanie have come to Blue Ridge to help them. The enchantments they bring upon them may, indeed, be helpful. At the same time, Captain Johnson and his Melanie understand that the enchantments they invoke may also initiate dangerous responses and surprising twists within the narratives that are unfolding inside the lives of these four persons.

"This one-day enchantment of Brett may bring trouble," Mr. Steerforth reminds Randall and Melanie when, as a fully embodied Spirit, he appears to them during the evening of this special day that Brett and Naomi have been sharing. He appears to them simultaneously, his rangy physique standing by their desks in the comfortable studies within their Georgian home.

"We understand that," Randall says, looking up from a legal brief that he was reviewing while he was alone inside the comforting silence of his study. "Enchantments often bring trouble."

"Lisa may become a part of the trouble," Mr. Steerforth reminds both of them, while his apparition continues to dominate both rooms at the same time.

"We understand that, too," Melanie says, looking away from the essay she is writing about the role that suppressed guilt plays in human behavior. She is unsurprised by Mr. Steerforth's appearance inside the privacy of her study. "You explained everything about this mission when we were in Sojourn."

"Good," Mr. Steerforth says. "I'm glad that you understand. Tonight, I came to remind both of you. That's all. I am pleased that you remember. Enchantments can bring danger. They can bring trouble."

No sooner has he spoken these words than he quickly vanishes from both rooms.

Now Melanie hurries to Randall's study.

"Robert came here to warn us," she says. "He wants us to be prepared. He wants us to know that trouble is coming."

Randall agrees.

"Yes," he says. "It's just as we expected. In fact, it's come sooner than we expected. Trouble is already here."

CHAPTER FIVE
TROUBLE

During the weeks that quickly follow, Brett looks at Lisa with new eyes. Now he perceives with deeper clarity the artifice that attends her. Her perfectly coiffed honey blonde hair that is pulled back to make a neat coil at the nape of her neck, her smoothly moisturized face with its light-skin delicacy, the natural tint of her lip gloss, and the disciplined slimness of her figure—all these emblems of her glamour intensify his awareness that everything about her contributes to the artfulness of her selfhood, the invention of her sleek personality, and the stratagems of her self-possession.

"We are all contrivances," he tells himself while searching for reasons that support Lisa's presentation of herself as the self-possessed woman that she wants business colleagues and close friends to see. "We invent our personalities, shaped though they are by random circumstance and by our private histories. Lisa is not alone in devising and exploiting the emblems that make her appear authentic. But she is all performance. With her colleagues and her friends, she is rarely capable of a true gesture or an honest word. In this respect, she is like me."

He is not ready to let her go. He is not especially interested in resolving the question of whether she really loves him. Their mutual need of each other's body, the shared ecstasies of their carnal alliance, and the thrill of their clandestine meetings fire his senses and quicken his acceptance of who they are together.

"When she is with me, Lisa is everything I want her to be. We break the rules. We are willing to smash up other people's lives to get what we want. We are no good. We deserve each other."

Yet, as passionate as their lovemaking remains, some fundamental change with sinuous tentacles and a tight hold upon his conscience is overtaking his perception of her. No longer does he casually dismiss her betrayal of Tate's trust of her. No longer does he shrug off his complicity in that betrayal and his wily exploitation of Tate's regarding him as a son. Nor does he treat with sardonic detachment their betrayal of Naomi. Way back in the most secret corner of his mind—way, way back so that the press of its reality cannot at this time disarrange the quiet order of their behavior—Brett is beginning to imagine that his fidelity to Naomi will yield safer and more lasting rewards. He does not want to violate the promise of faithful love that he has made to

Naomi. He does not want to hold back his love for her or negate the probability that he will love her even more profoundly as he comes to know her well.

He does not refrain from the sequestered meetings with Lisa. He is not ready to suppress his erotic need of her. Yet there are times during their lovemaking when he imagines that he is stroking with vigorous ardency not the voluptuous Lisa, but the equally receptive Naomi. One time, at the pitch of ecstasy and with a raspy groan, he calls out Naomi's name. He isn't aware that he has called her name until Lisa questions him the next morning. They have managed to steal away to his lakeside cabin in Vermont when Tate is spending that week in Washington, D. C.

"You were thinking of Naomi, weren't you?" she remarks, her question tucked within the folds of an assertion.

He does not answer her at once. Nor does he look away. Wily and manipulative, he gazes into her eyes and speaks smooth-sounding and understated words.

"If I called out her name, it was a conditioned response. After all, she and I *are* sleeping together."

"You were thinking of her when you were inside me."

"I wasn't thinking," he says. "I was fucking. I was shooting my brand inside *you.*"

For a moment, her blue-eyed gaze—hardened then and glowing still—studies him. He has risen from their bed, naked and swaggering toward the patio door that will lead him out to the sun-warm waters of the lake. When he reaches the door, he turns back as though with careless and preening abandon he wants to remind her of his rugged muscularity, the well-honed manpower he represents. Standing there, with full frontal authority, he throws out an invitation.

"Let's go for a swim," he says. "The lake's always good for a swim in the raw and for making love."

His words, sensual and venturesome, disarm her. The anger that has touched her because of his coital mention of Naomi quickly leaves her. With quick-witted words that carry the hint of a teasing admonition, she hastens to join him.

"I'm game," she says, "as long as you remember my name."

On this day, they revel in their sensuality with apparently the same fervor. Their warm-bodied caresses, their excited kisses, and their prolonged copulation nearly convince her that nothing has changed between them. Yet there lives, haunting and insistent within a secret corner of her mind, the knowledge that something essential is changing between them. In the weeks that follow, no longer does he arrange discreet meetings between them. No longer does she arrive, love-drawn and breathless, within the luxurious décor of his townhouse in Blue Ridge during those weeks when Tate is away for legal conferences in New York, Chicago, San Francisco, or London. No longer do they arrange trysts at Brett's lakeside cabin in Vermont or at a beach resort within the Bahamas or at a ski lodge in Switzerland. Working his charm upon her romantic sensibility and upon her passionate need of his presence, Brett cautions her toward safe plans and careful plotting.

"We can't afford to take chances," he whispers to her during one of the rare times that they do meet.

They are sitting opposite each other in the visitors' room within Blue Ridge Children's Hospital. No one else is in the room. They have come to the hospital with Hayden, Kayla, and Naomi on a Saturday afternoon to bring to children whom they have never met gifts of books, iPads, educational video games, and solacing words. At the moment, Hayden, Kayla, and Naomi are conferring with an oncologist and two nurses in a private office within the west wing of the hospital. Exemplary volunteers that they are, Naomi, Kayla, and Hayden are reviewing with the surgeon and the two nurses on his team the best ways to proceed in this visit to ten children—ages seven, eight, and nine—who are convalescing from brain surgery. They—Brett and Lisa—had taken part in this meeting until they were called away to oversee the imminent presentation of the iPads, video games, and adventure books as well as a rainbow layer cake, a milk bar cake, a ring cake with pink icing, and strawberry, chocolate, and vanilla ice cream. They have come here to celebrate the children for their courage and for their ability to soldier through this precarious time in their lives. Fortunately, the prognosis for their recovery is affirmative.

But not even the plight of these children, when for days their lives were hanging in the balance, dissuades Lisa from focusing on her romantic problems. Brett notices and remains unsurprised. Her inveterate self-centeredness matches his own. Today, though, he has tamped down his selfishness. He intends to make a most favorable impression especially upon Naomi and upon Kayla and Hayden. He wants them to imagine that he is on their team. With subtle nuances and cheerful countenance, he is conveying the reliable character of a full-fledged altruist. He has played this game before. He has convinced so many people that he is the man he appears to be. He is honest. He is steadfast. He is on the level.

Here, in this hospital setting, he would like Lisa to project a similar persona. He wants her to draw upon her savvy understanding of the judgmental society they inhabit. He wants her to be someone that she is not: a generous-hearted woman who works for the wellbeing of persons less fortunate than she is.

He begins again. He reminds her of the value of playing well their game of pretense.

"Right now, everything is working in our favor," he tells her. "Naomi believes every word that I speak to her and all my romantic gestures. Tate still trusts you, and he treats me as if I were a long-lost son that some kind Fate has brought home to him."

His words do not ease her disappointment or her tension.

"Everything seems different," she says, a frown touching her brow and altering with melancholic implications the smooth glamour of her face. "You are different. You act as though you no longer need our love. You have Naomi's love. She's the safe plan that pleases you. She's the linchpin of your careful plotting."

"You're jealous," he says while maintaining an even-tempered disposition and the suggestion of a light heart. He caresses her shoulders and, as if he were an actor in a film or on a stage about to recite his duplicitous lines with precise credibility, he brings into his wily awareness the gleam of her blue-eyed watchfulness.

"I suppose I should be pleased," he begins. "But, frankly, I'm disappointed. I thought you and I had gone past being the playthings of our feelings. You and I have made a plan to get everything we can from this world that doesn't really care about what happens to any of us. I'm doing what I need to do to make that plan work. It is going to take time to get what we want, and both of us have to be patient."

On this afternoon in May, sequestered as they are within this solitary hospital room, he brushes her cheek with his light kiss and clasps her right hand with the warm flesh of his own.

"Don't give in to feelings, Lisa," he whispers. "They'll mess up everything for us."

She does not believe in his lightheartedness. She resists the rousing effect of his touch upon her. She regards his charming manner as another disguise meant to put her off her accurate understanding of him.

"It's *your* feelings I'm thinking about," she says while he holds her in his studious gaze. "It's what you feel for Naomi that may ruin things for us."

He softly laughs.

"Nobody knows what I feel better than I do," he answers her. "I'm setting up Naomi just as we planned. She believes in me, and that is the important thing. I have her in the palm of my hands. In just a few weeks, she and I will be married."

This talk of marriage displeases Lisa. She finds a reason to criticize him.

"You haven't followed the plan. You've fallen in love with her."

"I'm a good actor," he tells her, surprised that she has guessed his secret. "Even you believe that I love her. I'm a master of deception."

She resents his smoothness. She suspects his motives. She sees through his deception.

"Don't hold out on me," she warns him, angry and resentful. "I'd rather know the truth now and walk away from you."

A part of him is pleased to hear those words. A part of him is relieved that she might be willing to walk away. A part of him knows her too well to imagine that she could walk away without wreaking havoc upon him, some wild kind of vengeance, perhaps, or an impulsive killing. Nevertheless, he prods her further. He would like her to explore her feelings. He would like her to tell herself that she could walk away without doing harm to him or to herself.

"Could you really do that? Could you really walk away for good?"

Before Lisa can answer him, a middle-aged nurse comes into the room now. She has snow-white hair; soft green eyes; a cleft nose with a slight indentation at its tip; full lips devoid of gloss; and a round, cheerful face.

"You folks should come back to the children," she says with gentle voice and a bright smile. "The party is about to begin."

"In a minute," Brett tells her while offering her a beaming smile. "We'll be there in a minute."

"Good," the nurse says. "You'll have a fine time with the children."

No sooner does she leave than he turns to Lisa to ask once more the question that is goading his ambivalent feelings about his situation.

"Could you really do that? Could you really walk away for good?"

Lisa hesitates. She is tense. She looks anguished. His question has prodded her to examine her deepest feelings about him. She does not like what she perceives.

"I'm not sure. I'd try to walk away. I'll do anything not to be two-timed or humiliated."

"What if I did love Naomi more than you want me to? What if, quite suddenly and altogether unexpectedly, I fell in love with her goodness and her being straight up with me in everything?"

"I couldn't bear it. I don't even want to think about what I might do."

"Would you kill me?"

"Maybe."

"Then you'd be loving yourself more than you love me."

"Yes. Ironic, isn't it? I'd be killing someone who is exactly like myself—someone who is devious and two-timing. Someone who gets into trouble for trying at last to love completely."

Her dark thoughts make him uneasy. To dispel the darkness and to reclaim the lighthearted repartee he has initiated, he chooses to speak soft words as he takes hold of her hands. He gazes into her troubled eyes. He soothes her unhappy premonition.

"Never stop loving me completely," he tells her. "Never walk away from our obsession."

"I promise that I won't," she says. "You will not be rid of me so easily."

They rise from their chairs. He plants a light kiss upon her forehead just before they head out for the children's ward and the festive celebration of the children.

Their whispered conversation has left each of them with a punishing awareness of how far from the reality of honorable lovers they have traveled. Cynical and demanding, Lisa is willing to accept their situation. Theirs is a carnal love. It is a love of body pleasures and other worldly excitements. It is not the soulful love about which the ancient poets often sang. It is here-and-now sensation. It is a social signifier. It is proof of female seductiveness and of male potency. It is a secular bond that preens with self-regard. It has nothing to do with soulfulness or with the soul-cleansing ecstasies that might enhance its significance.

So Lisa believes. Believing so, she is not willing to forgive a betrayal by a man that she has really loved and that has loved her in return. Her betrayal of Tate is, she tells herself, an altogether different matter. Neither of them has ever loved each other. Earthbound and carnal though it has been, her love for Brett could push her over the edge. If Brett betrays her, if—despite his denial—he falls in love with Naomi, she might very well kill him. Then, with the madness that has seized every fiber of her being, she would kill herself.

Brett is beginning to view love in a more profound way. When he is with Naomi, he is discovering the Spirit Being inside her body, the soul that calls out to his capacity for loving not only her body, but also the same eternal soul that glows, luminous and enchanting, within her body. In contrast, the lust he feels for Lisa is merely finite and carnal. Though he cannot yet explain this still-evolving change in his viewpoint, he from time to time sees his relationship with Lisa for what it is: an alliance coiled around deception and selfishness, a bond for schemers, a pact that generates self-lies and self-disgust.

A few more weeks pass. Melanie and Randall continue to work their spells upon Brett. Invisible presences though they become, their precisely calibrated spells influence him to perceive his moral culpability and to regard Lisa as a woman trapped by her greed and her narcissism. They leave his will free to make the life choices that will determine whether he will become a good man or whether he will remain a man both lost and dishonorable.

Lisa notices the change in Brett. Now, his lovemaking seems too swift and even detached from the highest pitch of the ecstasy they once shared with sensual murmurings and with orgasmic sighs. Sometimes, when they are sailing or swimming or hiking together, he flinches at her touch. No longer does his ardent gaze caress her face. No longer does he speak romantic words when they are dining in a secluded bistro in New York City. No longer does he whisper erotic words while his lips caress her right ear.

"You've changed," Lisa tells him one afternoon after they have made love within the secluded amenities of his townhouse in Blue Ridge. "Your lovemaking is different. It isn't as urgent. It isn't passionate. It's an animal response. There isn't real love in it."

"You're talking nonsense," Brett answers her as he moves quickly out of the bed they have shared and heads for the shower. "You are still a fantastic adrenalin rush. You still make my pulse beat faster."

His lighthearted words appease her, though they do not dispel her doubts.

Melanie and Randall have observed all of these telling scenes, though Lisa and Brett have been unaware of their ghostly presence. At these times, Melanie and Randall as flesh-and-blood human beings disappear. They will their bodies to vanish. They choose to become Shadows. As Shadows that are indiscernible to human eyes, Melanie and Randall watch these increasingly tense meetings between Lisa and Brett play themselves out. They do not, as invisible Spirits, try to prevent these scenes or to mediate their aftermath or to baffle both Lisa and Brett with a too-sudden awareness of their adulterous dishonor and a clear-sighted resolve to change their self-serving ways. Though Randall and Melanie continue to create enchantments from time to time, they want to give Brett and Lisa the opportunity to redeem themselves without coercion and without supernatural intervention. These recent scenes, with their fluctuations of heart's ease and emotional turmoil, have intensified the probability that something volatile within Lisa—some unsuppressed fury, some wayward retaliation—may soon destroy the makeshift peace and the superficial concord that hover around her and around Brett and Naomi and Tate.

"Lisa is her own worst enemy," Melanie tells Randall one evening in the privacy of their home. "She has become addicted to Brett's lovemaking. She regards him as her husband. Tate is merely the multi-millionaire who bestows upon her all manner of luxuries and the security and prestige of his status on Wall Street and in so many other corporate locations. She sees herself as his kept woman. He is the man that she does *not* love. She does not see what you and I see. He is the beginning of her punishment for having chosen him because of her greed. With him, she has made a sacrilege of marriage."

Randall has something to say. He has looked into Lisa's future without yet having access to the final consequences of her deeds.

"More punishment is on the way for her, unless she changes," he tells Melanie. "I think that it is time for you to nudge her toward a better path. It's time for you—with your fully embodied human presence and without invoking any miracles—to offer Lisa some sound human advice."

For a moment, Melanie muses upon the problematic situation. Then, because she too has sighted the uneasy scenes that presage danger and even destruction for Lisa and Brett, she provides new impetus to Randall's suggestion that she nudge Lisa toward a better path.

"That moment may come during the party that Lisa and Tate will be hosting next month to celebrate the beginning of summer."

"Let's try to alter things as far as The First Spirit will allow us," Randall says. "Let's find out what happens."

What happens at the four-day celebration at Tate and Lisa's Blue Ridge home invites at first the freewheeling spirit of summer. The startling incident that involves Lisa and Brett and that will threaten to disarrange its precisely calibrated scenes will not occur at once. Within the festival atmosphere that Lisa and Tate compose for the first days of the partying, all goes well. The twenty-four guests enjoy jet skiing and hiking and sailing. They enjoy, as well, a chamber concert within the splendid music room. Actors from The Blue Ridge Theater Company play scenes from William Shakespeare's *As You Like It* and from the Arthur Laurents-Leonard Bernstein-Stephen Sondheim musical *West Side Story*. In addition, Randall as a violinist and Melanie as a pianist surprise all the guests with altogether admirable performances. Extraordinary violinist that he is, Randall enthralls his audience with the pure melody and the poignant longing of Rachmaninoff's *Vocalise*. At her piano, Melanie conveys with an equal conviction the emotional and spiritual distance of Schubert's *Piano Sonata in B-flat*.

As a capstone to an occasion that contrives to be celebratory and carefree, a sumptuous banquet quickens the merriment of the Sunday afternoon that will close the weekend festivities. This banquet, unfolding as it does within the expansive greenery of the south lawn, becomes even more vivid because of its panoply of a colorful tent, elegant dinnerware and antique silver, and a popular New York jazz combo. It is even more extraordinary than the grand lunches and dinners that Tate and Lisa hosted within their mansion-like home during the first three days of this summery weekend. The banquet offers so many delicious foods. There are fresh pastas with seafood; tenderloins with *bordelaise* sauce, artichokes, and asparagus; and peach *blancmange*. There is an omelet stuffed with spinach and crayfish; monkfish, ample and tasty, in white-wine cream sauce with vegetables; and rum *savarin* with kiwis and strawberries. There is a veal and pork *pâté* in a puff pastry crust, as well as fillets braised in lettuce, and pineapple *mousse*. There are potato and leek soup with sorrel; medallions of lamb, tangy with garlic cream sauce; zucchini *gratin*; and Alsatian pear tarts. The guests freely imbibe an assortment of cocktails: Prosecco and scotch julep; red wine and whiskey sangria; and a blend of bourbon, Triple Sec, and Prosecco. The Champagnes include Dom Perignon and Veuve Clicquot.

If, Lisa tells herself as she observes the kaleidoscopic energies of this gathering, the splendor of this weekend does not glow for her quite as luminously as it had during the parties that she and Tate gave when her secret affair with Brett was a new-found ecstasy, the glamour of the decor and the celebrity of the guests succeed nevertheless in subverting the gloom that is waiting to overtake her. American actors and musicians, a South African poet and an Australian playwright, a French diplomat and a British foreign ambassador, and a Japanese scientist enhance the stylized construct that has kept at bay—for this weekend at least—her awareness of the tumult raging within her and the bitter closing of her love affair with Brett.

The guests, dressed in pastel gowns and summer-white tuxedos, abide by all the rules that exemplify their privileged class. They wear their formality with decorum and with ease. Their hearts remain buoyant. Their repartee has the ring of conviviality. Everybody is having a good time. Even Lisa gives herself to the exhilaration that rises upon the sun-dazzled afternoon. Vivacious and apparently relaxed as she saunters across the paths bordering the wide expanse of the lawn, she chats with the poet and the ambassador and the scientist and with their good-natured wives. She waves affectionately to Blue Ridge country club couples, tennis partners, and business associates. She strolls with the dapper British foreign ambassador and his charming wife down to the sun-shimmering lake. There, with them, she watches a flock of gray-back gulls hurrying toward white, fluffy clouds and then disappearing within the balletic drift of cloud softness. She directs the gaze of the ambassador and his wife to the place across the lake where chalky cliffs rise jaggedly out of the luminous water as if they were the bones of a discarded, ancient world.

"The cliffs look magical," the ambassador's wife remarks.

"They look magnificent," the ambassador says, "and a bit eerie, too."

"Just right for our fairy tale party," Lisa says, fully aware of the artifice and the illusion that propel this weekend celebration. She is aware, too, that with steel-true resolve she has thus far maintained her equanimity. She is harnessing her emotional equilibrium to the poise and the propriety that are her stock in trade.

As they saunter back, they head for the voluminous Victorian tent that is supported by center poles and guy ropes along the perimeter. The top has white peaks with an exaggerated pitch that gives to the burnished interior of the tent high ceilings, added elegance, and well-modulated grandeur. The tent has window sidewalls that allow the sunlight to brighten the interior and to protect the guests from inclement weather. Capacious and well-structured, the tent offers three decorative rows of banquet tables and comfortable chairs, color lantern lighting, polished cedar wood flooring, ample staging and risers for the musicians, two well-stocked bars, a dance floor, and air conditioning.

Once they are inside the glamorous tent, the British ambassador and his wife accompany Lisa to the first of the long tables. The ambassador and his wife join Melanie, Randall, Hayden, and Kayla at the center of the table. Each of these couples is seated opposite one another. Lisa takes her seat at one end of the banquet table and observes Tate at the opposite end chatting amiably with the guests seated near him—a prominent lawyer, a stockbroker, and a neurosurgeon. Naomi is seated to the right of Lisa. Brett is seated at her left. Lisa arranged the seating. With quick-witted self-possession and an acute understanding of this rare opportunity to be near Brett without inviting suspicious eyes, she draws him into conversation.

"Tate has told me that on the fourth of July you and he will take turns piloting his Outerlimits power boat."

Congenial and articulate, Brett dives right into the conversation. He directs his words not only to her, but also to the other guests at the table. This afternoon, his eyes do not linger upon her face. She tells herself that he is being cautious. He is protecting her reputation. She is not disheartened. She is happy in this moment when they are exchanging words that are as courteous as they are friendly.

"I'm looking forward to the race," he answers her. "It will be a real adventure. The boat is an SV-52. It has been designed especially for superior high-speed performances and is known for its steady ride and soft landing even in rough and choppy waters. The cockpit has dual helm controls and a standard GPS chart plotter. The boat is a long beauty, and it easily records speeds of up to a hundred miles an hour."

"Tate says that you are an excellent pilot. You know practically everything that there is to know about speedboats."

"I like speed," Brett tells her. "I like to make life run faster."

"Good for you," she says with a decorous smile. "I prefer life to run faster, too. That's why I'll be a passenger in the Outerlimits when you and Tate are racing her."

For this moment, her voice is filled with the thrill of anticipation. She will be riding in the boat when Brett is there. She will be sitting so close to him. She will observe his brawny shoulders and arms as he pilots the boat with acumen that soars at the cusp of higher swiftness and at the swerving impetus of well-calibrated daring.

"I'll be there, too," Naomi says, her face beaming and her voice exhilarated. "I'll be experiencing the speed and the suspense and the entire adventure."

"Of course you will," Lisa briskly answers her. "The four of us will have a tremendous time."

If she is dismayed that Naomi will be in the boat, too, cheering Brett during the race with genuine fervor and with her heart filled with love because she is his fiancée, Lisa gives no clue. Instead, she fabricates a convincing smile that brings a beam to her face as well.

The banquet becomes a splendid occasion for all the guests. They enjoy the delicious food and the wine. They chat about various subjects, including the home run records in major league baseball of Aaron Judge, Bryce Harper, and Pete Alonso; the excellent performances of golf pros Tiger Woods, Brooks Koepka, Dustin Johnson, Matt Wallace, Patrick Cantlay, and Jordan Spieth; the supreme discipline of tennis greats Roger Federer, Novak Djokovic, Naomi Osaka, Rafael Nadal, Pete Sampras, Serena Williams, and Angelique Kerber; revivals of Tony Kushner's *Angels in America*, Harold Pinter's *Betrayal*, Edward Albee's *Who's Afraid of Virginia Woolf?*, and Rodgers and Hammerstein's *Carousel* in New York; the latest computers, iPhones, and smart phones; a current exhibit of Impressionist canvases in the Blue Ridge Fine Arts Museum; and the superb V-12 engine and four-wheel steering of the Rolls-Royce Phantom.

All goes well during these convivial hours. The engaging repartee, the radiance of the women young and older, and the affability and suppressed arrogance of the men quicken the freewheeling spirit of the afternoon. The party goes into full swing when the dancing begins. Accompanied by a first-rate jazz combo, a curvaceous Norwegian blonde and a handsome Latino sing light-hearted, romantic ballads as well as love-haunted blues. Lisa, Naomi, Melanie, and Kayla, as well as many other women, dance with several partners. Sometimes, they return to the banquet table to relax, perhaps, or to sip

Champagne, or to wait for another gentleman to ask them to dance. Every one of the women glows with happiness. Even the men give themselves to the exciting rhythms and the heady amusements of this gathering.

Carefully melding exhilaration to an attractive decorum, Lisa appears to be the perfect hostess. But never does she lose sight of Brett. Even when she is dancing with Tate or with a suave corporate executive from New York or with the British ambassador, she takes careful note of Brett and his dancing partners. He dances with many women. At first, he enjoys several dances with Naomi, his fiancée. Lisa finds his choice appropriate and acceptable. Later, his partners are married women: Melanie first of all and then the wife of the British foreign ambassador, the wife of the New York corporate executive, the wife of a patent attorney, and the wife of a pediatrician. That they are respectable married women pleases her. She does not regard them as her rivals for Brett's secret lovemaking. She breathes more easily. She laughs at her dance partners' witty remarks. She offers them, in turn, engaging repartee about jet skiing in Nantucket, hiking on Mount Mansfield Loop Trail in Vermont, and skydiving in Danielson, Connecticut.

All this while, she is waiting for the moment when Brett asks her to dance. After nearly an hour of dancing, she returns to her place at the banquet table, apparently serene after one of her dance partners, a best-selling American author of political thrillers who wears his roguish charm with well-calibrated masculinity, has escorted her there. She waits for Brett to make an appearance. Surely, now that he has danced with at least a half dozen partners, he will ask her to dance. His asking her will appear most seemly and will suggest to any curious onlookers that his partnering with her gives evidence of his respect for her and for her husband, who is Blue Ridge's most renowned attorney.

Then, quite suddenly and with jagged emphasis, discord flares its anger and threatens to overtake the party.

Brett does return. To her surprise, he does not ask her to dance.

He asks Kayla, whose face shines with surprise and with delight. Charming and decorous as usual, Kayla turns to study Hayden's face before she accepts Brett's invitation. Hayden, pausing in his conversation with Naomi, Randall, and Melanie, notices her gaze. He notices also Brett standing, tall and courteous, by Kayla's place. Hayden guesses at once that Kayla wants his permission to dance with Brett. Her deferring to his will is old-fashioned and conservative. In matters of etiquette, that is Kayla's way. Hayden understands and is pleased. Kayla does not care to embarrass her husband by dancing with a handsome young man who is engaged to Naomi and who also has the reputation of being a playboy.

Hayden returns Kayla's gaze as he offers her a happy smile.

"Go ahead," he tells her. "Dance with this big lug. Kick him if he steps on your toes."

Kayla and Brett laugh. So do Naomi, Randall, and Melanie.

Naomi is particularly blithe and carefree.

"Brett will have you soaring in space," she says. "You will feel that you are levitating!"

More laughter.

But Lisa is displeased as she watches Brett, with a courtly swagger, guiding Kayla to the dance floor.

Her face tightens with anger. A frown creases her brow. She lowers her eyes and purses her lips. She is reflecting on what she has just witnessed. Her secret lover has asked Kayla Ericson, a beautiful woman, to dance with him. He has ignored her, Lisa Caulfield Calhern, the married woman who has given him her heart, her soul, and her body. He has slighted her. His passion has cooled. He is getting ready to toss her aside. These thoughts, like sharp needles spewing their poison into her heart and mind, intensify her anger. No longer does she care to suppress it. No longer does she conceal her feelings from these guests who are seated near her.

"It is not well done," she says, her voice tremulous and resentful. "Brett should never have asked Kayla to dance with him. It is unseemly. It is inappropriate. He is engaged to Naomi, and Kayla is married to Hayden. Kayla is a young bride, and Brett should not have asked her to dance with him."

Her angry words surprise Naomi and Hayden. They have never before observed Lisa's anger.

Randall and Melanie are not surprised. They have been anticipating this moment.

Hayden is the first to assure Lisa that all is well.

"You are very kind to think about Kayla's reputation," Hayden says. "But you need not worry. A dance with a good friend is not necessarily a preface to a romantic tryst. Brett's a good sport. He and Kayla are pals. There's nothing more in it than that."

Lisa smiles, grateful for his encouragement. But doubt still creases her brow.

"I hope you are right," she says.

Naomi has something to say. There is laughter in her voice. There is exquisite happiness.

"Of course Hayden is right. Brett is being especially courteous today. He wants everybody to regard him as an outstanding and one hundred percent about-to-be-married gentleman. He's trying out his part as Prince Charming. On more than one occasion, he has remarked that, once he and

I are married, he will always be Prince Charming and only for me."

"What a romantic thing to tell you," Melanie says. "You are a lucky young woman."

For a moment, Naomi ponders her remark. Then, without further hesitation, she finds the words that reveal the truth of her feelings.

"Yes," she says. "I believe that I am lucky. Very lucky, indeed."

Randall is pleased with the generous feelings that Hayden and Naomi have expressed. Those feelings are anchored to trust, respect, and friendship. But, in spite of their authenticity, they do not dispel Lisa's doubts. With his military bearing and the precise ring of his wise counsel, Randall nudges Lisa's conscience with new, sensible words.

"You mustn't worry about Brett's fidelity to Naomi," he tells her. "Only Brett is responsible for that, just as he is accountable for his infidelity—he and the woman he might partner in an illicit relationship. This afternoon, we shall give him the benefit of our trust. Besides, the man would have to be a cad and a fool to betray a young woman as lovely as Naomi."

Naomi beams once more. Randall's remark gives her immense pleasure.

"You are a charmer, Randall," she says. "A cool, fantastic charmer."

"I'll vouch for him," Melanie says. "He is the genuine article, a magazine cover exemplar."

Everyone laughs again—everyone except Lisa. This time, though, she suppresses her dismay and her anger. This time, she offers her friends the hint of a smile and conciliatory words.

"Forgive me for becoming upset," she says while addressing the friends sitting near her and before she centers her gaze upon Naomi. "I was thinking of you, Naomi. I don't want to see you hurt or treated lightly."

"I'm not brittle," Naomi answers her. "Besides, I trust Brett. As far as I'm concerned, he can do no wrong."

"Well, then, there is no problem. You are a romantic. You are an idealist. You will always find the world and its people better than they really are."

"So should we all!" Hayden exclaims. "Romantics and idealists always find reasons to enjoy life."

There is more laughter. There are more happy faces.

But her fake laughter cannot conceal Lisa's uneasiness. Her simulated happiness does not hide her anguish.

Most of the friends who are seated near her, accepting completely the moment's exhilaration, remain unaware of Lisa's anguish.

Tate remains unaware, too, seated as he is at the head of the long table thoroughly engrossed by his conversations with West Coast moguls and East Coast matrons from his own class.

Only Melanie and Randall notice. With a knowing gaze and a nearly imperceptible nod, Randall signals Melanie to take the next step. She must do the thing that needs to be done. She waits for two hours, until the festive celebration has ended. The day has been a success. Everyone leaves the party feeling exhilarated. Women have pleased themselves by displaying their glamour with well-modulated gentility, by dancing waltzes, sambas, and rhumbas with aplomb, and by expressing their points of view with knowledgeable conviction in conversations with groups of arrogant men and their old boy sensibilities. The gentlemen attending these festivities have enjoyed their mercenary exchanges with stockbrokers, hedge fund managers, corporate CEOs, and New York lawyers. Young couples and older have accepted the artificial construct that this party has created for their wellbeing. For a few hours, this artfully devised afternoon has kept at bay the rough edges and ingrained liabilities of the real world.

After the party has ended and after Tate and Lisa have offered their guests courteous farewells, Melanie and Randall do not leave. Tate draws Randall into his study. He wants to discuss a controversial court case and the background of the Latino that Randall is defending. Lisa finds her way to the drawing room and, tense and unhappy all over again, sits upon a vintage carved French country floral needlepoint armchair. She is more convinced than ever that Brett no longer plans to be her lover.

At the threshold of the room, Melanie watches her. She pities this woman who has broken her marriage vows and who desires to disrupt Naomi's happiness with Brett. But she cannot excuse her immoral behavior. She will try to help her to redeem herself. She tells herself that, if this errant woman turned onto a better path, she might save herself.

To defuse the tension, Melanie calls to her and persuades Lisa to accompany her to the garden.

Lisa accepts the invitation. She is glad for Melanie's company. She trusts Melanie. She needs to unburden herself of her unhappy thoughts and her bitter response to the first signs of Brett's abandonment of her.

Despite the promise that she made to herself to keep silent about the most private episodes in her life, Lisa finds herself telling Melanie almost everything about her affair with Brett. Tormented by her doubt of her lover and her fear that their affair has burned itself out, she needs to confess her apprehension. She needs to tell her trouble-haunted story to this genteel and sympathetic woman.

That she and Melanie are alone in this garden prods Lisa forward. She is both eager and wary as she confides in her. She is also relieved that the fourteen friends who were Tate's and her live-in house guests during this weekend, as well as the ten guests who reside in the Blue Ridge area and did not become overnight visitors, have returned to their homes here in Blue Ridge or to their townhouses and apartments in New York, New Haven, Palm Beach, Paris, and London. They are also returning to their career obligations. Within the late hour of this afternoon, the magnificent Blue Ridge house with sudden impetus seems lonely without the guests. Lonely though the house may seem to her disarranged senses, Lisa is nevertheless pleased that she can confide in Melanie, here in the privacy of the garden and safely apart from her staff who have begun the complicated process of dismantling the ornamental props of the banquet and of bringing the south lawn back to its traditional order.

When she and Melanie enter the garden, Lisa at first walks away from her. Her quickened gait seems natural, because she is focusing her gaze upon the blue-rimmed well and upon the colorful efflorescence that surrounds her. She seems very pleased to be here, partaking of the beauty of the garden and allowing the scene to calm her at least a little.

For her part, Melanie is equally pleased that Lisa may at last confess the wrongness of her relationship with Brett. From time to time during this festive weekend, she sensed what other guests might not have noticed. Lisa is very unhappy. Melanie knows Lisa well enough to perceive the sorrow that is imprisoning her within its mysteries. On every one of the four days of this long weekend, Melanie saw that beneath Lisa's glamorous appearance there lives—as though it is a variant imagery or a will-o'-the-wisp that discloses its nature only in temporary flashes—a sorrow that binds itself to both guilt and remorse.

It is this same imagery that she notices upon observing Lisa standing pensive and solitary at the blue-rimmed well in the rose garden. All about them are the harmonies of floribunda and hybrid teas, delicate rosemary and damask and blue moon surfaces. Cloistered here, within the shadows of the late afternoon, Lisa appears tentative and melancholic, silently debating perhaps how she will begin to confess her adulterous relations with Brett. Not even the orange, yellow, and white splendor of rhododendrons and the red, lavender, and cream petals of camellias can dissuade her from her sorrow. Nor, Melanie imagines, can the golden-leaves and glossy, rounded red fruits of the pomegranate tree ease Lisa's troubled awareness that the confident woman she has always been is now becoming—to herself most of all—an uncertain stranger.

Melanie continues to observe her, enveloped as she is by the blue-gray mist of the oncoming night. She can see, even from the dusk-laden distance that separates them, that, despite the temporary solace she takes from the scene, Lisa is lost inside sullenness and recrimination.

With the assured poise that gives to her carriage a grace both straight-backed and feminine, Melanie hurries to join her—there, by the blue-rimmed well within the dusk-shaded splendor of the rose garden. They take their places on a comfortable bench not far from delicate topiaries of a doe and her fawn. For a few minutes, they sit together without uttering a word. To a casual witness, they might appear as two stylish women who have come to the garden to breathe the crisp air and to savor the variety of breeze-tossed colors that, in their scanning glance, wear the fleet emphases of a montage or the animated imagery within a kaleidoscope. Before their contemplative eyes, the oncoming night is altering the colors of ferns and flowers and of shrubs and trees, disguising in subtle ways the reality of their forms. A soft breeze with tactile energies caresses these forms even as the slowly vanishing light keeps translating them into vigilant and shadowy presences.

In these moments, Melanie regards the imagery around her as a disguised play upon her senses. Only after she has pondered the shrouded implications of these garden forms does she turn to observe Lisa sitting beside her and the taut stillness that holds her to its steadfast ordinances. Sorrow is working as a shadow upon the artifice of her beauty, redefining the rigorous discipline of her poise and of her pensive manner. Warmhearted as always yet called here to be judgmental, Melanie finds herself moved by the onrush of anguish that Lisa is struggling to keep at bay. Her unease at witnessing this struggle pushes her forward now as she dispels the silence that has held them to its powers.

"I've been noticing how sad you are," she tells Lisa. "Perhaps you may want to tell me why. Sometimes it's wise to bring these suppressed feelings into the open."

Despite Melanie's sisterly manner and her equally kind words, Lisa at first remains silent. With keen and questioning eyes, she studies Melanie's gentle face. At the same time, she weighs the consequences of telling her about her love affair with Brett. She trusts Melanie. In all of their exchanges, this friend has shown herself to be honest and prudent.

Without further hesitation, she begins to tell Melanie nearly everything about her involvement with Brett. At first, she speaks of their mutual respect. Even before they met, each of them was aware of the impressive law school credentials and the hard-driving courtroom manner that accelerated their journeys to the top of their profession.

"In those first months of our friendship, Brett and I came to feel that we are counterparts of one another," Lisa says. "We are divided souls who make each other whole and complete. Brett and I are *simpatico* in so many ways. We are like-minded and ambitious. We want the same things. We want to achieve so much. We want to make our lives run faster. When we are together, the world seems like such a wonderful place. It feels so good to be alive!

"'Isn't it lucky that we have met!' I told him on more than one occasion. 'From now on, we can't possibly live without one another.'"

Melanie notices the exhilaration in her voice. It is that and something more. Its joy yokes itself to melancholy and loss. The joy sounds tattered and hurt-filled. Once more she feels a tinge of regret that this vain woman whose beauty seems as hollow as her success has betrayed her troubled husband and her trusting stepdaughter. She has also betrayed her better self. Now she hurries to say the careful words that may persuade Lisa to tell more and, despite her waywardness, to tell the truth.

"You are lucky," Melanie says. "Making a life-long friend is a very special thing."

To this remark, Lisa does not respond—at least, not with words that clarify her feelings. Instead, she studies Melanie with deeper interest and with a more pressing inclination to tell her all the important things about her relationship with Brett.

She tells her more.

"Brett and I are more than friends," she says. "We are much closer than that."

The modulated spell that Melanie has set upon Lisa is working its harnessed power. The magic spell will not overtake Lisa's free will, nor will it instantly vouchsafe her regeneration. But this magic spell may nudge Lisa toward reformation. It may inspire her to change for the better. Everything depends upon Lisa's admission of wrongdoing and her willingness to make amends for her errant ways.

Hearing Lisa admit that she and Brett are more than friends, Melanie calmly urges her to tell more about this relationship that has cost her both her peace and her fidelity to her marriage.

"Tell me about it," Melanie says. "Tell me all of it. I'm not brittle. The truth will not break me into little pieces. Nor should you allow it to break you."

Lisa hedges. She inches toward the truth.

"A few months after we met, Brett confessed that he loves me," she says, "and I told him that I feel the same way about him."

In the face of her news, Melanie remains impassive. Her composure interests Lisa and persuades her to say more. She wants to tell her all of the truth. She needs to admit to someone other than herself that she has enjoyed her affair with Brett. She needs to say clearly and without hesitation that Brett is the only man that she has ever truly loved. The magic spell continues to work its influence upon her. It suppresses her deviousness. It awakens her willingness to tell the truth.

"Brett and I have been sleeping together for more than a year," she confesses. "He is my lifeline. He is my reason for living. Without his love, there can be no light in my life. There will be only darkness and despair. There will be bitterness and desperation. I need Brett. I need his acceptance and praise and protection. I need his vigorous lovemaking. I need the sperm that he shoots inside me. Without his love, I am empty. I am a pretty mannequin. I am a savvy lawyer. But I am not a complete woman."

Only when Lisa starts to explain the intensity of her sexual relationship with Brett does she pause in her telling.

Melanie nudges her forward.

"Tell me all of it, Lisa. You may see things more clearly after you've told me."

Lisa begins again. This time she makes an appeal to Melanie's life with Randall.

"You are a happily married woman," she begins. "You know the joy of loving and being loved. You can understand what I mean when I say that Brett is the mate to my soul. Without him, my life will become a slow dying. The woman who came into this world as Lisa Caulfield will no longer exist. The Lisa who married Tate Calhern will merely drift through her makeshift life. There will be no joy. There will be only simulated feelings. There will be merely an imitation of life with Tate and a punishing forfeit of the life with Brett that excites and exhilarates and fulfills."

Melanie ponders these words, calculating their implication for Lisa's fall away from goodness. Then she proceeds to ask the questions that may challenge the perversities of Lisa's willfulness.

"What about Tate? Where does he fit into the picture?"

"He's not in the picture," Lisa says with the hardheartedness that she has often made her stock in trade. "He never really was. I married him without loving him. Our relationship has been a smooth routine for both of us. I'm the glamorous badge he wears to prove to himself and everyone else that he's still alive, even though he lost his first wife. He's a blue-chip stock that pushes me up a notch or two in our social circle. He's the investment that will always yield high dividends."

Lisa pauses once more. She has told the truth. She has placed her trust in this exemplary woman who is gazing upon her with eyes that are sorrow-filled and judgmental. She waits for her to speak.

"I am wondering," Melanie says. "It must be a terrible thing to know that you have betrayed your marriage vows and all the good people who believe that you are doing your best to rescue a lost man, a widower whose grief has imprisoned him."

Lisa makes an emotional appeal. There is anger in her voice. There is defensiveness.

"Before Brett, I was dying. There were many other men in my life. But none of them meant anything special. We played our games. We gambled playfully with our feelings. We accepted our wins and our losses. We waved our goodbyes and went forward to new games. But Brett is different. He is more than a game. He is everything. Without him, I will have no life. Without his love, I could never be happy."

Melanie throws out another question.

"What about Naomi's happiness? Doesn't her happiness count?"

"Brett doesn't love her."

"He is learning to love her," Melanie says. Her voice is soft yet insistent. "He will love her if you don't get in the way."

This truth brings Lisa new apprehension. The hardheartedness that still coils itself around her soul pushes her to repudiate the advice that Melanie is offering her. Her face flushes with anger and fear. Her tremulous voice is heavy with protest and pleading.

"I tell you that I need Brett. Without him, I may as well die."

Maintaining always her ingrained decorum, Melanie speaks the words that Lisa needs to hear.

"You are too soft on yourself. You are forgetting that in matters of love there are things that we can never forgive.

The only way a married woman can exonerate herself from the crime of falling in love with a man meant for another woman is to turn away from that man. She must be her own instrument for saving herself. Only in that way can she belong to herself again."

Lisa begins weeping. Her voice sounds strange and raw now. It is a long time since she wept.

"I can't turn away. I can't stop loving him."

Melanie's words become even more insistent.

"You must do it. You must stop loving him. Otherwise, you will be harming Brett and Naomi and Tate. And you will destroy yourself."

Lisa raises her voice in new, anguished protest.

"I love Brett. I can't stop loving him."

Melanie refuses to back down.

"You must stop loving him. If Brett marries Naomi and if you stay with Tate, Brett will still be in your life. But you must be strong enough not to be in love with him."

Her eyes filled with tears and her voice raspy with sobbing, Lisa makes a new appeal.

"I thought that you would be on my side. I thought that, of all the people I know, you would understand the torment I have been going through. But you are like all those other people. You want me to play by your rules. You don't really care about the grief that those rules will bring to me."

"I care about you," Melanie says. "I also care about Brett and Naomi and Tate. You should care about them, too. You should care about the grief that your willfulness will bring them."

Lisa is not ready for the truth. With her monogrammed handkerchief, she dries her tears. She feels cornered. She becomes wary. Willful and determined once more, she scoffs at Melanie's counsel.

"There is nothing wrong with my leaving my husband to marry the man that I really love. Women do such things every day."

Now Melanie warns Lisa against her worst enemy— herself, the lost woman named Lisa Caulfield Calhern.

"You are not meant to do such a thing. Neither the Kind Fates nor the Good Spirits want you to steal Brett's love from Naomi. Nor do they want you to betray Tate. They want you to be strong enough to do the right thing."

Lisa spurns this news.

"I'll be strong for my own purposes. I'll leave Tate. Brett can forget about Naomi. Together, we can make our own happiness."

Melanie makes a prediction.

"You and Brett will never be happy together. I know. I have seen some of your future."

These words startle Lisa. For an instant, she ponders their meaning while she observes Melanie with eyes that question and that seek an explanation.

"I don't understand," she says. "What is this talk of Kind Fates and Good Spirits?"

"Those Fates and Spirits are my friends," Melanie tells her. "They have shown me some scenes that may belong to your future. Each one of these scenes is different, yet all of them end in tragedy."

Once more, Lisa scoffs at Melanie's words. She rejects them, and she rejects the possibility that the Kind Fates and the Good Spirits might help her.

"I don't need their predictions," she says. "I don't need to know about those scenes. I'll make my own scenes."

"Of course you will. Those are the scenes that the Stern Fates and the Punishing Spirits have in store for you. None of them ends happily, and all of them convey the same message."

"What message is that?"

"Trouble is coming to you. It is trouble of your own making. It is trouble that you cannot avoid unless you change your ways."

Lisa becomes even more impatient. She does not want to hear the truth. She regrets having told Melanie about the affair with Brett.

"How do you know the future? What makes you so special?"

"I am one of the Kind Spirits who are Secondary Spirits. The First Spirit Who knows everything and sees everyone has sent me here to give you a fair warning."

"I don't believe you."

"You *will* believe after I show you those unhappy scenes that may destroy you."

Now, quite suddenly and with a quick wave of her hand, Melanie creates an enchantment. A giant Spirit wall rises upward to surround the wide expanse of the garden. The wall becomes a panoramic video upon which Lisa's future unfolds its mysteries.

As though she is caught inside a dream, Lisa watches herself within a whirlwind of images—layer upon layer of montages and fast-paced scenes that play out their tensions, their obsessions and betrayals, and their varied tragedies.

As the scenes unfold, Lisa begins to comprehend her fate. The trouble that is coming has always been hovering around her. Until now, her deviousness and her wild luck had kept trouble at bay. Now the fiercest kind of trouble like a grim Phantom or a threatening Shadow or the eyeless skull of a cadaver has come to claim her.

CHAPTER SIX

THE FIRST SHOOTING

"I don't want to see your wall videos," Lisa says. "I haven't asked for your storm-predicting forecasts. I don't need your rescuing speeches. I'll make my own way. I'll get the things I want on my own terms."

She is angry. She sounds imperious. Her raised eyebrows bring a hint of *hauteur* to her tense features. She is directing her words to good-natured Melanie and to formidable Randall, who suddenly—and as if emerging from the hidden layers of air—joins them.

"You will have to see the wall videos," Randall tells her.

In this moment, his tall stature, his well-honed muscularity, and his brusque manner serve him well. His no-nonsense demeanor indicates that he will not tolerate the perversities of her willfulness. His husky voice tells her more.

"The videos are your only chance to save yourself."

This time, Lisa cries out her protest. Her voice is no longer imperious, though it still carries the harsh sounds of her anger. Her words enter the air as a tremulous lament that is yoked to a bitter appeal.

"I can't bear to look at what may happen to me," she says. "Let it happen. Let come what may. I'd rather not have it in any other way."

Melanie, influenced by a tremendous capacity for pity and for helpfulness, offers her new, counseling words.

"You must watch the wall videos," she advises Lisa. "What you do in the near future will influence not only your life, but also the lives of Naomi, Brett, and Tate. Surely, you do not want to bring harm to any of them. Yet, if you do not do the right things, if you do not make the correct choices, you *will* bring harm to them and to yourself."

Lisa, apprehensive and resentful, still hesitates.

Melanie prods her further.

"Randall and I want to help you," she says. "You are lost, and we want to help you recover your better self."

"By watching these wall videos?"

"Exactly."

"It all sounds so fantastic."

Randall comes into it again.

"It's very real," he tells her. "In truth, the videos are more than real. They are supernatural."

Lisa reconsiders the implications of his words. She reflects upon the trajectory of their meaning. Her tough-mindedness cancels none of her doubts. Her cynicism, her distrust of most people, and her contempt of the world that she has learned to navigate with wily nuances and well-calibrated betrayals push her forward. This news of supernatural sightings goads her disbelief even as it inspires her apprehension.

"In that case," she says, "I will watch the videos. I have nothing to lose."

Now, with her gentle manner and her soft voice that intends to counsel her well, Melanie has more to say.

"Oh, my dear, you do have something to lose. In fact, you have everything to lose."

"Everything?"

Randall comes into it again. Steel-true and insistent, his words tell her what she needs to hear. They tell her what she may lose.

"Everything that matters to you," he says. "Everything. Yourself."

Once again, Lisa's eyes are drawn to the giant Spirit wall that, with a wave of Melanie's hand, has risen upward and surrounds the wide expanse of the garden. The wall has become a panoramic video upon which Lisa's future unfolds its mysteries.

Once more, as though she is caught inside a dream, Lisa watches herself within a whirlwind of images—layer upon layer of montages and fast-paced scenes that play out their tensions, their obsessions and betrayals, and their varied tragedies.

As the scenes go on unfolding their lacerating revelations, Lisa comprehends her fate with grim-faced rancor. Her strong-minded awareness of her fallible self tells her the punishing truths that in the darkest corners of her soul she has often concealed from herself. The trouble that is hastening to reveal itself has always been shadowing her. Until now, her duplicity and her shrewd calculations have kept trouble at bay. Now the fiercest kind of trouble like an accusatory Phantom or a prosecuting Shadow or a hostile Specter has come to claim her.

There, on the video wall, right *there* inside the flurry of scenes that impart their wayward meanings, Lisa sees herself hurrying from her Mercedes-Benz on a rain-swept summer night into the private elevator that will bring her to Brett's pristine townhouse. She is wearing a Marc Jacobs metallic blue vinyl trench coat that has a long, oversized design punctuated by strong shoulders. A concealed button closure keeps the focus on the style. A cinching self-tie belt, belted cuffs, and a pleated back yoke add glamour to this rain-serviceable coat. Beneath the coat, she is wearing a powder blue jersey, a navy belt, and white slacks. She is also wearing waterproof garden shoes that gleam with a design of delicate blue and white leaves. She is carrying a navy-blue Yves Saint Laurent medium matelassé calf leather shoulder bag with its iconic YSL logo in silver-toned metal. Inside the bag, she has concealed a Colt Cobra .38 Special— a reliable snub-nosed revolver with a nickel finish and a round-butt grip frame. The revolver will protect her from the highway thieves who have lately been plundering and raping lone female drivers on dark, stormy nights such as this one that she has managed to navigate without any violent incident. She carries, too, a white leather overnight case that matches her slacks.

She looks young and alive. There is an urgent rhythm in her step. The elevator is carrying her upward to the only man that she will ever love.

During the past week, Brett has been away in Brussels for an international conference of lawyers. In all that time, they exchanged three or four email messages. None of them specified the day of his return. But she knows that some of their colleagues returned from the conference two days ago. She does not understand why Brett has not answered her most recent email messages. She imagines that his commitments to the conference and his additional meetings with new lawyerly friends have kept him very busy. At any rate, she is abiding by the plan they made before he left for Europe. Exactly one week from the afternoon of his departure, she is supposed to meet him here in his penthouse. They will have hours and hours of being together. They will revel in passionate nights together, and they will enjoy wonderful days afterward.

Tate is in Chicago. He will not return for several days.

She enters the apartment quietly so that she will not waken Brett. It is more likely, of course, that the storm will waken him. The rumbling of thunder, the heavy rain lashing against the panoramic window, and the surreal flashes of lightning have already disturbed the quiet of the living room. Still, she sees the room, with its rich furnishings and precisely selected amenities, as a solacing refuge. In the distance, at the bar located within the southeast corner of the room, she notices a gold-rimmed tumbler containing a few drams of scotch. The tumbler was not there a few days ago, when she brought a fresh arrangement of red and yellow roses to trumpet-shaped white opal glass vases that brighten the right and left corners of the bar. The roses are still blooming. The motherly woman who cleans the apartment twice a week has seen to that. The roses please Lisa. They meld with the painted flowers that adorn the vases, and they enhance the gold decoration on the neck and feet of the vases.

She leaves her shoulder bag on the counter of the bar. The glamour of its matelassé calf leather smoothly conceals her Colt Cobra .38 Special.

Brett is not in this room, but the tumbler tells her that he is in the apartment. Even though he is not right here, standing next to her, she feels his sensual presence. Within this hour, after she bathes and powders and covers her perfumed body with a cobalt blue negligee, she will slip into Brett's bed. She will not stir him awake. But, as he has done in the past, he may turn in his sleep and become aware of her presence. Perhaps the touch of her scented body next to his nakedness will rouse him out of his sleep. He will begin by kissing her. He will notice her blue, consenting eyes and understand that she has been waiting for him. He will come fully awake and make vigorous love with her.

On entering the apartment on this stormy night, she imagines that all these things may happen.

She does bathe, powder, and perfume her body. She covers herself with the cobalt blue negligee that has always increased Brett's pleasure. She sips some brandy to allay the late summer chill that has suddenly taken hold of her, as though her ghost or some invisible Phantom is hovering uneasily near her. The howling wind, the lashing rain, and the booming thunder intensify her need to be with Brett. Now she hurries to the master bedroom and pauses before the closed door. Its being closed convinces her that Brett has sought the privacy of sleep after spending an exhausting week in Brussels.

But when she opens the door, Lisa sees an altogether different scene from the one that she has been anticipating. The soft lights of the lamps on the night tables that flank the oversize bed reveal Brett to her eyes first of all. He is lying on his back, asleep. His naked body catches some of the lamplight and glows with an otherworldly, rugged handsomeness. Leaning into a galaxy of pillows, he looks contented. There is no trace of the sullenness or the dismay that has sometimes touched his face when he is with her. He looks like a young man that, for this night at least, has reclaimed the happiness he has sometimes squandered.

Naomi is lying next to him. She, too, is naked, and her soft-skinned, fragile beauty glows as if she too is otherworldly. She is sleeping as peacefully as Brett. A smile touches her lips, and her right hand touches Brett's left arm.

For a moment, as though she is held prisoner by what she sees, Lisa freezes at the threshold of the bedroom. Her astonishment at finding Brett in bed with Naomi sets her senses reeling. The room swirls and swoops away from her. The walls and ceiling fold into one another, tilt and slant and pitch and then slope and scatter. In almost the same instant, the capacious room hastens back to reassemble itself and then lists, careens, and keels over, throwing away with a spinning velocity the vividly textured paintings, night tables, and lighted lamps, and the oversized bed with cobalt blue Egyptian cotton sheets, bear-skin blanket, and a galaxy of colorful pillows.

So Lisa believes, as she leans against the door and struggles to find her proper balance. She closes her eyes and, like a self-centered woman who has experienced for the first time the harsh betrayal of her romantic assignations, she waits for the vision that has flashed before her seeing to disappear. She waits once more for the room to reassemble itself. As soon as she opens them, she sees that her eyes have not confused her. Brett and Naomi are lying in bed, their naked bodies erotically connected by Naomi's caress of Brett's arm and by the mutual touch of their legs. Once again, Brett has lied to her. Before he left for Brussels and right after one of their frequent copulations, he assured her that she was the only woman that he loved. His being here with Naomi, carnal and duplicitous, instantly spurs her anger. Tense yet self-protective, she compels herself to stay in control. She invents reasons for Brett's willingness to sleep with Naomi. Possibly, Naomi threatened to break their engagement. Perhaps, Brett had a few drinks and had no will power to resist his need of a woman. Maybe he was lonely. Maybe he missed *her*, Lisa Caulfield Calhern, the woman he sometimes referred to as a desirable voluptuary because, before Tate and before him, she had seduced many men. Maybe he was thinking of her while he made love to Naomi.

In her haste to be gone, Lisa turns from her sighting of them and, with her back to the light, gropes for the doorknob. She intends to enter the private corridor and retreat, sixty feet away, to the guest bedroom. But she stumbles, and her hand brushes against the switch that turns on the central lights. At the same time, the key falls out of the lock and tumbles across the hardwood floor. Over and over, it rolls, its metallic clink rising up to declare itself even while the wind and the rain keep swirling and reeling their powers outside the panoramic window.

The echoing tinkle of the fallen key and the dazzle of light shooting out of the ceiling's crystal bulb pendant awaken Brett and Naomi. Startled and disconcerted even in their languor, they lift themselves away from their pillows and with searching eyes survey the room. The key has ceased its tinkling and has come to rest near the plush Egyptian rug that covers the area around the bed. But the central light shines with modulated warmth and coaxes the two lovers out of their languor.

At first, Lisa cannot bear to look at them again. Instead, she wills herself to concentrate upon the crystal bulb pendant, with its hand-carved patterns that replicate those found on whiskey glasses and decanters. To maintain her self-control, she focuses her gaze upon the gold silken fabric cord from which the lighting fixture is suspended. She recalls traveling to Italy to confer with the famous glassblower who designed and created the pendant. Despite her attempt to keep her gaze on the pendant, she steals another glance at Brett with Naomi. She stiffens at the sight of them. Her hatred of Naomi is a new and fierce sensation. Naomi, with her various neuroses spawned from her mother's early death and her father's inveterate disdain of her, is her adversary. This thought grounds her to the complicated situation into which wild chance and bad luck have plunged her. It takes only a moment for her to recover herself and, without flinching, to face amorous and needy Naomi and utterly faithless Brett.

Brooding and slowly coming awake, Brett leans against a colorful array of pillows and, with wily interest, observes the scene that unfolds its complications.

Naomi is the first to speak as she hurries out of the bed and covers her nakedness with a lacey, pink clay kimono robe. With her tangled titian hair; her long, slender legs; and her tall, slim figure, she looks lovely and seductive. In this problematic moment, a frown mars her beauty, and her impatient voice yokes her displeasure to a blunt protest.

"You shouldn't be here," she tells Lisa. "You are way out of line. You are forgetting who you are."

Instantly, Lisa has a wild impulse to rush across the room and slap Naomi's face until she draws blood from it. But her fear that she might strike her so hard that she will kill her holds her back. If she makes a violent scene, she will destroy forever her chance to maintain her affair with Brett. She will also destroy the marriage to Tate that enhances her status and makes her an heiress to part of his immense fortune if she remains married to him for another year.

Instead, she speaks soft words.

"You know about Brett and me," she guesses aloud. "He's told you everything."

"Yes," Naomi answers her, with words both ironic and matter of fact. "He has told me. It's a surprise, isn't it? Lately, he's had some rough bouts with his conscience. Maybe he's becoming a new man."

Now it is Lisa's turn to choose ironic and matter-of-fact words.

"Don't you believe it," she says. "Pangs of conscience are not Brett's style. He smashes lives and never bothers with the wreckage."

Naomi chooses insinuating words that point Lisa the way to her own folly.

"What about you?" she asks. "What do you do after you smash up lives?"

Her words give Lisa pause. But they do not dissuade her from her selfish motives. She is not willing to abandon the pact that she has made with Brett.

"I go on living," she says. "This time I'll go on living with Brett."

"What about my father? You told him that you love him. You married him."

"Maybe I loved him—a little—when I married him. But I don't love him now. I love only Brett."

Naomi turns pale. Hearing Lisa's brazen confession, she is sorrow-filled and angry and despairing and all at the same time.

"So, you'll go on lying to my father," she says, her words coming fast and accusatory. "You'll stay in the marriage so you can share his fortune. You'd even go on sleeping with Brett, if you had your way."

With a contemptuous glance toward her and with blunt, cold-hearted words, Lisa quickly answers her.

"Brett needs me. He needs excitement and mystery and adventure. You don't do any of those things for him."

Naomi ignores the harsh language and the pride-wounding insult. Instead, she reminds Lisa of the wrong she is committing.

"You'll go on betraying your husband. Just like that."

"Plenty of women have done so," Lisa answers her. "Now it's my turn."

"Brett won't give you that chance," Naomi tells her, caustic now and admonishing. "He has his flaws, but he also lives on the realistic level. Without me, he won't have any share in my father's fortune. Brett's dumping you. You'd better get used to the idea."

"We don't need your father's fortune," Lisa says, uneasy because the idea is new to her. "We have successful careers. We can make our own fortunes together."

At once, Naomi spurns this idea. Her awareness of Brett's betrayal of her trust and of Lisa's betrayal of her and of Tate activates her capacity for tough-mindedness and for blunt appraisals of the man that she plans to marry despite his moral failings.

"That won't be enough for Brett. He's a greedy man. He wants a share of my father's fortune, too."

The truth of Naomi's words stings at Lisa's apprehension.

"I'm not letting him go," she says. "Brett will be making a big mistake if he thinks that I'll let him go."

Naomi fires new words at her.

"You are the one who is making a mistake," she says. "Brett has let *you* go, and that is the end of your wretched affair with him. Count yourself lucky that I'm not telling my father about your betrayal of him."

These words surprise Lisa.

"You are not telling your father? Why not?"

Once again, Naomi glares at her with new and irrevocable hatred.

"I'm not doing it for you," she says. "I'm doing it for me. You and my father deserve each other. You are the punishment that my Good Fates have brought into his life because of all the years that he refused to love me."

Willful and rebellious, Lisa delivers a warning.

"I'll still see Brett. He's not going out of my life."

Naomi delivers her own warning, its implications even more troublesome.

"If he starts sleeping with you again, I'll know it. So will my father."

She hurries to the bathroom to shower and to cleanse her body with expensive lotions.

During this exchange of words, Brett has continued to lean into the comfortable array of pillows while he goes on observing Naomi and her with cynical detachment. Now, when he is alone with her, he brushes aside his betrayal of the pact that he had made with her.

"Stuff happens," he says, as he leans away from his pillows and takes a cigarette from the gold case on the night table next to him. Only after he brings a gold lighter to his cigarette and takes a drag on it does he cover his nakedness with a blanket. There is no modesty in the gesture or any concern that in this troubled hour his nakedness may offend her. He does not care what she thinks. He cares only for himself and for the pleasure that he has taken from Naomi.

A churning hatred surges inside Lisa's mind and soul. The hatred alarms her. She does not want to hate this vigorous man who, even now as he leans against his pillows, excites her. Yet she does hate him. She hates herself even more because he expects her to forgive his careless disregard of the love that she has been offering him.

"This wasn't supposed to happen," she says. "You promised that you would rarely sleep with Naomi before you married her. You said that you were saving yourself for me alone."

"Naomi is needy. She likes the way I make love to her."

"Bastard," Lisa says. "You bastard. I should call it quits with you. I should turn away from you and never look back."

"You're stuck with me, baby, even though we won't be sleeping together. I'll be around all the time because I'm marrying Naomi."

"You told me that you do not love her."

"I'm beginning to love her. I love her because she adulates me. I love her because she regards me as her hero. She's a foolish romantic, and I love her for that, too. She's my biggest fan. Lately, I get a hard on every time she praises me."

"Bastard. You are enjoying this mess because you are a devious bastard."

"With you, I've never pretended otherwise. We've always leveled with one another. We are self-centered and manipulative. We use people. We hurt them and never count the cost. We never pay for our wrongdoing. You and I have had a good time together. I thought I loved you as much as I could ever love anyone. But something's changed. I've changed. The big surprise is that I'm beginning to love Naomi—really love her. I care about her. I want her to be happy. I want her to be happy with me."

"She's your lottery prize. That's why you love her. That's the reason you won't let go of her."

"Maybe. But maybe that's not the reason. I'm already becoming a success on my own terms. I don't need her money."

"What about us? What about the plans we've been making?"

"We've got to let them go. We've got to let go of each other. We have to make a clean break. It won't be easy. I admit that. After I marry Naomi, she and I will be in Tate's and your company on many occasions. Maybe Naomi will learn to forgive you. Maybe she won't. But she's not going to tell Tate about us. Naomi loves me. She has already forgiven me my various transgressions. Intuitively, she knows that I'll be traveling a straight-and-narrow path. There will be no other women for me. There will be only Naomi. She is the is the only woman that I will ever love."

"You can't get rid of me so fast. I won't let you."

"We've got to make a clean break. Everything's different now. There's no going back. We can't play our games anymore. There's nothing permanent in them. There is only cheating and lying and hurting other people."

"I don't care how many women you sleep with, as long as I'm one of them."

Brett meets her remark with a husky laugh.

"You are a good sport, baby," he says. "You've always been fun to be with because you've known that we have been playing a game. But the game is over. It's ended. *Finis.*"

After saying so and without waiting for her to reply, he leaves his bed quickly and covers himself with a burgundy robe. With a cigarette perched in the corner of his mouth, he looks like a street tough. The shadow of a sneer suggests a callous nature and a ruthless disposition. He takes one last drag on his cigarette, snuffs the remains in an ashtray, and heads for the bedroom in the east wing of the townhouse. There, Lisa imagines, he will use the shower in the adjoining bathroom to wash away Naomi's scent and his own carnal odor.

Without offering her any other words or indicating that her being here is of any importance, Brett leaves Lisa standing alone at the foot of the bed. Dressed in her cobalt blue negligee, she appears to his eyes as an intruder. From now on, she will have to keep her distance. Otherwise, with guarded reserve and courteous words, he will nudge her away from any contact he deems too personal. That is the way their lives will play out. Until the end of their time, they will have to keep their distance. Brett will see to that. All these things Lisa comprehends with new anguish and the beginning of a fury she struggles to suppress.

Her shrewd instinct that has always protected her during those darkest hours when her life seems disarranged and hollow warns her to hurry away from this scene. But something keeps her here—some brooding need to bring harm to Brett and to Naomi, some implacable desire to avenge herself against the lover who has betrayed her and the girl who has stolen that love from her.

Bitter and despairing, she waits for Naomi to emerge from her bathing, fully awake now, freshly scented, and revealing no evidence of her intercourse with Brett. While she waits, she stands at the rain-spattered window and observes the new flashes of lightning, the wind-sieged branches of trees, and the quickened rivulets of water flowing across the wide, empty street. A pale moon is peering behind an ominous cloud, and thunder is still booming over the sweep and swirl of the rain. In spite of the torrential rains and the punishing winds, the brownstones that line the affluent street stand formidable and resilient. She needs that kind of strength. She needs to reactivate the tough-minded capacities that have always persuaded her to endure without flinching the raw bruises and scalding betrayals of life. If she capitulates to the self-centered terms that Brett has invoked for their relationship, she will forfeit her best defensive capacities. By deferring to his will, she will lose her own will. The thought makes her bristle. Never will she become weak-willed and petitioning. Never will she surrender her unbridled freedom and her self-possessed individuality. If she places her iron will in his keeping, Brett will make a chain of it to bind her to his arbitrary and self-serving inclinations.

To dispel these bitter thoughts, Lisa hurries into the living room and heads for the bar in the southeast corner of the large, richly appointed room that overlooks a terrace and, beyond that, another dimly lighted street that appears to be moving, at least for an instant, because of the rivulets of rain that are scurrying along the street and off the curbs.

She pours herself a snifter of brandy, her second that night. She leaves the bar and takes a seat on the richly upholstered sofa in the living room. She drinks this brandy more swiftly than she had the first. The liquor warms her and brings a semblance of pleasure that momentarily pushes away the disheartening effects of the past half-hour. The brandy revives her belief that she can change Brett's mind. She can persuade him to abandon his rigid, moralistic plan. She can win back his love and stoke his desire to continue their affair. But no sooner has this makeshift conviction, with its fantasy implications, convinced her that happiness is once more within her reach than Naomi comes into the room. An undercurrent of tension does not eclipse her glamour or diminish her titian-haired beauty. She wears a navy-and-white stripe top, white jeans, and navy ankle boots. On her arm, she carries a beige double-breasted trench coat that navy buttons make even more stylish. The look is absolutely right for her. It enhances her feminine appeal even as it intensifies the forthright manner and no-nonsense certainty that now attends her.

Naomi is carrying a beige overnight duffel bag. It has loop handles and adjustable shoulder straps, and its zippers and clasps are colored in gold. This duffel bag completes the elegant image that Naomi means to impart. As fraught with tension as she is and with new combative willfulness, she will not betray the careful presentation of herself to anyone observing her.

Now, as she enters the room, Naomi is the first to speak. She brings to her words both insolence and enmity. She is confronting the woman who has betrayed her trust and made a fool of her father. The offense against her father, she can easily forgive. The affair with Brett, illicit and duplicitous, she will never forgive. There is a harder edge to her voice as she addresses her. No longer does she care to imagine that Lisa is her friend. By sleeping with Brett, Lisa has declared that she is her adversary. Naomi chooses harsh words to declare once more how things stand between them.

"Keep in mind my warning to you," she says. "Stay away from Brett. Get used to the idea that he will be your son-in-law, not your lover."

Lisa grows very still. Her face turns pale with the anger that is rising inside her. Her eyes narrow their gaze and glare their hatred. She will not cower before Naomi's warning or accede to the staid rules that she is summoning as her allies. She will flout every one of those rules. She will be herself, Lisa Caulfield Calhern, a twenty-nine-year-old woman who has fallen in love with Brett Robinson and will never let him go.

She heaves blunt words at Naomi.

"Even if I stay away from Brett, he will never stay away from me. We are meant to love each other. Maybe we are even meant to die together."

Naomi lodges another protest, more vehement and abrasive.

"I don't believe that. You shouldn't be speaking those words. Those words are meant for two people that love one another honestly, without any complicated plotting or subtle deception."

"I won't give him up," Lisa insists. "Never!"

Naomi scowls. For an instant, she looks like a woman capable of murder. Lisa sees her own face in that scowl, in the hate-filled eyes, and in the angry curve of the lips. In so many ways, she and Naomi are unlike each other. But in their capacity for killing their rival and in the likelihood that they will go over the edge and kill that rival and even their traitorous lover, they are very much alike.

Restrained yet threatening, Naomi hurls another warning.

"Stay away from Brett."

Lisa fires back her refusal.

"I'll never stay away, and neither will Brett. Just wait and see."

Lisa returns to the bar, pours herself another brandy, and lights another cigarette. This time she drinks the brandy more slowly while she stands by the window and once again peers at the storm-laden street. Though Naomi remains in the room, Lisa no longer acknowledges her presence. Only when she hears Brett's voice does she turn to see that Naomi has taken a seat on the sofa and has withdrawn to her own private musing.

When he enters the room, Brett studies them with his wily assurance and his playful arrogance. He looks refreshed and complacent. He is wearing a collarless blue shirt, gray trousers, black tailored trench coat, and black ankle rain boots.

"Let's get on with it," he tells Naomi as he smiles through the tension that she and Lisa have brought to the room. "I'll get you home safe and happy in a few minutes."

He grins at her with casual affection. She, in turn, rises from the sofa and plants a kiss upon his lips. The sight of him has dissolved nearly all of her tension, at least on the surface.

"I'm ready," Naomi tells him. "This is one time that I won't keep you waiting."

The kiss inspires him to help her with her raincoat. After tying the belt in the front without buckling it and retrieving her duffel bag from the sofa, she is ready to leave.

"What about me?" Lisa asks him.

In this moment that will be a revelation for her as well as for Naomi and him, Brett offers her blunt, dismissive words.

"It's over, Lisa," he says. "Let's end it with style. We are grown-ups. We've been around the block a few times. We know the score. We know when an affair begins. We know when it ends. Let's walk away from each other. Let's never look at each other in the same way even when we are in one another's company."

"You don't mean the things you're saying. You can't mean them—not after what we've meant to each other, not after all the secrets we've shared with one another, not after all the promises we've made for the days and months and years that are yet to come."

"Things change," he says. "People change. I've changed. I'm getting what I want. Don't stand in the way. Don't make trouble."

Lisa's voice is harsher now as she delivers a warning.

"You'll never leave me. I won't let you."

Brett, insolent and cynical and brash, fires back at her.

"But I am leaving you. Just move on. You'll get over it. An affair like ours never lasts. It blazes quickly. It burns brightly and burns out fast."

Lisa suddenly looks frightened. Her voice loses its harshness. She makes an appeal, yet her words still convey a darker edge.

"Don't try to leave me. I'm warning you."

Brett wants no more of her.

"You are history, Lisa. You belong to my past."

Lisa becomes unstrung. She grabs hold of his shoulder. She wants to keep him from turning away.

"Don't leave me! Don't!"

Brett breaks away from her touch. This time, he doesn't look back. This time he starts to leave the room with Naomi.

Lisa senses herself evaporating from herself, becoming someone other than herself, becoming lost in an altogether alien scene, a disoriented reality somersaulting into still another and even stranger reality. She screams a furious and heart-breaking scream that stops Brett in his tracks and compels him to look back at her.

Instantly, the room rises up and scatters all its properties. Walls curve and slope inward, hurry toward her and just as quickly rush away. Space hurls itself apart from her. Sofas and chairs, panoramic window and cathedral ceiling, chandelier and paintings and wrap-around bar pitch and waver and fling themselves forward, catapulting through chasms of rising darkness. Swaying now, as if in unison with the lift and drift and propulsion of the room, her body starts to keel. But something, some force or fury raw and alive inside her, pushes her back to her ordinary stance, tall and willowy and confident. In this here-at-last minute, here in this electric minute that in the back of her mind she has been anticipating, she catches sight of her shoulder bag on the counter of the bar, where she left it when she entered Brett's townhouse. She lifts out of it her snub-nosed revolver and—quick as a flash of motion—points the pistol at Brett and fires it again and again. The bullets crash through his heart and his forehead and his face and, as if in the same instant, his body falls backward. His dead eyes and his ruined face glare their surprise. Blood trickles out of his nose and out of the left corner of his mouth and spills out of his chest.

She hears Naomi's scream. It is more than a scream. It is a woman's lament. It is an agonized wailing.

"No! No!" she screams as she kneels by the crumpled body. "No! No!"

"I warned you," Lisa says. "I warned both of you."

Now she shoots Naomi in the back of her head. Blood and brain tissue swoosh from Naomi's forehead and from her mouth. The body slumps over and arrives at a place just below Brett's shoulders. From a distance, the dead bodies resemble two lovers caressing each other upon a gleaming hickory floor.

A strange silence, eerie and mysterious, overtakes the room. Not even the lashing patter of the rain and the booming thunder and the flickering lights displace the strange silence that draws Lisa into its labyrinth. Once again, she swoons. She passes out. Her body crumples across the floor, not far from the bodies of this arrogant man and this foolish woman that she has killed.

After she awakens and slowly sifts the meaning of the violent look of the room, after the strange stillness melts away and her terrified eyes notice the gleaming revolver and catch sight, too, of the dead bodies lying one upon the other in the center of the room, Lisa becomes aware of what she has done. There is no escaping the grim reality of the scene. The stare of Brett's bleeding eyes and the crushed look of his face and his slightly open mouth declare, voiceless and irrevocable, that his life is over. The twisted expression that deprives Naomi of her genteel loveliness and the left brown eye that bulges from its socket are signs of her violent dying.

The shock of the two corpses jolts Lisa into a screaming admission.

"I've killed them! I've killed them!"

She turns from the sight of the bodies. She intends to hurry to the bedroom, change into her street clothes, and flee from the house. But no sooner does she take the first steps into her flight, than ghostly shadows rise up before her. At once, she sees that these are no ordinary shadows. They are otherworldly Shadows. They are Apparitions. In the same instant, the scene within the wall video, anchored as it has been to malice and horror, vanishes away. As though she is waking from a nightmare, she finds herself once again in the here-and-now reality of the dusk-shaded splendor of the rose garden. She is sitting on a comfortable bench not far from the delicate topiaries of a doe and her fawn.

In this same familiar reality, ghostly shadows continue to rise up until they pause before her.

One of the Apparitions slowly emerges as a beautiful woman from a fairy tale—a princess, perhaps, or a young queen. In less than a minute, she becomes Melanie.

The other Apparition comes forth from its Shadowy existence as a luminous Shape Shifter—a warrior archangel, first, and right afterwards as a heroic World War Two bomber pilot. Just as swiftly, the Apparition becomes Randall Johnson.

Stern and commanding, Randall steps forward. In this instant, he is once more the prosecuting attorney. He is the captain of a jury of stern Spirits. He is the Spirit Executioner who has always been waiting for her.

"You want to flee," he says. "But you won't be able to run away. There is no escape. You are a cold-hearted killer now. You have stopped the lives of two human beings."

Melanie joins him. With her ingrained decorum and her large capacity for pitying the downtrodden and the errant, she whispers words that sound as though they are carrying all her sadness and all her tears.

"Oh, my dear. Why did you do it? Didn't you consider the punishment that awaits you?"

Randall, as if sentencing her, tells her more.

"Here on Earth, you will be tried and convicted. You will spend the rest of your life in prison—but not for long. One morning, just before dawn, you will hang yourself in your prison cell. After you die, you will come to Sojourn. There, a jury of formidable Spirits will review your case. I will be the judge who pronounces sentence upon you. I already know the verdict the jurors will reach. I already know my final judgment upon you. We will condemn you to eternal vanishment."

Lisa, bewildered by her crime and embittered by the folly of her love affair with Brett, pauses after the brusque sounds of Randall's words.

"Eternal vanishment?"

Without sympathy and without softening the message that he is bringing to her, Randall tells her what she needs to know.

"All traces of you will be deleted from the Earth's memory and from Heaven's, too."

Now Lisa begins to implore Randall and Melanie with words of regret and with an awakening capacity for pitying the two persons that she has murdered.

"I don't want it to end in this way. I don't want to kill them. Please give me another chance. Please tell me that this is not the way things will end."

Impassive in this moment and disinclined to impart any new words except those encompassing a stoic interrogation, Randall pushes blunt questions before her.

"Are you really willing to change? Or do you pity yourself rather than Naomi and Brett? Have you begun to confront your wrongdoing, even apart from the murders?"

After entering a long silence and after reflecting upon his questions, Lisa answers him.

"I don't know. I'm not certain. What I do know is that I don't want to murder anyone, not even Brett, who has betrayed me, and Naomi, who has stolen the only man that I will ever love."

"Look to your own sins," Randall admonishes her. "Keep in mind all the moral errors you have committed."

"I want to forget them."

"That is the easy way out—to forget, to deny that your wrongdoing even existed."

Wary now of Randall's hostile presence and fearful of her murderous impulses, Lisa chooses new petitioning words.

"I want a chance to live differently."

Melanie comes into it again. She is warmhearted as usual, yet tension and melancholy touch her words.

"You will have that chance, Lisa. You'll see."

With a wave of her right hand, Melanie brings forth another enchantment. A new video flashes upon the celestial wall that surrounds the full expanse of the room. New sightings of the wily and turbulent episodes involving Lisa, Tate, Naomi, and Brett begin to unfold. Before they impart their conflicted narratives, Randall offers her a clue about their meaning.

"You will find that nobody changes overnight. The rewards of sin last only a moment, but the consequences of evil last even after our judgment day."

CHAPTER SEVEN

THE SECOND SHOOTING

"Once again, you are being tested," Randall tells Lisa. "Once more you will have the chance to identify who you really are."

"I know who I am," Lisa says. "I don't want to kill anybody. I only want Brett to love me."

Melanie comes into it now.

"What if he doesn't love you?" she asks. "What will you do then?"

"I'll soldier through," Lisa answers her. "I'll do what is right. You'll see."

The three of them are standing not in the Calherns' garden, but in in the middle of the reception room of their Georgian home, with its French Provincial plushness; its needlepoint, amply upholstered sofas and chairs; its Aubusson carpet; and its pale gold walls on which are placed four Impressionist canvases. One of these paintings shows a teen boy and his girlfriend sauntering hand-in-hand along the yellow sands of an afternoon beach, oblivious of the crowd of exuberant summer people swimming or cavorting with adolescent assurance there in the teal-blue waters of the French Riviera. Another canvas reveals the pensive face of a nineteenth-century French ballerina in a red tutu with its layers of pleated net and delicate lace ruffles as she stands with disciplined poise at a dancer's handrail. A third canvas portrays a tuxedoed, sandy-haired youth with a beatific expression as he plays upon a violin, the left side of his chin and his shoulder firmly holding the violin stable as his left hand begins to move from a high-pitched note far up on the keyboard to a low one nearer to the peg box. The fourth canvas shows a lovely blonde-haired woman in a white chiffon dress and a dark-haired man in a World War Two pilot's dark brown bomber jacket and light brown trousers. They look exactly like Melanie and Randall. They stand side by side by a lake—this Air Force captain and the love of his life—while they bring to the canvas a heavenly radiance and while, with searching eyes, they peer out at the viewer.

Sunlight glows not only within the canvas. It shines through the panoramic window and brings into the room a luminous, otherworldly ambiance. Melanie and her captain are wearing the same clothes that their lookalikes are wearing in the Impressionist canvas. Lisa is wearing a white sleeveless shift maxi dress, with a V neck and butterfly patterns in blue, red, orange, and yellow. She also wears blue flower sandals.

"We do see what you are going to do," Randall tells her when she urges him to believe that she will do everything that is right if Brett does not choose to return her love. He speaks for himself as well as for Melanie.

His captain's uniform intensifies the militant appearance that has always been an authentic presentation of who he is.

"Though the First Spirit has not permitted us to know what choices you will finally make about your life, He has allowed us to know the mistakes you will continue to make before He tests you for the last time."

As soon as she hears these words, Lisa lodges another protest, one that she prefaces with a question.

"What mistakes are those? Tell me. I want to know. I have a right to know."

Unmoved, Randall issues a new directive.

"You will continue to struggle through the destiny that your own willfulness is creating."

Suddenly, though with no surprise for either Randall or Melanie, Lisa's expression hardens. Her taut features stiffen. Her eyes become clouded with resentment and with her pent-up anger. She no longer petitions Melanie or Randall for their pity and their help. She understands that, despite their earlier counsel, she is on her own. Only she can finally determine her fate.

"So be it," she tells them. "I'll run my own race. I'll pilot my own ship. I'll be in charge of what's going to happen to me."

Having said so, she watches Randall and Melanie carefully observing her within the stillness of a minute. Now, quite suddenly and with a quick wave of his hand, Randall permits the new enchantment to unfold. A giant Spirit wall rises upward to surround the wide expanse of the room. Vivid and clarifying, the wall becomes a panoramic video upon which Lisa's future unfolds its mysteries.

Now, in a flash and without any words to signal their departure, Randall and Melanie vanish away.

Lisa stands alone now—vulnerable, exposed, and indeterminate. She waits for the next minutes to unfold their surprises and their dangers.

Those minutes arrive. The surprises and the dangers begin.

Once again, standing as she does at the wall video as though she is caught inside a dream, Lisa watches herself within a whirlwind of images that belong to her future— layer upon layer of montages and fast-paced scenes that play out their tensions, their obsessions and betrayals, and their varied tragedies.

In this next instant, she finds herself in the bedroom of a ski home in North Conway, New Hampshire. Tate owns it, but he is not here with her. Nor is Brett. During this weekend, she has invited Jake Boldwood into her bed. They go back a few years. Mired by hedge fund scandals, disinherited by his unforgiving father, brought low because of his links with New York racketeers, and struggling to regain his footing after serving four years in an Arizona prison, Jake has lost none of his streetwise inclinations and his willingness to enter nefarious deals that bring him substantial profits.

Jake has lost none of his physical prowess or his sensual magnetism. At thirty-two years old, he stands predominant and assured at six foot two inches. His blond crew cut gives him a clean-cut, trustworthy appearance. His handsome features, his athletic build, and the congenial gleam of his smile win him many admirers. Women admire his charming manner and his understated way of making them feel that each of them is the only woman in the room. Men respect his ingrained authority and his genuine-seeming comradeship. But even these amiable people are wary of associating with him in any business matters. The scandals that have weighed him down have left large stains upon his reputation as an attorney. Currently, Jake makes a modest living by selling luxury cars and by sleeping with debutantes and with the bored wives of rich husbands who are willing to pay him well for his vigorous and furtive companionship in and out of bed.

Before she married Tate, Lisa and Jake went a few thrilling rounds together. Except for Brett, Jake is the lover who excited her most of all. In those days, five years ago and more, he was one of the most successful hedge fund attorneys on Wall Street. But his greed overtook his quick-witted awareness of the punishing way the world works. His wily disposition failed him in crucial episodes that called for keen-sighted planning and fail-safe chicanery. Surreptitious and overconfident, he stole millions from his clients and left them stranded when hedge funds bottomed out. His four years in prison—harsh though they were to mind, body, and spirit—reinforced his plan to steal from the world again and this time to run scot free with the plunder. His prison sentence might have been longer. But, with his lawyerly connections, a payback of ten million dollars, and four years of prison already served, he secured his early release.

Right now, he has been biding his time. He has primed himself to move forward, away from the luxury car front that satisfies his parole officer and away from the escort service that has turned him into a male prostitute. He is ready to win the equivalent of high-yielding blue-chip stocks or of a grand, once-in-a-lifetime lottery.

Sly and self-serving, Lisa has been paying many of his bills. She has set him up in a fashionable apartment in one of the tonier sections of Blue Ridge. She has given him a substantial bank account. She enjoys being his benefactor. The money she gives him derives from her large income as a successful attorney and from an even larger inheritance from a wealthy uncle. Her occasional trysts with him are her secret revenge against her loveless marriage with Tate and her troubled relationship with Brett.

On this here-and-now November morning, when they have awakened from their pleasurable nighttime copulation, Lisa and Jake are conversing in an oversized bed that wears navy blue sheets, a brocade comforter with navy, gray, and burgundy patterns, and a matching galaxy of shams and pillows.

"I like you because you are athletic and because you are as young as I am," Lisa casually remarks to Jake on this Sunday morning when they are spending one of their furtive weekends in a secluded, two-storied ski house in North Conway, two hundred miles away from Blue Ridge. On this weekend Lisa has not been partying with Tate's and her married friends. Nor has Jake involved himself with a vain and deceptive heiress or an unhappy divorcée. During this weekend, he has renewed his passion for Lisa, whose worldly instincts and jaded soul match his own. The world they have fabricated from this weekend tryst has a population of two—Lisa Caulfield Calhern, a clever woman who uses the world with perfect timing and precise negotiations, and Jake Boldwood, a tough-minded man whom the world has knocked about and who—though battered and bruised—hurries in for another combative round.

"I like you especially because you are very good in bed," Lisa tells him. "You really enjoy sex. You are an altogether different specimen from my high-and-mighty, uptight husband who has a severe case of compunction because he's screwing *me* instead of his first, very dead wife."

"You and I think alike," Jake tells her. "We *are* alike. Sex and money—they are what we are made for."

Lisa laughs a lighthearted laugh. This morning she is working the world in her favor.

"We are not afraid of telling the truth to one another. We call a spade a spade."

"Of course we do," Jake says. "We make a good team. We want the same things."

He rises from his bed now and, swaggering across the expansive room, draws open the curtains to the panoramic window to allow the sunlight to float its radiance into every corner of this well-appointed bedroom that is sequestered within the second story of Tate Calhern's country house that Lisa uses whenever she wishes. He can feel the warm glow of the sun touch his naked muscularity and bring to its strength an attractive sheen and an iconic emphasis. In the far distance, the snowcapped mountains rise, proprietary and massive, toward a cold, pale-blue sky and toward wind-pushed wispy clouds. Men and women are skiing down curving slopes of the faraway mountain, their spiraling forms so many flashes of color within the wintry scene. The painterly motion of the scene—its flare, its vitality, and its speed—pleases him. The night just past has brought him gifts. Lisa's perfumed body, open and generous with her favors, is one of the gifts. The other gift, equally compelling to his need, is the plan to make Naomi fall in love with him.

Remembering Lisa's words as she described in detail all that he must do to win Naomi's favor, he turns to gaze upon his loyal friend once more. Their nighttime sex has left him contented and even newly energized. The prolonged thrill of their consummation has eased the festering wounds of his bitter life. Lisa is lolling against a galaxy of colorful pillows, while the scented sheets that she tossed about her only partially conceal the seductive curves of her naked body. She looks like a life-loving woman posing for a museum canvas or like a carefree debutante whose evening copulation has left her satisfied.

He walks back to the bed, his tall and husky manhood a strutting emphasis upon her steady gaze. After climbing in next to her, he fondles her ample breasts and then with his adept hands gently caresses her face. Only after that does he plant a firm kiss upon her lips.

"Tell me about it," he says, right after the kiss. "I want to hear it all over again. Tell me when and why you want me to make Naomi Calhern fall in love with me."

She pulls away from him now. The bluntness of his remark does not disconcert her. She maintains her composure because of her hardheartedness and her jaded acceptance of all the wrongdoing from her past and the wrongdoing that will belong to her future. She grows very still. The stillness that comes upon her neither surprises nor disturbs him. He knows her well. Her stillness is a strategy for taking control of the moment. He watches her reaching for one of her imported cigarettes from the gold cigarette case on a bed table nearby. After bringing it to the flame of a gold lighter, she leans once more into the galaxy of pillows that, in a compatible way, extend the comforts of the morning. She takes a few drags on her cigarette and watches the smoke wafting around them. Once or twice, she peers at him. The intensity of her blue eyes and the warmth of her soft flesh is a vivid presence beside him. All this while she lingers within this stillness that seems as natural as it is reflective. He joins her in the stillness, unwilling to hurry her into the words that he is waiting to hear. When she does speak, she offers her appraisal of where they stand with each other.

"I am using you," she says. "But you don't mind. You and I use each other, and the games we play always leave us happy. This weekend, though, isn't about us—at least, not all of it. We are here together because you need information about Naomi and about the best strategies for gaining her trust and her love. We are here because we both stand to win a big prize."

Jake is not surprised by her cold-hearted appraisal or by her refusal to romanticize their association. With him, Lisa has always been on the level. If she were less honest with him, he would see through her dissembling. She is willing to bring him into her plan because he has leveled with her about his hedge fund crimes and about his Wall Street schemes that drove three weak-willed, pampered heirs to suicide.

"How big a prize is it?" he asks her. "You haven't told me that yet."

Before Lisa answers him, she takes another drag on her cigarette and once again studies the wisps of smoke billowing around her and around Jake. Then she turns to him because she wants to study his reaction. She speaks the words that he is ready to hear.

"You will be fifty million dollars richer," she tells him. "That's the money that Naomi's mother has left her. That sum doesn't include the big money she is raking in from the sales of her books or the inheritance she will receive after Tate dies."

"What will my marrying her get you? Why do you want Brett Robinson out of the picture?"

"He's no good for her. He will only make her life miserable."

"There's more to it than that. I know you too well to imagine that you want to play Fairy Godmother to Naomi. What's in it for you, besides pushing Naomi away from Brett?"

"Brett is better for me. At first, I wanted them to get married. That was my way of keeping Brett near me. But things have changed. Brett has changed. He's gone noble. He wants to become a faithful husband. He no longer wants me around as his secret paramour. When Naomi marries you, Brett will come back to me. I'm as sure of that as I am of anything."

"Are you planning to leave your husband?"

"No," she answers him without any hesitation. "Tate wields a great deal of power. I like being inside the center of that power. It thrills me. It gives me the kind of pleasure I never get when he's in bed with me."

"Do you really believe that Brett will come back to you if Naomi decides to marry me?"

"Of course," Lisa says. "After Naomi marries you, Brett will be lonely. He'll drift. He'll sleep with a few debutantes and some nightclub girls and quickly tire of them. He will keep in mind that Naomi has spurned him, and he will grow to hate her. He'll remember all the times that I've defended her from the tyranny of her father. He'll remember the risks I've taken to sleep with him. He'll remember the gifts and the stock market tips. He'll come back to me because we are so much alike. We belong together. We are very selfish. We are too ambitious. We are deep-down-and-forever rotten."

"Just like me," Jake says.

"You and I know how to play the game even more than Brett does. Lately, he's turned soft. He's become moral. But he's good in bed. He's what I want this year and maybe for many years to come."

"What about me? Where do I fit in your life?"

"In the most secret part—that's where you belong. I'm not letting you go, even when you marry Naomi and not even when Brett comes back to me. We'll always have our trysts—you and I. Besides, I really want to help you. I'm going to introduce you to all the right people—celebrities and other big leaguers who have moved through a few scandals and who have become even richer afterwards. They are our kind of people. They scoff at convention, and they ride roughshod over adversaries. When they back you, Tate will fall in line. He owes them a few favors. They know the skeletons hiding in his closet."

Hearing her words, Jake offers her a sly smile. His pulse quickens. His wind-burned face becomes flushed. It takes him a few moments to harness his feelings. When he speaks, he chooses streetwise words to deflect the excitement that is rushing through him. Before he finds the right words, he leans toward Lisa and kisses her. He takes hold of her cigarette and enjoys a few drags upon it. Its coiling smoke rises and hovers around him, as though it has come there to conceal his face. Only now does he speak the words that keep him anchored to his realistic understanding of who Lisa is.

"You are quite a babe," he tells her. "You are not afraid of getting hurt or of hurting other people."

"I won't get hurt, because I'm going to make everything work for me—and for you."

"I like what I'm hearing," Jake says. "I like it fine. I've struck a gold mine—a treasure trove, the mother lode."

Lisa laughs. It is not the first time that she finds Jake's sly wit to her liking.

"You are a cool hustler," she says. "You know an opportunity when you see one. Naomi Calhern doesn't have a chance of escaping you. Not that she will want to. You will be Mister Right because you and I are going to make her believe you are."

Jake hands Lisa her cigarette and, while he watches her take a drag on it, he speaks matter-of-fact words. As he speaks, he watches her keen-eyed gaze upon him and her knowing smile. He remembers the brazen promise of her words that has revived his self-belief and his plans for climbing to the top of his mountain after all.

"This time, I'll do everything right," he says, his remark a pledge more to himself than to her. "This time I'm going to win the prize."

"You *will* win the prize," she tells him. "But be ready to pay for it. Nothing comes free."

As he stands inside this scene that flashes its tentative reality across the celestial wall, Jake accepts Lisa's words as a reflection of her guarded realism.

Lisa sees more.

Standing outside the supernatural wall and inside its future reality as a suddenly here-and-now influence, Lisa with keen-eyed awareness observes herself in this revealing scene that may or may not enter the future as it unfolds its mysteries, pleasures, and tragedies here on Earth. She wonders whether her admonition to Jake derived from her own thoughts or whether, with a wave of a hand or a snap of fingers, Randall or Melanie or some other watchful Spirit sent the thought to her mind and voice and speaking lips. The thought becomes an echo that stays with her, stays way back in the most secret corner of her mind.

"You will win the prize. But be ready to pay for it. Nothing comes free."

Suddenly, as though all of the space around her is shifting and whirling and spinning into mysterious spheres beyond her knowing, the scene floats and ascends and vanishes. New scenes hurry into her view and, freed from present time, carry her into their future reality—an eddying fury of images, a swirl of familiar faces and dangerous episodes, a revolving series of dramatic complications, and a bleak montage of actions and consequences that flare their betrayals and obsessions and their fatal consequences.

The first of these scenes calls forth a conflation of agreeable events. Lisa sees herself introducing Jake Boldwood to Tate within the seclusion of his study in their Blue Ridge home, an impressive and voluminous surround with long wide windows and stately beige drapes that look out at a landscape of December snow, a topiary of a doe and her fawn, and a giant elm tree. The study imparts a well-calibrated sheen because of its polished oak walls; canvases by Edward Hopper, Grant Wood, Andrew Wyeth, and John Singer Sargent; and a coconut cream carpet. Lisa refers to Jake as the son that the real estate tycoon Glenn Boldwood has abandoned—a son who possesses a first-rate work ethic. After he shares a rugged handshake with her husband, Jake confidently works his well-honed muscularity and his canny insights about patent and hedge fund laws, Wall Street trading, and thriving foreign stocks. Tate likes the precisely modulated aggressive look of him and the understated assurance. He wants to know more about his background.

Without a hesitation and following Lisa's advice about how to proceed, Jake tells him the truth.

"I made mistakes. I disappointed some people. I've paid for the mistakes. Now I want to move forward. I need a push in the right direction. I need your push. I won't let you down."

Lisa comes into it now, discreet and petitioning.

"He's served his prison sentence. He's had four long years to prepare himself for a new beginning. Let's give him that chance, Tate. Let's pitch him a fast ball and find out whether he can hit a home run."

Tate enjoys the moment. Arrogant and proprietary, he can nevertheless promote this moment of good will and generosity. He is making Glenn Boldwood, Jake's father, look like a shabby soul, a poor excuse of a father who is failing his troubled son in his hour of need. He, Tate Calhern, will be the power link for Jake Boldwood. He will bring him into his thriving law firm.

"I won't let you down, sir," Jake promises. "You are bringing me back from the dead. I'm going to live. I'll be strong and successful. I won't let you down."

Tate sees in Jake a rapacious heart similar to his own. The sight pleases him.

"I'm a good judge of people," he says. "I know a winner when I meet him."

The scene quickly fades away, leaving the after-images of smiling faces that approximate the gleam of temporary happiness and that nearly conceal the devious plot makers behind those smiles.

Images continue to overlap each other. Scenes rise up, pause uncertainly, and scatter away without disclosing their significance.

One scene stays long enough to reveal its ongoing duplicity. Lisa and Jake are meeting once again in the secluded country house in New Hampshire. Tate is not with them. He is in Chicago for a week of conferences with some of his most influential clients.

"We are on our way," Lisa is telling Jake a week after their earlier meeting with Tate.

They have been cross-country skiing, snowmobiling, snow tubing, and zip lining. They have strapped on snowshoes and have gone for a walk among waterfalls, meadows, riverside views, and hills along the forty miles of groomed trails at a ski touring center in northern New Hampshire. They have savored steaming soup and hot chocolate in warming huts along that trail. When they return from each of these minor yet exciting adventures, they make love in the comfortable bed within the seclusion of this splendid country home.

"Get ready to meet Naomi," Lisa tells Jake on the morning that they are leaving New Hampshire and returning to Blue Ridge. "Put your sensuality to its best uses. Win her, and you win a fortune."

"I'll be firing on all cylinders," Jake says. "Naomi Calhern won't be able to resist me."

"I'm counting on that," Lisa reminds him. "I'm counting on your being top grade whenever you are with her."

In the next instant new scenes throw forward their pictorial narratives with revolving impetus and with the twists and turns of here-and-now reality. Caught inside a swift montage of tensions, triangles, and complications, Naomi and Jake and Brett play out the drama in the real time that will be the future, a time that pushes them onto a path from which there is no returning. Both men are courting Naomi. Both men are walking on a tightrope. They are accommodating Naomi's every wish while maintaining their proper balance as vigorous and proprietary men who make their own decisions about the next step that needs to be taken if they are to remain the keepers of their destinies.

Months swiftly pass and suddenly it is early summer. On every weekend of that June, they sail in the regatta of boats that journey smoothly over blue-green, sun-crested waters across the lake behind the Calherns' three-story house in Blue Ridge. They swim in the heated pool within the west wing of that same house in Blue Ridge. They dine inside the glamorous banquet tents that rise from manicured lawns and that look out upon the breeze-stirred waters of the lake. They water ski and scuba dive while they visit the oceanfront property of Naomi's Aunt Marguerite in Newport, Rhode Island. They skydive in Danielson, Connecticut, about one hundred twenty-five miles from Blue Ridge. They skeet shoot at a Blue Ridge firing range, and they race their favorite automobiles on a drag strip twenty miles from Blue Ridge. Naomi pilots a Porsche 944. Brett races a Camaro Firebird. Jake takes the wheel of a Mazda MX-5 Miata. Always, they represent a trio of friends. Sometimes, they suggest the undercurrents of a romantic triangle.

Often, Randall and Melanie accompany them in these adventures. Occasionally, Lisa and Tate join them. It is Lisa who has brought the three of them into the complexities of rival courtship and the surprises imparted by a too-casual young woman caught in a plot that she, devious Lisa Caulfield Calhern, has devised. The complications are becoming even more entangled because Randall and Melanie have once again wrought upon Brett a spell that inspires him to love Naomi with a deeply felt obsession that makes his love of her a strange compulsion, an erotic thrill, and a mind-racking need.

Melanie and Randall also draw Naomi into an enchantment. This quickened spell makes her more self-assured and more knowing about the world's wily gestures and ambivalent suitors.

One time, when he is alone with Naomi, Brett asks her the blunt question that for days has been haunting him.

"Why are you doing this? Why are you flirting with Jake when you are engaged to me?"

"I haven't made my mind up," Naomi answers him. "Marriage is a big step. I don't want to stumble into it. I want to be certain that I really love the man I'm going to marry."

"Your loving me was never a problem before," Brett tells her. "More than a few times, you've told me that I'm the only man that you will ever love."

Naomi, transformed by a spell that Melanie and Randall have placed upon her, responds to Brett's questions without any compunction and with a confident manner that makes her appear altogether different from the submissive woman whose attention he was taking for granted—an emotionally deprived woman's expression of her adulation for him. Now, her regard of him seems careless and even perfunctory.

"People change," she explains with a flippancy that gives her a hard edge. "Things change. Everything is different now that I've met Jake."

"Does that mean you love him?"

"I don't know yet," she answers him. "But the three of us being together is a wonderful way to find out."

"I don't like the setup," Brett says, brooding and dissatisfied. "I don't like being played with."

"Be patient," Naomi tells him. "Lisa and my father think that I'm doing the right thing. I'm not rushing into anything."

"Your father and Lisa have nothing to do with us."

"You don't really believe that. Besides, I'm waiting for you and Jake to make up my mind for me."

"How do we do that?"

"By being yourself. Right now, for instance, you are very much yourself. You are a loose cannon. You are a trip wire waiting to explode. I'm not holding that against you. I like a dangerous man."

Brett grabs hold of her shoulders and pushes her body toward his chest. His angry brown eyes meet her blue, suddenly apprehensive gaze.

"Don't play with me," he says, while his big, strong hands press down hard upon her shoulders. "I'm warning you."

She winces at the pain rushing through her shoulders and shooting through her entire body.

"You're hurting me," she says, her voice a mere whimper now and a frightened protest.

"I'll do more than that if you betray me," Brett tells her. "That's a promise."

The scene flashes away from the video wall. Lisa, outside the wall looking into this scene that is yoked to her possible future, hurries toward the wall as though she is trying to apprehend it. She calls it back so that she can alter its dark implications. A bitter scream leaps from her throat.

"Bastard!" she shouts. "Lousy, rotten bastard! I won't let you marry her. She will marry Jake. She will! She will!"

Despite her exclamation, the scene does not return. Instead, another scene leaps into her view.

Another month has passed. The future that is hurrying toward her belongs to a sun-misted day at the end of July. From her place outside the video wall, she watches it with steely perceiving. Without leaving that place, she or her doppelgänger or her spiritual double has already entered the video.

A festive wedding celebration in the sumptuous ballroom of The Blue Ridge Country Club is bringing a more-than-ordinary elation to the faces of the hundred guests that Tate and Lisa Calhern have invited to Naomi Calhern's wedding to Jake Boldwood. These favored guests include Wall Street executives and government officials, film stars and television celebrities, two seasoned astronauts and three Nobel Prize-winning scientists and their wives, and some of their most affluent Blue Ridge neighbors. Women young and older, with slender or full-bodied figures, have adorned themselves in pastel gowns and dresses. Brawny men and scrawny men with handsome or cragged features wear white dinner jackets with black shawl lapels and black trousers, white shirts, and black bow ties. Some men wear two-piece medium blue suits with notched lapels, basted sleeves, flap pockets and two-button front. They also wear azure blue shirts and paisley jacquard silk ties.

One hundred twenty-five guests are having a good time. Many of these guests are sitting at the six long banquet tables that dominate the south corner of the ballroom. Everyone appears affable. Everyone looks privileged. Everyone seems carefree and articulate and even elated. These guests talk of many things, including their recent visits to the Bahamas or Hawaii or Palm Beach; their thrilling experiences water skiing, skydiving, and sailing; and their piloting their private planes—a Bombardier Challenger 350, a Cessna Citation Latitude, and a Boeing VIP Dreamliner. They speak of the recent merger of three global corporations. They mention top-performing stocks; controversial happenings in Washington, D.C.; the imminence of commercial flights into space; medical breakthroughs in the treatment of brain tumors and heart maladies; and the current season's most promising baseball teams. Young waiters, proficient and agile, have cleared away pristine chinaware and delicate crystal from the long, ornate tables where, two hours earlier, the guests partook of a five-course meal that included split peas soup with bacon, sorrel, and lettuce; puff pastry shells with salmon, asparagus, and lemon butter sauce; stuffed loin of veal with artichokes; orange sorbet; and a four-foot-tall, strawberry-filled wedding cake.

In the east corner of the ballroom, an orchestra is playing romantic ballads. A young blonde woman, glamorous in a chartreuse gown, is singing about the happiness and the adventure of love. In this specific moment that Lisa is observing from her place outside the wall video, couples young and older are giving themselves completely to the flowing movements of a waltz. Jake and Naomi lead the dance, the groom in a blue tuxedo and his bride in a white, appliquéd wedding gown that has lace over satin, a scoop neck, and half sleeves. They look as though they have stepped out of a fairy tale. They dominate the room, and they revel in this once-in-a-lifetime moment. Tate, tuxedoed in summer beige and genuinely ebullient, is dancing with a distinguished French ambassador's red-haired, fashionable wife who looks stunning in a pleated, emerald-green gown that is trimmed with ruffles and has a jacquard belt. Lisa—looking lovelier than ever in a pale-mint, lace gown—partners with a Wall Street broker, a stately white-haired charmer in a cobalt blue tuxedo. Hayden, handsome in a light gray tuxedo, and Kayla—beautiful in a floral watercolor gown made of silk chiffon and enhanced by an A-line silhouette, a spread collar, three-quarter sleeves, a button front, a self-sash at the waist, and a floor-sweeping hem—are circling the dance floor with easy, rhythmical turnings. Randall, dashing in a navy tuxedo, and Melanie—exquisite in an azure blue gown that has a scoop neckline, pleated shoulders, long balloon sleeves, and beaded cuffs—sway and lean into the music with poise and precision.

Everything about the room seems sumptuous and pristine. Everything about this wedding imparts a festive atmosphere. The splendid scene has a fairy tale glow to it. So Lisa believes as she continues to peer at the video wall. Round and round the ballroom the apparently happy couples whirl. As though they are actors in a dazzling film that want to draw her notice, the essential persons in her life and the friends who have proved themselves loyal dance before her astonished seeing. She recognizes all of them. Yet the one person who is most essential to her happiness is missing. Why has Brett gone missing?

Surely, Tate would have insisted that he attend Naomi's wedding. Though he is not the groom, Brett is an important part of The Calhern Law Firm. In the spirit of *noblesse oblige* or good-natured camaraderie or disciplined sportsmanship, he should be here. What has kept him away—unbridled jealousy or hardhearted betrayal or trouble-haunted memories of the thrilling year he was engaged to Naomi? Lisa wonders. When Hayden and Kayla dance by her once again, she extends her right hand, imagining for an instant that she can enter the scene and halt their progress. She needs to speak to them. She needs to ask them why Brett has failed to attend the wedding. But, try as she does, she cannot enter the scene. She cannot halt Hayden and Kayla's dancing.

Now, sensing that someone is standing behind her and observing her responses, she turns away from the wall video. She notices at once that Randall and Melanie are standing behind her. He is wearing his World War Two pilot's uniform: a dark brown bomber jacket and light brown trousers. She is wearing a white chiffon dress. Turning quickly back to the wall video, she sees that Randall and Melanie are also inside the video, dancing. The time frame is different. It represents the future that might be. In that potential future, they appear exactly as she noticed them a few moments earlier. He is wearing a navy tuxedo, and she is dressed in an azure blue gown.

Once again, she turns away from the video wall and gazes upon Randall and Melanie. Then the questions that are goading her curiosity and her tension leap from her lips.

"Why isn't Brett at the wedding? Why hasn't he accepted the invitation that Tate and I sent to him?"

At first, Randall and Melanie stand silent before her. There is no happiness in their faces. Randall shadows his handsomeness with tightlipped contempt. Melanie brings a frown of disappointment and melancholy to her lovely face.

When Randall does speak, his voice is filled with brusque words that are accusatory and bitter.

"You want it all. Tate and his money aren't enough for you. You want your illicit affair with Brett, too. You want him at the wedding as a sign of his bond with you. You want to imagine that he is not only your lover. He is the man you regard as your real husband, even though he has never married you."

Lisa doesn't want to hear any more of his words. She flings her own harsh words at him.

"I love Brett! I'll never stop loving him. He belongs to me and to no other woman!"

Melanie comes into it.

"Oh, my dear, don't you know what you have done? Can't you see the wrong that you have plotted? Can't you imagine what is going to happen now that you've pushed Naomi into Jake's arms?"

"Brett will come back to me. Without Naomi, he'll see that I'm the only woman who really loves him. He'll also realize that he loves me more than he could ever love any other woman."

"It's pretty to think so," Melanie tells her. "But it's only wishful thinking."

Randall, grim-faced and insistent, has more to say.

"Turn back to the video wall. Look at the scenes that are rushing relentlessly toward you. You can't stop them. Nobody can. Your plan to keep Brett has loosed its powers, and Brett, Naomi, and Jake are caught in its undertow."

Lisa turns her gaze back to the video. The music has stopped. The musicians are taking a break. Merry voices and lighthearted laughter are influencing the atmosphere. The dancers have returned to their places at the banquet tables, or they have sauntered onto the terrace or wandered to the bar. Everything about this moment seems jubilant and life-affirming. Happiness has found a place here with all these guests and plans to stay with them even after they leave this wedding celebration.

Lisa wants to believe in such a scenario, despite Randall and Melanie's troubling prediction. As she looks at the wall video, she sees herself chatting amiably with Hayden and Kayla. A television celebrity and a Washington senator join them in quick-witted repartee about the best ballroom dancers, the most recent medical breakthroughs, and the fastest thoroughbreds. Jake and Naomi are holding court at the opposite end of the long table. Guests young and older are greeting them with genuine well-wishes and, at the same time, sharing with them the afternoon's *joie de vivre.*

All the other guests are also giving themselves completely to camaraderie and exhilaration.

Suddenly yet inevitably, Brett has entered the wedding banquet. He is wearing a steel gray tuxedo that intensifies his handsomeness. His brown-haired crewcut, his broad-shouldered muscularity, and his straight-back posture give him the appearance of a well-trained Army captain or a battle-tested Air Force major. His brown, gleaming eyes show the weariness of sleepless nights and brooding anticipation. He searches the room with steadfast and accurate gaze. Many of his friends notice him and wave to him. Invariably, they call out to him. They would like him to join their tables. Though he waves back, he moves past them and, with athletic agility, continues to make the journey that some unkind Fates or his own conflicted nature have devised for him. He hurries toward Jake and Naomi. They are his chosen quarry. They are part of his fatal destiny. As he approaches them, he brings a smile to his lips. The Fate that cuts the fragile thread that measures each of their lives is making the final cuts. He is the instrument. He is the messenger of death—their deaths and his own.

Peering at him from her place outside the video wall, Lisa knows his thoughts. She perceives his bitterness and his murderous hatred. She wants to warn him against his self-destructive intentions. She wants to save him from his violence and his wretchedness. She wants to save Naomi and Jake, as well.

She does call out to him. She screams her warning.

"Don't do it, Brett! Don't do it! You will ruin everything for them and for yourself! You will never come back! Never! Never!"

Brett doesn't hear her cries. How can he? He is locked inside a future that has not yet unraveled the intricacies of these happenings that Lisa is now watching. He arrives at the table where Jake and Naomi, the dashing groom and his lovely bride, are holding hands as they converse with their friends. As soon as they and their six friends notice him, a hush falls around them. His being here in this specific moment astonishes all of them. Though the three young men give him a good-natured military salute and their girlfriends offer him a cordial smile, nobody speaks. Jake stares at him, guarded and tense. Only Naomi nudges the silence away. Only she speaks the words that are meant to ease the tension that suddenly has come to watch them, here at their festive wedding table.

"How good it is to see you, Brett," she says. "I'm glad that you are here to wish us well."

Brett stands before her and Jake, the smile never leaving his lips. He finds the ironic words that will serve as a preface to his wrongdoing.

"I've brought you a present," he says. "It's a special present that you and Jake and I can share. Each of us deserves it."

As he speaks, he opens his jacket, removes a Ruger Super Redhawk revolver from a leather chest holster, and swiftly fires .44 magnum rounds into Jake's and Naomi's brain and heart. Only after he watches the dark red blood and the brain cells and the jagged pieces of flesh and hair spilling out of their heads and their hearts and spilling, too, across their startled faces—only then does he point his revolver inside his mouth and fire. His head explodes with blood. His left eye spills out of his head. His face becomes warped and distorted. His rugged body drops down upon its knees and stays kneeling for a few eerie moments. Then, swaying uncertainly, it leans forward and slowly falls upon the gleaming hardwood floor.

The six guests who have witnessed close-up these cold-hearted murders and this swift suicide draw back, horrified and speechless. Two of the young women begin screaming and wailing. One of the men, an intern at Blue Ridge Medical Center, quickly attends the bodies of Naomi and Jake that have slumped inertly against the back of their chairs. Randall assists him. Melanie, sorrow-laden but holding back her tears, kneels by Brett's body. She notices the Ruger semi-automatic revolver with its brushed stainless patina, its redwood grips, and its length of approximately thirteen inches. The revolver lies inches away from Brett's right hand. She whispers a prayer that asks The First Spirit for His mercy upon this tormented man, this lost soul, this crazed sinner. At the same time, the entire ballroom is seized with terror and amazement. There is a rushing toward exits. There is a crescendo of fear-ridden and screaming voices. There is the genuine sobbing of women and the tight-lipped sorrow of men who have witnessed death intruding upon a wedding celebration and scattering its happiness into a fathomless darkness.

Outside the wall video, Lisa is screaming a new protest.

"It won't end this way! It will be different. I'll make it so."

Randall and Melanie, no longer observing themselves in the video, turn their attention to Lisa in the present time that is hastening towards its varied rewards and punishments.

Melanie is the first to speak.

"You will need to change," she tells Lisa. "You will have to become a different person."

"I will, I tell you," Lisa says. "I will. That's a promise."

Randall has more to say.

"You have lost your soul," he tells her, stern and judgmental. "You lost it not all at once. You lost it gradually. You began to lose it when you made avarice and infidelity your intimate friends. Finding your soul again will be a rigorous test for you. The journey of a soul-seeker is always hard and sometimes terrifying. Only time will tell whether you can make that journey successfully."

Melanie, with her forgiving nature, asks Lisa a question.

"What is the next step you plan to take?"

Lisa ponders the question before she answers her.

"I'll begin," she says. "I'll begin my journey."

CHAPTER EIGHT
LOST SOULS

"Finding the soul that you have lost may take you a lifetime," Melanie tells Lisa. "You must not give up your search. You must not give in to wild impulses or fearful doubts or unanticipated disappointments."

These are the last words that Melanie speaks to her before the enchantment that has overtaken her here-on-earth fallibility instantly evaporates. It floats away like magical vapor or a clouded dream or a strange reality spun from secret yearnings, pent-up desires, and guilt-laden impulses.

Melanie and Randall disappear as well. So also do the wall videos disappear, vanishing inside the layers upon layers of reality too obscure for ordinary seeing, too formidable for finite perception.

On her own now, Lisa finds herself without Melanie's wise counsel to keep her on the right path of her journey and without Randall's far more abrasive words to warn her of her imminent follies. Only intermittently do their enchantments influence her behavior. For more than a year, she remains true to her promise to redeem herself, to change for the better, and to recover whatever goodness once lived within her blemished nature. She has been doing what she tells herself are all the right things. Without benefits of enchantments of any kind, she has willed herself to journey through the hard road of self-reformation. She has sometimes stumbled, particularly during those moments when she has focused upon her own anguish. Sometimes, she has succeeded, especially during those times when she has helped other persons who are trapped by their own sorrows and betrayed by their own misdeeds.

At the same time, she brings to her assignments as a top-notch lawyer in Tate's firm both expertise and authority.

During these transformative days, the heft and impetus and significance of her altruistic efforts become vivid and clarified as they unfold within her new-found moral awareness. She sees herself as a young woman who, if not altogether different, has added new facets to her character, even as she sometimes sees with clarified vision and heart-wrought empathy the persons whose lives she strives to affect in positive ways. But the clarity of her perceiving and the honesty of her empathy are merely intermittent. They cast a temporary glow upon her deeds. They do not expel her waywardness or expiate her past offenses. Nevertheless, her intermittent compassion toward others and her understated helpfulness become steadying influences upon this new version of Lisa Caulfield Calhern, fallible and tentative though that version remains. Compassion and helpfulness keep at bay her selfish motives, her illicit yearnings, and her devious plots.

Even when she is compassionate and helpful, though, she cannot free herself completely from an ingrained detachment that keeps her emotionally distanced from the persons she tries to help. Detachment is an inveterate part of her nature. The arrogance of her toughminded father and the animosity of her disappointed mother, the bitterness of her mean-spirited husband, and the rapacious nature of her lawyerly associates have hardened her character. On her best days, recalling as she does Melanie's counsel and Randall's warning, she manages to summon the necessary compassion and dutiful helpfulness that bring credibility and competence to her service to others.

To Elena Montalban, she brings not only compassion and helpfulness. She also brings new hope. Elena is a twenty-one-year-old woman who has lost her husband, Alejandro, a brawny Marine who died a hero's death in the war within Afghanistan. When she first meets her, Lisa finds that Elena has no hope. So overwhelmed is she by the tragedy that has killed her brave husband and killed, too, the life-force that had pulsed so vibrantly within herself, so disheartened has she become because the Fates have declared their indifference to her sorrow, that she has more than once attempted suicide. Pale and care-worn, she looks beaten down and sorrow-laden.

"You have made yourself a prisoner of your misfortune," she tells Elena, not without at least a particle of impatience concealed inside her solicitous approach to her. "You've got to spring free of your prison. You've got to declare your courage to the wretched Fates that have chained you to their prison."

This time, Elena takes notice of what she is telling her. This special time, she listens with a glimmer of anticipation and a faint light of hope showing themselves in her questioning eyes.

"How do I do that?" she asks her. "How do I escape from my prison?"

"Start helping other people," she answers her. "Focus on their pain and disappointment. Rescue them, if you can."

Her words make Elena pause. A frown creases the younger woman's brow. Tremulous and uncertain, she rises from an embroidered floral armchair in her parents' living room and slowly walks to the panoramic window. As though she is standing alone in the spacious room, she peers out at the sun-misted blueness of the sky and the snow-white clouds and the gray-haired man who is her father driving a tractor across the yellow-gold farm field. Only after that, after two or three minutes, after she has observed the sky and the clouds and her still-rugged father on the tractor does Elena turn to her. Studying her face with pensive care, she makes an open confession of her uncertainty.

"I wouldn't know where to begin," she says.

"You can proceed with your nursing program in Blue Ridge College," Lisa tells her. "You can become the nurse that you promised your husband you were going to become."

Hesitant once more, Elena searches for the words that will tell her what she is feeling. After a minute, she finds the words and quickly speaks them.

"I'm not certain that I can do that. I'm not the same person that I was when Alejandro was alive."

"Of course you are not the same person," Lisa says. "The Fates have knocked you about. They are testing you. You've got to show them and everyone else that you have grit. You must show that to yourself, too. You have the courage to get up after you've been knocked down. Your Alejandro is watching you. He's counting on you to do the brave thing. Move on to the next chapter."

By persuading her to enter the nursing program in Blue Ridge College, she guides this grieving widow onto a life-affirming path that will make the days and years that she has not yet lived both meaningful and productive. But the journey is a rugged one. Despite Lisa' encouragement, Elena's doubts and fears keep holding her back.

"I've been having terrible dreams," she confesses to Lisa on a chilly November day when dark-gray clouds, flashes of lightning, and the rumbles of thunder disturb the quiet of Lisa's meticulously appointed study where they are meeting.

Elena blurts out the confession as though she must choose swift words to describe her feelings. Otherwise, her fear of them might suppress her telling. Her unwillingness to admit the truth and the reality of these words might push her off her proper course. Now, in this very instant, she hurries to say them.

"I've been dreaming that I see Alejandro in a beautiful garden. I hurry to greet him. But he does not recognize me. I have changed too much. No longer am I the shy girl that he married—the girl who leaned on him to make all the important decisions in our marriage. I'm more certain of who I am—more confident and self-reliant. Even the way I walk is different. I'm in a hurry because I want to accomplish so much."

Lisa chooses words that may calm her.

"There is nothing wrong with that," she tells her. "You are hurrying to do the things that need to be done."

Lisa's words comfort Elena only a little.

"If I change too much," Elena explains as if lamenting, "Alejandro may never recognize me as the woman he married. I will be a stranger to him."

Lisa ponders her words. She finds them poignant and urgent. Now she summons the words that can allay Elena's fears.

"Does a man ever really understand the woman he marries?" she asks. "In essential ways, we women remain a mystery even to the husbands who give us all their love. Besides, a man expects a woman to surprise him at least some of the time. Keep on changing. Alejandro will always recognize you, whether he appears to you here on Earth in a dream or meets you eventually in whatever comes afterward."

With cautious attention, Elena listens to these words. Imperceptibly at first and then visibly, her sullen face alters its features. Her frown disappears. Her brown eyes light up. Her mouth consents to a gleaming smile.

"If you are right in all that you are telling me, maybe I can go forward. Maybe I am not betraying Alejandro's expectation that I will always be the same Elena for him."

"You will never be anyone except Elena Montalban," Lisa reminds her. "Alejandro will understand that, even though you are discovering new facets of your identity."

In that storm-roiled November time, she draws Elena away from her fears and from her nightmares.

Other uncertain days follow. But always she is there to talk things out with Elena and to guide her back to the proper path for self-discovery.

In the spring of the following year, Elena consents wholeheartedly to the changes that the various events and her independent decisions are bringing into her life.

"I'm in it again," Elena tells her after her auspicious beginning in the nursing program. "There is a reason for me to go on living. I will be able to help other human beings at the same time that I am advancing in this program."

For the first time in the year and more since they met, Elena beams with elation that is anchored to self-trust and renewal. Her young features rediscover their radiant beauty: jet black hair and glowing brown skin that enhance her confident manner; heart-shaped face that has a wide forehead and narrow chin; dark green eyes that meet your own gaze with honest cordiality; and a gleaming smile that instantly puts you at ease. It is not difficult to accept her remark that she has found new reasons to go on living.

"There will be other reasons for you to go on living," Lisa assures her. "A new home, different friends, and a young man whom you will grow to love. All that will be a part of your future."

"How do you know?" Elena asks her, both surprised and pleased by her remarks.

"I can't quite explain it," Lisa answers her. "It's just something I feel. I'm certain it will happen. Call my certainty intuition, if you want. Call it second sight or clairvoyance. But way back in a nearly hidden corner of my awareness—way, way back so that it rarely influences my conscious thinking, my mind tells me that good things will be happening to you."

Elena, as charming as she is elated, beams with delight once again. She wants to believe her. She wants to keep journeying on this long, winding road that may lead her to new friends and new places, new challenges and rewards, and new happiness that is both earned and life-rescuing.

"I'll work hard," she tells Lisa. "I'll work every day to bring some happiness to others. Maybe I'll find happiness in that way."

"You *will* find happiness," Lisa says while reinforcing her previous remarks. She cannot explain her certainty even to herself. She does not yet understand that her contacts with Melanie and Randall have deepened her perception. Her good deeds have begun to awaken her insight. She guesses at Elena's future even as she glimpses the reality of its possibilities.

Lisa's altruism brings her into other territories.

She continues to visit the children's cancer wing within Blue Ridge Hospital—that part of the hospital that bears the name of Tate's first wife, Amelia, and that receives the generous financial support that Amelia's will has established. Without hesitation or a desire to be noticed or praised by her friends or by the hospital staff, she helps the hardworking family of a seven-year-old girl, Gabriella Rossi, who has waged a brave battle against brain cancer and is now recovering from that malady. She helps the trouble-torn parents to find an attractive townhouse that will provide a more comfortable home for Gabriella as well as for themselves.

"Nobody has helped us as you are helping us," Mrs. Rossi tells her. "You are a saint."

Her words carry thick Neapolitan inflections and emotion-laden rhythms.

The praise pleases Lisa, even while she resists it.

"I am not a saint," she says. "I'm doing what is right. That's all."

Now Mr. Rossi comes into it.

He has a brawny, blue-collar physique; an olive complexion and dark, curly hair; blue, searching eyes and an aquiline nose; and a husky voice.

"That's everything," he says. "Everything."

He takes her hand and shakes it heartily.

She accepts the handshake as a gesture of genuine friendship.

"I'm happy that you think so," she tells him. "I'm happy that I can help your family."

Her empathy surprises and pleases her. Perhaps, after all, she will recover the innocent, hopeful young woman that, years ago, she was becoming.

She enrolls this bravest of girls—this delightful Gabriella who has curly black hair, brown eyes alive with natural merriment, an olive complexion, bee-stung lips, and scientific interests—into a private school that will carefully influence her academic advancement and connect her to the social groups that will become a part of the girl's future success.

"I want to be a brain surgeon," Gabriella tells her with confidence that makes her announcement seem like a realistic goal. "I want to be an oncologist. I am going to help other children who have brain tumors."

"Work hard," Lisa advises her. "Then, one day, I'll be calling you Doctor Gabriella Rossi."

Her words bring a smile of delight into Gabriella's face. Noticing the effect of her words upon the girl, Lisa feels motherly, helpful, and protective. Once again, she feels like someone other than the Lisa Caulfield Calhern who has made self-centeredness and wily schemes friends of long acquaintance.

Despite her motherly and helpful feelings, she experiences only the surface of these episodes. She has not yet located the soulful part of her nature.

She goes on searching.

She attends a frail ninety-two-year-old woman, Judith Kenyon, who has outlived all her relatives. Alone in the attractive Georgian home that she has refused to leave, Judith has braved all kinds of misfortune, including the early deaths of her two sons in the Vietnam War; the killing of her only daughter, a twenty-four-year-old teacher, during a shooting massacre at Blue Ridge Elementary School; and the natural deaths of her husband, a respected pediatrician, and of her older siblings and their children. Indomitable for so long a time, this Judith Kenyon, this aged woman—with silver hair; upturned nose with a dent in the middle of the bridge and a protruding tip; time-creased, delicate skin; and courteous smile that gives her a patrician dignity—was preparing herself to die. Her pale blue eyes seemed haunted. All her hard battles were behind her. So this nonagenarian began telling herself during the months preceding their casual meeting at a fashionable tea party one winter afternoon in the Blue Ridge Country Club.

When she, troubled Lisa Caulfield Calhern, first meets her, Judith speaks of many things, including the journeys that she and her husband had made to Hawaii, South Africa, Australia, and Europe. She mentions her organic gardening, her *Cordon Bleu* cooking, her painting in a neo-Impressionist manner, and her six books of poems that a university press has published. Most revealing of all, she mentions that for the first time she believes that she has finished everything that she needs to do. She has completed the work that some God-spun destiny or the Fates have assigned her.

"For the first time, I am willing to let go," she remarks as they sit at the country club table sipping herbal tea and tasting the chef's lemon cakes. "All of it is behind me now. I've finished my tasks. I must not overstay my welcome."

"Nonsense," she answers this patrician woman with lighthearted, corrective words. "There is so much more that you can do."

"I wish that were so," Judith says.

There is a wistful timbre to her words that is struggling with her belief that she must close all her transactions with life, all her yearnings, all her strivings, and all her expectations.

"I'll prove it," Lisa tells her. "But you will have to help me."

Judith does help her.

Together, they resurrect Judith Kenyon. They guide her forward to new, creative life. As Mrs. Tate Calhern, she uses her influence and her publishing contacts to bring forth new editions of Judith's poems. She arranges an exhibit of her beautiful neo-Impressionist paintings. Equally important, she inspires her to become Judith Kenyon all over again. She must leave behind the aged woman that is convincing herself that she has finished all her tasks. She must explore new facets of her belonging to life. She must embrace that life. It is not yet time for her to embrace death. There is still time to create new artworks and new poems.

"I'm beginning to believe that you are an enchanter," Judith tells her. "You are working your wonderful magic. You are bringing me into life again."

"You are doing most of the work," she answers her. "You are creating your own enchantments. You are doing it right now."

"Perhaps that is true," Judith says. "No matter what misfortunes I have endured, I have always kept my soul. I have never lost that. It is easy to bring enchantments into your life when you have your soul to help you."

Having said so, Judith quietly observes her. Then, after a moment's reflection, she tells her more.

"I also have a dear friend to help me," she says. "You are that friend. Enchantments come more easily when you have caring friends."

Judith's praise delights Lisa. It lifts her spirit. Momentarily, the praise strengthens her belief in this new version of herself that she has so carefully been composing. Yet this experience of helping this aged woman cannot completely dispel Lisa's resentment about her own new situation that is imprisoning her to life choices and a lifestyle that seem alien to her restless and self-involved nature. Not even her success persuading Judith Kenyon to go forward to new challenges, not even rescuing Elena Montalban from her young widow's grief and guiding Gabriella Rossi into a promising future, not any of these things at all or any of her other successes with the needy and the nearly forgotten can convince Lisa that her own rigorous journey toward a morally centered life will eventually bring her once again the happiness that the guilt of her past misdeeds and a vague premonition of disaster have prodded her to fling away. The guilt that has attended her for more than a year has, with subtle increments, been wearing down her wayward inclinations. Even now, that guilt compels her to help other human beings and to suppress her narcissistic impulses. Yet her compassionate involvement in the lives of others, her guardian care of them, and her momentary elation at being their rescuer cannot displace her yearning for that other version of herself, devious and ambitious and carnal.

She has no recollection of the violent scenarios that Randall and Melanie allowed her to witness as she stood outside and at the same time appeared inside the supernatural wall video. That experience has merely stirred her intuition, goaded her unease, and wakened her moral awareness without providing a map or a chart or a compass that will show her how to save herself and save, as well, the imperiled lives of the four persons who have become essential to her own life and who are as lost as she is. The

First Spirit has allowed Randall and Melanie to place enchantments upon her so that, by means of a supernatural wall video, she can witness the destruction into which her errant life has been pushing her. But those enchantments have served as merely temporary influences upon her nature. They have predicted her bitter end and the equally wretched end of the four persons whose lives have been entangled with her own. No vivid memories of the enchantments have stayed with her. Only shadowy recollections of those end-of-life scenarios stay with her. Although Randall and Melanie will continue to observe her behavior here on Earth and sometimes advise and encourage her while she journeys toward her self-reformation, she will have to make that journey alone. She alone needs to earn her salvation. Alone, she must discover the correct path to her moral transformation.

She has tried so hard to make the best of things. She has, with a rigorous suppression of her willfulness and the sacrifice of her worldly desires, brought new hope and continuing solace to the sick, the despairing, and the lost. She has brought hope and solace not only to Elena, Gabriella, and Judith. In this year-and-a-half, she has also assisted many other needy individuals. The roster of persons that she has rescued include Nora Paige, a weeping thirty-eight-year-old woman, dowdy and already over-the-hill, whose husband—a successful hedge fund manager—

has left her; Shawna Leigh, a hard-luck, girl-young competitive swimmer, a lovely Asian, who broke her leg in a skiing accident that threatened to deprive her of her agile gait even after her recovery; and Neal Hardy, a jealous lover, a nineteen-year-old college youth—dark-haired and ruddy-handsome—whose fiancée was sleeping with his best friend, whom he shot with a snub-nose revolver and nearly killed.

She advises Nora, the dowdy and despairing woman, to remake herself. She coaches her in the stylish ways that she can capture once again a semblance at least of the slim and attractive brunette she used to be. She persuades her to return to the working world as a real estate agent. Through her own success as a lawyer for a large corporation, she "models" the way an accomplished woman should participate in the world and, with acumen and self-assurance, negotiate for the best terms as she makes her journey to self-knowledge and solacing rewards.

She brings Shawna Leigh, the award-winning swimmer with the grievous fracture of the femur, the longest bone in her leg, into the care of a prominent Blue Ridge surgeon. After three surgeries, after the eight weeks of enduring a metal rod that keeps the healing bone in place and enduring, too, the plates, screws, and pins that support the fracture, and after more weeks within the rehabilitation wing of Blue Ridge hospital, Shawna recovers her agile gait and her well-honed swiftness in the water. She reclaims, as well, the hard-edged discipline that has always proved her mettle—the vigor and strength of her spirit, her ingrained tenacity, and her fierce refusal to admit defeat no matter what adversary stands in her path.

Neal Hardy is a different case. Enraged and heartbroken at the same time, he tried to kill his rival for the affection of a beautiful girl. Lisa draws to his case Wesley Thompson, a savvy criminal lawyer who works for her husband's law firm. A plea of temporary derangement and genuine remorse work in Neal's favor. The jury agrees that Neal— an honor roll student at Yale, an acolyte in his church, and a volunteer in a nursing home—need not spend time in prison. Instead, he should be placed on probation after he has spent months in a psychiatric unit within a clinic in Massachusetts.

That she remembers the names of these persons whom she is rescuing and the specific problems that beset them surprises her. Never before has she made empathy her stock in trade. Never before has she permitted herself to feel any emotion toward human beings whose lives were not closely intertwined with her own.

She lives through the swift months of this year-and-a-half with cautious discipline and with an equally cautious awareness of this new self that with rigorous determination she is composing. At times, the Lisa Caulfield Calhern with whom she is most familiar returns to subvert her new-found altruism. She yearns to break free of this vague enchantment that overtakes her, this mysterious spell, this magic-seeming power that keeps on subduing her cynical nature and her self-centered ways. This new version of herself, this self-sacrificing alter ego, infuses the minds of so many troubled people with positive anticipation of the good years ahead of them.

She remains emotionally connected most of all to Neal Hardy, the Yale University athlete who for a shocking instant turned murderous because his girlfriend prefers a young, ambitious banker. At some profound level, she identifies with his anguish. She understands his response. She imagines the terror of his girlfriend's abandonment of him, the searing pain of his girlfriend's betrayal, and the wild hatred and despair that drove him to shoot his rival. His girlfriend's betrayal robbed him of his pride. It killed the self that, with discipline and confidence and joy, he had been creating. So she clearly perceives. She wonders that Neal did not shoot his false lover, too—the redhaired narcissist with the gleaming blue eyes, the voluptuous figure, and the carefully glossed lips. She regards Neal as a lost-soul mate. In a happier, freewheeling time when she was not held back by rules and duties, she might have drawn him into her bed—no matter that he was eight or ten years younger.

There are others, too, whose griefs and disappointments she carefully redresses. They are the lost souls whom she strives to rescue. They are the fallible persons whose resilience and courage the stern and unyielding Fates are testing. They include an impoverished Black man arrested for petty theft; an idealistic college youth suffering with broken arm and painful concussion in the aftermath of a protest march that supported beleaguered immigrants; a traumatized blonde, an innocent girl of sixteen, who was raped by a neighbor's drinking pals; a thirty-year-old man who has left the priesthood, married a lovely widow with two children, and brought upon himself the wrath of his tyrannical father; and the beautiful Latina framed for a banker's murder that two neo-Nazis committed.

Once again, the vague stirrings of enchantment that Melanie and Randall placed upon her persuade her to do the right things.

In a nearly empty courtroom, she successfully pleads with a judge to place the Black man on probation because the petty theft was his first offense, because she has found him adequate lodgings in a housing project, and because she has coaxed him into joining a job-training program.

She uses her friendship with cable news reporters to publicize and activate the idealistic college student's efforts to help hardworking immigrants to become American citizens who will offer their varied skills to their new-found country.

She works with a team of detectives, state troopers, and a district attorney to capture and imprison the three men who raped the innocent girl.

She convinces the former priest who is journeying on a different path with a wife and two children to embrace his new life and to leave behind him the tyrannical father who has never wished him well.

She also hires top-notch detectives to apprehend the two neo-Nazis who murdered a Jewish banker and left false clues at the scene of the crime that implicated the banker's secretary, an innocent Latina whom an upscale and racist community wrongly condemned as the killer.

Lisa's success as a generous woman who has made her guardian care of others a primary goal convinces her that she has reclaimed her soul. She is a thirsty seeker who has learned to drink Creation whole. She has cast off her imperfect self. She has become somebody altogether new. She has learned how to be a Soul. So she tells herself, with wishful thinking that makes her inaccurate appraisal of her reformation appear reliable and honest. She also tells herself that it is time for her to befriend her stepdaughter Naomi and her former lover Brett in upright and acceptable ways.

In those moments when she confronts the truth about herself, she admits that she must not revive her plan to destroy the imminent marriage of Naomi and Brett. She must abandon her plan. She must disown it by turning completely away from it. Yet, try as she does, she cannot turn away from it. If she is to go on living, really living with her heart beating faster and faster and her desires inordinately satisfied, she must cling to her plan. With subtle increments and modulated impetus, she must use her plot to draw Jake Boldwood into a triangle that involves Naomi, Brett, and himself.

Only on her worst days do these dark thoughts assail her. Only then does she feel utterly lost.

These wayward thoughts set her adrift. She might be an arrogant mariner who has ventured into a storm-tossed sea and into the heave and fury of mountain-high waves that will swallow her whole. Her vague remembrance of the grievous revelations within the wall video, all the mayhem, blood-shedding, and death, does persuade her to pause before the wrongness of her yearnings for Brett. But not even the flashes of awareness that rise from the hidden corners of her brain, not even those omens of murderous revenge and horrific endings, can dispel her revived craving for Brett or dissuade her from her desire to steal Brett away from Naomi.

At first, she does not give in to her desire. During these eighteen months after the wall videos have left upon her conscience the vague residues of their messages, she has willed herself to make the right choices. She has compelled herself to help the neglected, the sick, and the disheartened. She has discovered reserves of empathy within herself that her self-serving past had often suppressed. In profound ways that surprise her, she has comprehended the deep-seated anguish, the physical suffering, and the festering despair of these troubled individuals. With clarified awareness, she has looked upon their pain as if it were her own. Only after her rescuing deeds diminish that pain and at times send it scattering, only then does she calculate her positive influence upon the brave, the needy, and the lost.

At the same time, she calculates once again the price she is paying because of her good deeds and the cost to her selfhood. Those deeds, with their rigorous demands and their necessary sacrifices, have suppressed the Lisa Caulfield Calhern that, through all the days she cares to remember, she has with wily aptitudes and ruthless plotting carefully devised. Insidious and influential, her carnal desire for Brett gradually overtakes the fragile compunction that has inspired her good deeds and her regeneration. She begins telling herself that without Brett she is utterly lost.

She tells herself that she must test herself in even more personal ways as she struggles through her journey toward moral transformation. She must place herself in the company of Naomi and Brett. Only then will she know for certain whether she will be able to endure life without Brett as her husband or as her lover.

At first, she never allows herself to be alone with Brett. Always, Tate is a part of the quickened scene. The private dinners that she and Tate share with Brett and Naomi; the exuberant afternoons that the four of them experience while skydiving from a Cessna Super Grand Caravan in Danielson, Connecticut, fifty miles away; the glamorous party that she and Tate host for sixty of their most influential friends in their Manhattan penthouse; and the swift, sun-misted hours of riding golden-colored Palominos along a lakeside trail and across miles of greenery within a horse farm in nearby Avon—all these occasions become extraordinary and compelling to her keen-sighted awareness of handsome Brett, the only man that she will ever love. Almost always now, he stays in romantic proximity with his fiancée Naomi, the young woman she calls her stepdaughter who lately appears exhilarant and satisfied. Almost always, Brett stays within the safe boundaries of decorum.

During one evening that is different from all the other evenings and most of the afternoons, too, when she discreetly places herself in Brett's company, surrounded as they are by dozens of guests or by six or eight visitors, or when they—she and Brett—are held to careful proprieties in the presence of Naomi, who now fully embodies the new, exhilarant version of herself, and when they exchange casual pleasantries under the watchful eyes of Tate, who now more than ever enjoys his role as a canny business leader whose fortunes keep burgeoning—during this one special evening that is different from all the other evenings that have left her feeling love-spurned and anxious, she joins Brett when he is alone on the terrace of the Sutton Place penthouse that she and Tate make their home for special occasions and for a change from their more familiar activities in Blue Ridge.

She guesses why Brett has come to the terrace where in this moment, at least, no other guest has sought temporary solitude apart from the lavish party that she and Tate are hosting. Weary on this evening of having to fulfill the role of Tate's goodwill ambassador, he has stolen away from the party, colored though it is with glittering surfaces, buoyant personalities, and extravagant appurtenances. He intends to absent himself only long enough to calm his vague dissatisfaction by lighting up and inhaling one of his Treasurer Aluminum Gold cigarettes, the most expensive cigarette brand in the world favored by Tate and by himself. The autumn breeze wafting across the wide expanse of the nighttime terrace quickens his senses and mitigates, in part, the melancholy that appears to be overtaking him despite the festive occasion. That he has temporarily abandoned not only the party, but also the lockstep rules that tie him to his courtship of Naomi intensifies the rush of satisfaction that stirs his awareness of the vivid moon and the star-filled sky in the vaulted space above him and the efflorescent panorama of New York City that sparkles below him. So she tells herself, imposing as she does her own desires and wishes upon this supremely handsome man, this passionate lover, this prodigious influence upon all her senses.

When he hurried away from the ballroom in the east wing of this penthouse, Brett did not elude the party completely. He was merely moving into its outer margins, within the privacy of the expansive terrace that overlooks Sutton Park and the East River. From her place on the dance floor, partnered as she was with a tall, silver-haired gentleman who years earlier had inherited his family's Philadelphia steel corporation and more recently had acquired ten million shares in ExxonMobil, she had watched Brett's every move. Even before her dance with the dashing executive ended, she knew as though it were a certainty that Brett was doing what he had often done at parties. His restless nature required fresh air and private breathing space. He was heading for the terrace. With the polished assurance that always gave him a courtly manner, he was leaving Naomi to dance the next set with altruistic Hayden, inside the wide circle of other couples. Brett was making his way with equal assurance and with brisk gait away from the dance floor and on to the rim of the crowded dining room, filled as it was with couples in tuxedos and gowns and made painterly by the yellow gold of dahlias, the lavender of camellias, the red of hibiscus, and the peach hues of roses that flared their beauty in precise arrangements at the center of each table.

When she first noticed him entering the skyline terrace that had been temporarily abandoned by the partygoers who have given themselves over to the exhilarated camaraderie of the dance, she imagined the sounds of the party following him. Behind him, as a faraway impression, the melodious rhythms of a Cole Porter love ballad was navigating the blue-jazz sounds of piano, trumpet, and violin. The smoky voice of the woman who was singing it floated across the air with aptitudes both seductive and poignant. The voices of the guests, intermittently hushed or cacophonous, were another riff upon his senses. She knew what he was seeing and hearing. All these impressions, these sounds and their rhythms, were married to her own awareness of the scene that was unfolding around Brett and, as though in unison, around herself as well.

Brett's withdrawal from the party happened only a few minutes ago.

Now the merriment of the party floats away from her hearing, too, as she moves into the terrace and, just beyond the entrance, places herself within the shadows of a marble column not more than ten feet from where Brett is standing. For a moment, she debates whether she should stay or go, so disinclined is she to appear as an intrusive woman or as a lovesick paramour. Yet her need to speak with Brett quickly cancels her doubts and her hesitation. When she moves forward, out of the shadows that even now partly cover her tall, slim frame, he turns and notices her blonde hair, blue gleaming eyes, and the black chiffon gown that enhances her glamour. She watches him watching her, even while with the taut harmonies of determination she maintains her composure.

He offers her a gentleman's nod that bonds its cordiality with ambivalence. He calls forth no lighthearted greeting. Nor does he offer her a kiss or permit his hand to caress her shoulder or to guide her to the place where he has been standing, pensive and moody and alone. He is wondering why she has intruded upon his privacy and why, by leaving the party, she has possibly drawn attention to their being here together in some casual assignation or some careless declaration of their illicit relationship. That these thoughts are rankling his calm, she feels certain. She knows him well.

The furtive months they spent as lovers showed her his face when pleasure rouses him. Those same months showed her his face when dismay and disappointment brought vague traceries of displeasure to his handsomeness.

Despite her knowing all these things, her need to be with him pushes her forward. In this moment that quickens its reality by the excitement of being here alone with him, she moves toward him and plants a light kiss upon his lips.

"I've been missing you," she tells him. "This is the first time in many months that we are alone together."

Brett carefully studies her. Even now, he is not smiling. Instead, a frown creases his brow.

"We have a lifetime before us of not being alone together," he answers her.

Startled by his brusqueness, she peers upon his face. His husky, matter-of-fact voice makes her uneasy. She was not anticipating his aloofness or, for that matter, his blunt dismissal of the intimacy they had once shared with so much joy and with so many plans for their future.

With the cool detachment that she recognizes as the armature of his self-possession, he chooses other words that with whiplash accuracy explain the change that has overtaken their relationship.

"We are finished, Lisa. You need to accept the way things are now. I'm going to marry Naomi. I intend to be faithful to her. I owe her that much. She believes in our love.

She believes in me. She is the first woman who has ever made me want to be a solid citizen."

"What about us? What about me?"

"There is no *us*. Not anymore."

"You love me. I know you do."

"Of course I love you. But what does that matter? Our sleeping together can only bring ruin to all the people who should matter most to us."

"You are not yourself. You are somebody else. You act as though somebody has cast a spell upon you."

"I don't need a spell to change me. Just common sense. Naomi is my ticket into the big time. I'm not letting her go."

"You are using her."

"Maybe. Isn't that what love is—people using each other for pleasure and for other rewards? Naomi and I are making a fair deal, a sensible exchange. I give her my love and my fidelity. She points me toward the once-in-a-lifetime opportunities with the big boys, the old boys who include the man who happens to be her father and your husband."

Confronted by the low-keyed abrasiveness of his remarks, she shrouds herself in silence. Beneath the artifice of her composure, she struggles to find the words that will call him back to her. Never before has she felt so uncertain of him. She does not know whether she should explain the profound nature of her love of him. Now, as if to clarify the person that his brooding demeanor represents, she looks upon him with a more studious gaze. Only then, while choosing carefully measured words that keep in check the anguish that she is experiencing, does she declare herself to him.

"You and I belong together," she tells him. "We can leave Tate and Naomi behind us. We don't need them to make our happiness a lasting thing. We are already building solid careers. We can make a good life together. All we need to do is to walk away from them and from our makeshift attempts at happiness. We can be together always. We can leave our unhappy days behind us."

With a steady gaze of his own that has made a pact with truth as well as with melancholy, Brett quietly observes her. Once again, she watches him watching her. She examines the world-weary manner in which he takes a drag on his cigarette. With more incisive comprehension, she notices the frown that creases his brow as he carefully observes her. If these frowns are signs of his thoughts about her, she has no way of knowing with any certainty. She guesses her way into his thoughts. He will not allow his romantic emotions to subvert his tough-minded realism. He perceives her as she really is—a woman who has fallen in love with the wrong man. Or, perhaps, he is willing to admit that he might have been the right man for her, but he came into her life too late. When he resumes speaking to her, she parses every word that he chooses to tell her. She analyzes every look and every gesture. She interprets the timbres of his voice. His saddened eyes, his tense manner, and his deepening frown become visible clues to his conflicted feelings. Yet, despite her recognizing all these outward signs of his conflicted feelings, the words that he chooses to speak in the next instant take her by surprise.

"It's wrong," he says. "Everything between you and me is wrong. I don't know why I didn't see it before. I can't even explain why I am seeing it now—*really* seeing it, the whole sordid mess of it."

Suddenly, reality as she understands it spins away from her. She tells herself that she is caught inside the vortex of a terrifying dream.

The glass-enclosed terrace—stately and glamorous with marble columns, potted multi-colored exotic plants, navy-linen-covered tables, Noritake polished platinum china, and delicate crystal—seems to float away from her. The moon and the stars, like giant will-o'-the-wisp amulets presaging imminent disaster, spin away from her momentary gaze. Even the crowded city below, all dazzling lights and excited motion, sways, soars, and levitates. She feels her body swaying, too. Her reeling senses confuse and alarm her, but only for a swiftly passing moment. In the next instant, Brett sways as well, teeters, wavers, and undulates—or so it seems to her confused senses. She closes her eyes, her way of escaping the pitching and sloping and scattering of the ghostly face of the moon and the ominous blaze of the stars and the elegant artifice of the terrace. Then suddenly, quite suddenly, as though she were after all anticipating its ghastly presence, she comprehends the message that this moment is bringing to her. An enchantment has overtaken her and has caught in its powers as well the enigmatic Brett, the lover who altogether bluntly and astonishingly is repudiating the pact that they made with sensual urgency.

The sloping stops. The spun velocities that appear to be the runaway moon and the scattering stars and the somersaulting terrace hurry back to their natural-seeming positions. Whether Brett has apprehended the world floating away, she cannot with certainty tell. Nevertheless, enchantment has worked its magic upon him. He no longer wants to make his life with her. Of that she is most certain. The new words that he chooses to speak carry with them a finality too lacerating to bear. Randall and Melanie have worked their spells upon him. Their influence has wrought this astonishing transformation upon him.

So she tells herself while she waits for Brett's next words and for the news of the honorable life he is choosing to live.

When he does speak, his words are forthright and decisive. Yet always he maintains control of his feelings. Always, he imparts compelling and earnest counsel. She tells herself that he is not himself. He does not sound like the Brett Robinson that she thought she knew so well. The flippant tone, the cynical asides, the sly grin, the sometimes-hooded eyes that conceal his schemes—all these emblems of his approach to the world that has often left him bruised and bitter are missing. Now the tone of his voice is matter of fact. There is no sly grin or cynical asides. Gone, too, is the hooded look of his eyes. His gaze is direct, and his words carry honest conviction. He is no longer the Brett Robinson with whom she made furtive and illicit pacts. He is himself and yet someone altogether different. He is Randall Johnson or a ventriloquial stand-in for him. Randall has cast a spell upon him, a warning signal meant to draw him to a rescuing path.

This thought, this eerie awareness, makes her bristle. So do the next words that Brett speaks to her.

"I tell you that we have to let go of one another," he says, willful and adamant. "We have to stop making messes of our lives. We can't go on hurting other people."

"You can't mean what you are saying," she tells him as she cries out a raw plea to him. "You can't throw away our love as though it were a temporary sensation. We need to save our lives together. We *have* to save us. Everything will work itself out as long as we stay together."

He lowers his voice, as though he is whispering a secret. The words come fast and carry with them a relentless message.

"Everything between us is over."

Once again, she cries out to him. Her voice sounds panic-stricken and desperate.

"Never. It will never be over."

"It was over a long time ago. It was over the moment that you brought Naomi into my life."

"You don't love her. You love *me*. You've told me so, not only tonight but also on all the other nights that we have been together."

"I do love you," he says. "But I don't need you—at least not in the way that I need Naomi. With her as my life partner, my wife, I'll get everything that I want out of this crazy, brutal world."

"Is that it? Is that all you can say to me."

"That's all of it, except maybe 'goodbye,' without any kisses or promises or fanfare. It's a strange 'goodbye,' because we will often find ourselves in each other's company. Maybe eventually I will get used to thinking of you as my mother-in-law, even though we are the same age. You will have to keep remembering that I am Naomi's husband. We can never be lovers again, not if we want our world to stay intact. Our rock-like determination will be our ballast against confusion. That determination never to be lovers will be our steadying force. It will keep our world from spinning away from us."

"Randall has been talking to you. He's turned you against me."

"Randall and I *have* sat down and talked out things. He has set me on a better path. Because of his advice, I see things more clearly. But not only Randall's words have persuaded me to change my point of view and the way that I conduct my life. Something else, something more, has made a difference—has made *me* different. Maybe Randall is connected to this something else. I had a strange dream a few weeks ago. I dreamed that he cast a spell upon me. I dreamed that he bound me to some enchantment. Lately, I've come to believe that it wasn't a dream at all. An enchantment is guiding me to do the right things, think the right thoughts, and lead an honorable life."

"Then there isn't anything more we need to say to one another. You have made your choice. You plan to spend your life with Naomi. You are heeding Randall's advice and maybe Melanie's, too."

"You should heed their advice, too. They want only what is good for you. They know that, together, we could only be lost souls. They will help you find your soul. They want you to learn how to be happy with Tate."

"I don't need Melanie or Randall. I'll find my own way to happiness."

"Is that a promise?"

"Yes," she answers him. "It is most certainly a promise."

She turns away from him now and starts to make her way back to the ballroom alone. When she reaches the threshold that separates the terrace from the ballroom, she turns back just for an instant. She peers at Brett with inquisitive eyes. He is looking out at the glittering city below and at the yellow-gold moon hanging in the sky like a dazzling amulet. He is looking ahead of him. He is imagining his future. He is eager to take possession of it.

He expects her to take a merely incidental part in that future. But she has a different plan. More than an ordinary plan, her plot to win back Brett will alter his future as well as hers. Devious and self-protective, she will draw Jake Boldwood into the romantic triangle that makes him Brett's unexpected rival and Naomi's ardent lover. Not even the vague memory of the wall video that warned about the tragedy spawned by this triangle stops her from moving forward with her plot. Possibly, she and Brett *are* lost souls. But some special insight, her intuition perhaps or a magic spell influencing her awareness or some momentary enchantment, tells her that her soul and Brett's met long before they were born.

CHAPTER NINE

DANGER SIGNALS

Suddenly, Lisa awakens on a sun-misted morning in late August. Quite suddenly, because she was not anticipating it, she comprehends with a new and more bitter awareness the consequences of her dark plotting and her selfish schemes. Those consequences are hastening toward her and toward Brett, Naomi, and Jake. Their unravelling powers, their unharnessed fury, their unleashed violence—all their lacerating punishments are already stalking her and disarranging, as well, the lives of those three human beings she has tried to control.

No new enchantments have intensified her awareness of the perilous situations that her scheming has wrought. Nor have Randall and Melanie appeared to her recently in a troubled dream or inside a wide-awake, summer afternoon scene that keeps unfurling its pleasures when she with Tate, and Naomi with Brett and Jake are experiencing the sweep and lift of a sailboat race, perhaps, or while they are riding upon the swift velocities of Tobianos, Appaloosas, and

Palominos along a four-mile horse trail. Randall and Melanie have left her to her own devices, as troubling as those devices may become. She has no clarified memory of the supernatural wall videos that Randall and Melanie have, with a wave of their hands, summoned from a perilous future. But a vague thought, some nebulous after-image of their enchanted visits, stays with her, leaving her at times puzzled and apprehensive. She cannot explain to her most private, inquiring self why these two affable persons with busy lives of their own could be intertwined with her fate. Her fleet and occasional sightings of them in dreams seems natural and even pertinent, because of the kindness and encouragement that they have always extended to her and to Naomi, as well.

No, their enchantments have not influenced Lisa's newly profound awareness. Instead, a fearsome reality has overtaken her perception of her life that all too suddenly, when she has not been expecting it, is spinning away from her control. Whether an implacable Fate or an avenging Angel has been working against her happiness, she cannot say. Perhaps, Blind Chance or her own willful nature has betrayed her, setting on her path acrimonious scenes and volatile implications. So she imagines as she sits up in her canopy bed, trying to draw comfort from its tulip-print fabrics and from the plush carpeting, button-tufted chairs, and walls in warm shades of apricot that make of this room a luxurious privacy.

Finding no comfort, she hurries out of her bed and heads for the shower, where she washes her body with aromatic soaps and with the warm spray of soothing waters. Because she wants to feel cleansed, she rubs her body harder and harder. She wants to clean away all traces of Tate's scent several hours after he visited her bedroom for the first time in weeks and, with his rough pinioning of her receptive femininity and with his brute strokes, shot his sperm inside her vagina. After he was finished, after his gruff, coital moaning and after his quick departure from her bedroom, she lay very still—too bitter to rise from her bed and quickly wash away Tate's scent as she had so often done. She lay awake, staring through the moonlit darkness and waiting for the dawn to signal that a new day was arriving and that she might serve her purposes well if she hurried to meet it.

The scenarios that, eighteen months ago, flared their ambivalent meanings inside the wall video have flashed anew their twisted implications. During the weeks since her unhappy meeting with Brett on the terrace of Tate's and her Sutton Place townhouse, she has worked her own magic upon the episodes that even now are still unfolding their mischief and their danger. There is no enchantment in her magic. Her magic is all too human, composed as it is of a jugglery of words and deeds that carry forth the doubleness within her scheming. Hers is a magic of trickery and skullduggery, a pact between subterfuge and guile. It is artifice, manipulation, and gamesmanship. It is her tenacious willfulness overriding the plan that would marry Brett to Naomi. It is her inveterate wiliness prevailing over Randall and Melanie, over Tate and his daughter Naomi, and over the stern Fate that would steal Brett's love from her. The magic encompasses all these things while it keeps conjuring unexpected alliances and furious surprises.

With only a vague recollection of the complicated scenes within the wall video—a memory that she tells herself was merely a dream—Lisa has carried forward her plot to bring Jake Boldwood into Naomi's life. Ambitious and avaricious, Jake needed no prodding. He reveled in the challenge, finding a special joy in his displacing Brett as the lover who fulfills in every way Naomi's schoolgirl expectation of romantic passion and of lifelong happiness with the man of her dreams.

In this swift and kinetic year-and-a-half, the scenes from the wall video that disclosed the triangle involving Jake, Naomi, and Brett have thrown forward their pictorial narratives into here-and-now reality with the same revolving impetus and with the same twists and turns. Caught inside a swift montage of tensions, triangles, and complications, Naomi and Jake and Brett have been playing out the drama that pushes them onto a path from which there is no returning. Both men have been courting Naomi. Both men have been walking on a tightrope. They have been accommodating Naomi's every wish while maintaining their proper balance as vigorous and proprietary men who make their own decisions about the next step that needs to be taken if they are to remain the keepers of their destinies.

On every weekend of this deceptively jubilant summer, they have been sailing in the regatta of boats that journey smoothly over blue-green, sun-crested waters across the lake behind Tate's and her home. They have been swimming in the heated pool within the west wing of their three-story house. They have dined inside the glamorous banquet tents that rise from manicured lawns and that look out upon the breeze-stirred waters of the lake. They have water skied and scuba dived when they visited the oceanfront property of Naomi's Aunt Marguerite in Newport, Rhode Island. They skydived in Danielson, Connecticut, about one hundred twenty-five miles from Blue Ridge. They went skeet shooting at a Blue Ridge firing range, and they raced their favorite automobiles on a drag strip twenty miles from Blue Ridge. Naomi piloted a Porsche 944. Brett raced a Camaro Firebird. Jake took the wheel of a Ferrari 488 Pista that Tate had lent him. Always, they represented a trio of friends. Sometimes, they suggested the undercurrents of a romantic triangle. Often,

Randall and Melanie accompanied them in these adventures.

Occasionally, Tate and she—Lisa Caulfield Calhern, at that time newly elated by the success of her plot—joined Naomi and her two ardent suitors. Even now, at the summer's end and with a troubling awareness of the fury with which her plot is unraveling, the memory of how well her schemes were at first succeeding revives for a brief moment the happiness that she then felt, as well as the certainty that she was going to win back Brett. There were solid reasons for her believing in that certainty. Some of those reasons still exist. With streetwise perceptions and his masculine assurance, Jake has won not only Tate's fatherly allegiance. He has also won Naomi's love.

On this sun-brightened, August morning, though, the rising consequences of her plotting steal away her ease and her sense of empowerment. Brett is the problem. He refuses to back away from his relationship with Naomi. He refuses to concede that Jake has won Naomi's love and has won, as well, her promise to marry him. Never did she imagine that Brett would fall so profoundly in love with Naomi. It is as though a spell is inspiring him to love Naomi with a deeply felt obsession that makes his love of her a strange compulsion, an erotic thrill, and a mind-racking need.

Temporarily safe within the contrived harmonies of her luxurious bathroom, Lisa peers at the recent past while her memory with its revolving images reveals the complications and the tensions spawned by her plotting. Though she remains here, caught as she is in the uncertainty of the present moment while she cleanses her body in the shower, her mind transports her—swiftly and altogether suddenly—to an earlier day. Before her imaginative seeing, one scene in particular comes swiftly back to her, as though it is happening for the first time.

That specific time, when he is so tormented by his need of her acceptance and by his awareness that she might give her heart to Jake, Brett asks Naomi the blunt question that for many days has been haunting him. That she—Lisa, his former paramour—is there with them in the eighty-foot catamaran that is carrying them across wave-crested Newport waters does not deter him from speaking out his dismay.

The three of them have been sunning on the yacht's full-beam terrace. The sun gleams like a sacred, golden medallion in the vaulted space above them, way up there within the immaculate blueness of the sky and the soft whiteness of the clouds. In this tense moment, only Lisa notices the sun and the clouds and the vaulted, faraway space. Brett, with brooding emphasis, and Naomi, with too-casual regard, take note only of each other.

"Why are you doing this?" Brett asks her. "Why are you flirting with Jake when you are engaged to me?"

"I haven't made my mind up," Naomi answers him, too quickly and too lightheartedly. "Marriage is a big step. I don't want to stumble into it. I want to be certain that I really love the man I'm going to marry."

Surprised and uneasy at their openness before her in this matter that is so personal and so complicated, Lisa starts to leave.

"You two need some time alone," she says while maintaining a genteel and caring manner.

She starts to leave, heading for the flybridge, where she can swim in the long expanse of the pool there or sip a cocktail at the wet bar while conversing with Raoul, the well-travelled bartender—tall, rugged, and sleek even at forty-five—who will offer her new, exciting stories about his adventures in the many countries where he has lived.

Brett eyes her with wary interest.

Naomi, all courtesy toward her and all hardened resolve in this problem involving Brett and Jake, chooses words that hold her back. Even then she does not know about Lisa's adulterous relationship with Brett.

"Don't go," she tells her. "With you, I've never made my life a secret. I won't start now. Stay here. You may as well know what's going on with Brett and me."

Demure within the boundaries of her artifice, Lisa says more.

"I'll stay as long as Brett doesn't mind."

To these soft words, Brett says nothing. For a moment, he glares at her. On that day, as on all of the other days of their relationship, he knows her well. Already, he has begun to suspect her complicity in this plan to marry Naomi to Jake.

Then, he quickly directs new, blunt words at Naomi.

"Your loving me was never a problem before," he tells her. "More than a few times, you've told me that I'm the only man that you will ever love."

Naomi responds to his remarks without any compunction and with a confident manner that makes her appear altogether different from the submissive woman whose attention he has been taking for granted—an emotionally deprived woman's expression of her adulation for him. Now, her regard of him seems careless and even perfunctory.

Observing her, Lisa wonders whether Naomi is playing with and even punishing the two men who are courting her because of the unjust way that her father has treated her. Perhaps, she perceives the shadow of her father in these men. For that reason, possibly, she cannot allow herself to trust them.

"People change," Naomi explains with a flippancy that gives her a hard edge.

The flippancy helps her to parry Brett's reminder that she once told him he was the only man she would ever love.

"Things change," she says. "Everything is different now that I've met Jake."

"Does that mean you love him?"

"I don't know yet," she answers him. "But the three of us being together is a wonderful way to find out."

"I don't like the setup," Brett says, brooding and dissatisfied. "I don't like being played with."

"Be patient," Naomi tells him. "Lisa and my father think that I'm doing the right thing. I'm not rushing into anything."

Once again, Brett glares at Lisa. Now he is more convinced that she and Tate have conspired against him. Nevertheless, he shrugs away their involvement. He is not going to be made a plaything of their treachery or of Naomi's whimsical desires.

"Your father and Lisa have nothing to do with us."

"You don't really believe that," Naomi says. "Besides, I'm waiting for you and Jake to make up my mind for me."

"How do we do that?"

"By being yourself. Right now, for instance, you are very much yourself. You are a loose cannon. You are a trip wire waiting to explode. I'm not holding that against you. I like a dangerous man."

In this angry moment when he is heedless of Lisa's startled presence, Brett grabs hold of Naomi's shoulders and pushes her body toward his chest. His angry brown eyes meet her blue, suddenly apprehensive gaze.

"Don't play with me," he says, while his big, strong hands press down hard upon her shoulders. "I'm warning you."

She winces at the pain rushing through her shoulders and shooting through her entire body.

"You're hurting me," she says, her voice a mere whimper now and a frightened protest.

"I'll do more than that if you betray me," Brett tells her. "That's a promise."

With a shove, he pushes her away from him and heads for the flybridge and the bar.

Naomi goes on whimpering, her body hunched and vulnerable.

Lisa holds herself steady and observant, careful to remain apart from Naomi for a minute or two. Then, hurrying to her and, with the gentle touch of her hand upon her shoulder, she murmurs encouraging words to her.

"These things happen," she tells her, "even to people who love one another. Try to forget what happened just now. Brett is not himself today."

Still weeping, Naomi speaks bitter words.

"These things don't happen if a man really loves a woman."

These words please Lisa. They presage further discord between Naomi and Brett and their final separation. So Lisa tells herself while she chooses false, solacing words that intensify Naomi's distrust of Brett.

"Brett does love you."

"Maybe he does," she says, after silence comes to watch her new frown and her rankling sorrow. "Maybe not enough."

Still Lisa plays the roles of the caring stepmother and the loyal confidante. Still she imparts words that sound heartfelt and sympathetic.

"You are too hard on him and on yourself."

The words make Naomi pause. They coax Naomi's thoughts to self-blame and to forgiveness of Brett's rough handling of her.

"Maybe I pushed him too far," she says and says it again, as though her words are an echo of her fear. "I pushed him too far."

Lisa is displeased, though she does not show it. Naomi's forgiveness of Brett is not in her plans. Nevertheless, she offers her more makeshift, solacing words.

"He'll get over it," she tells her.

"Not this time," Naomi answers her. "He won't get over it this time."

Secretly pleased that Naomi is downcast, Lisa offers ambivalent words that anchor their comfort to the imminence of danger.

"Maybe you are right," she says. "Maybe Brett won't get over it. Wait and see what happens."

This tense scene, fraught as it was with Brett's angry suspicion and a foreboding of his furious retaliation, occurred a week ago. Ever since that afternoon when Brett, Naomi, and she were cruising across Newport waters, the scene has been revolving over and over within Lisa's memory. It is a warning. It is an alarm. It is a signal of danger. Recognizing its harnessed furies, Lisa has become apprehensive. Naomi's having called Brett a loose cannon, a trip wire ready to explode, seems like a realistic appraisal of that formidable man.

Now, on this Thursday morning, after she emerges from her shower and after she selects the smart business suit and the appropriate accessories that she will wear to her office, she initiates the plan that might resolve her apprehension and her fear of the fury that may be rising within Brett. She arranges to meet him for lunch at a country club in Greenwich, about fifty miles away. Tate is once again busy with corporate executives in New York. That Brett is willing to spend a lunch hour alone with her pleases and surprises her. For weeks, he has avoided being alone in her company. He has been working hard at being faithful to Naomi. Hard task it must be for him to practice fidelity to a romantic partner. Faithfulness has never before been one of his virtues. But these uncertain months in which Naomi has turned her romantic gaze upon Jake Boldwood have disconcerted him. The presence of a rival threatens his plan to win the boss's daughter and to accelerate his journey to the top. That presence, nearly a mirror image of his own duplicity, has ignited his anger. Lisa tells herself that their meeting within the luxurious amenities of the country club may soften the edges of Brett's anger.

The exterior of the club makes a privileged setting of its Georgian mansion, enhanced as it is by garden efflorescence, manicured lawns, and an undulating golf course. Inside, the impressive building defines itself by peaceful tones of rich mahogany, neutral walls with abstract paintings, gleaming floors, and Karastan-beige carpets. Inside the main dining room, more mahogany adorns solid tables and upholstered chairs. Centerpieces flourish with red and yellow roses. Immaculate-white, hand-embroidered linen covers these tables, and Baccarat crystal and porcelain china rimmed with gold offer other emblems of elegance. This luxuriant setting, Lisa tells herself, may soften the jagged edges of Brett's anger.

This time, each of them drives into Greenwich alone— she in her Mercedes-Benz and he in his Camaro Firebird.

When she enters the club and after a waiter guides her to the wrap-around bar, Brett greets her with guarded courtesy. His tanned handsomeness and his summer-friendly silk-linen gray suit complement his casual-seeming manner. Solaced by the setting and by his favorite Glenmorangie scotch whisky, he soon reveals the degree to which Naomi's rejection of him will incite his vengefulness.

"I don't like being pushed aside," he says. "For more than a year, Naomi and I together were a sure thing. We were inevitable. Jake's coming into the picture has messed things up. That bastard needs to be set straight. He needs to be punished."

"Punishing Jake won't change things," she tells him. Her voice is soft and calm. In this tense moment, she bonds her sympathy with matter-of-fact counsel and with carefully chosen words that convey the sounds of truth and of loyalty. "Punishing Jake won't change Naomi's feelings for him. It won't stop her from loving him."

"I've got to win her back," he insists. "I've got to kick Jake back to the hell that spawned him."

To this remark, she at first says nothing. She sips her *Veuve Cliquot* while she cautiously studies his face. His casual-seeming manner has vanished. Now his words sound hard-edged and bitter.

"I'll have to settle the score with him," he says. "I'll make him see that, if he wants to go on living, he'd better back away from Naomi."

She notices the scowl that makes his face look suddenly dangerous. She sees his brown eyes, nearly glazed with the effects of the four or five whiskies that he quickly swallowed even before she sat at the bar and began conferring with him. He looks not only dangerous. He looks careworn and unhappy.

"You will do nothing like that," she tells him. Once again, her words sound helpful and encouraging. "You don't need Naomi. You are getting everything you want from life. You are the golden boy in Tate's law firm. You are hurrying to the top. You have already entered the big time. In a year or two, you will be a mega-millionaire. And you have Tate on your side. You need him far more than you need Naomi. Tate regards you as a son. It's Tate who is pushing you to the top."

Her quiet words, leavened as they are with clarifying ideas and realistic optimism, make Brett pause. For just an instant, his face brightens. The possibility of new hope lingers with familiar radiance and just as quickly vanishes, though not completely. That Tate remains his powerful advocate is all to the good. Jake Boldwood's winning Tate's favor need not diminish his own standing with Tate. A man like Tate craves the allegiance of many sons.

So, Lisa imagines, Brett is telling himself. Whatever the cause, the brooding stare that dimmed his brightness takes leave of him. Husky laughter rises from his throat and quickens his next remark.

"You are absolutely right," he says. "I've got Tate on my side. I can still play the winning hand."

An hour later, after a waiter had with careful proficiencies guided them to a table by a panoramic window that looks out at the breeze-tossed ocean, the brooding stare returns. By that time, they have dined on trout braised in Riesling wine, Brett has comforted himself with more tumblers of Glenmorangie Scotch whiskey, and she has nursed a few more tulip-shaped crystal glasses of *Veuve Cliquot*. They have spoken of many things, including lucrative hedge funds; the latest Rolls Royce; the Nubra Valley within the Ladakh Himalayas; and skiing in Vail, Colorado. Brett has laughed or smiled many times, his gleaming white teeth enhancing his exuberance and his willful capture of the happiness that had begun to outrace him.

But all too soon this same, nebulous happiness once again runs away from him. Happiness as he perceived it is a false light in the darkness. It is an *ignis fatuus,* a will-o'-the-wisp, a flame-like luminescence that with wily proclivities conceals the dismay and disappointment that have shadowed him ever since Jake Boldwood caught

Naomi's attention. His new, bitter words send his forlorn hope scattering. The problem of Jake Boldwood is not going to vanish. It is no will-o'-the-wisp. It is a dark reality. It is a challenge calling him to its surprises and to its fatalities.

Suddenly, even though her intuition has in the hour just passed alerted her to this electric moment—quite suddenly because her wishful thinking has with temporary powers deflected its inevitability—Brett sends his casual remarks and his hope-laden expectations scattering. With blunt words and vengeful implications, he speaks the truth of his feelings.

"I want more than Tate's acceptance," Brett tells her. "I want more than his push to the top. I want Naomi."

With always quiet words and with heartfelt concern, Lisa urges him to retrieve his hope.

"Why? Why do you want Naomi? You don't really need her. You don't even love her."

Quickly, he repudiates her remarks. His eyes glow with impassioned certainty. That passion, bonded as it is with new-found poignancy and with honest feelings, rouses her envy and her dismay.

"I do need her. I do love her. Even against my conscious will, I love her. Besides, she's the badge I intend to wear. She's the prize that I aim to win."

"What happens if she doesn't love you? What happens if she loves Jake more than she loves you?"

"Then I'll kill Jake and her and, afterwards, I'll kill myself."

These blunt words startle Lisa. Stillness overtakes her, though only for an instant. She chooses careful words to make her protest.

"You don't really love her," she says, "not if you are willing to kill her."

"I'll kill her for not loving me. I'll kill her for killing me first of all."

Brett glares at her. But he does not really see her. He sees Naomi with Jake. So she imagines. A dangerous intensity overtakes his stare.

Quickly, Lisa finds words to calm him. There is a measure of truth in what she tells him. It is this truth that lends conviction to her words.

"Naomi hasn't made up her mind. She's testing you. She wants you to show her that your love for her is stronger and better than Jake's love."

"She's playing with me. She's playing a game, and I don't like it."

Genteel and self-controlled, she nudges his willingness to believe her.

"It's a serious game," she tells him with absolute conviction, "and the winner takes all. You can still be the winner."

"How do you know?"

"I know *her*. I know how she thinks. She's testing you, and she wants you to win the game."

"Maybe," he says. "Maybe not. I'll find out soon enough. When I do, I'd better find out that I'm the winner."

For an instant, Lisa becomes very still. She perceives the danger that anchors itself to Brett's remark. As though one of the stern Fates, invisible and implacable, has waved a hand and shown her the future, she witnesses a horrifying scene unfolding before her. Her cautious eyes recognize the scene. A shadowed memory pushes the scene forward—an after-horror rising out of a nearly forgotten enchantment, a murderous violence overtaking an equivocating future. Brett is firing bullets from a Glock revolver into Jake's forehead and heart. The impact of the bullets throws his tall, muscular body against Naomi, who is standing next to him within the sanctuary of the magnificent church where the aged priest officiating at their marriage has raised his hand to bless them. Blood is spilling out of Jake's forehead, mouth, and chest. Its deep red spatters Naomi's white bridal gown and spills across the hands of the priest as he catches hold of the falling body and utters a prayer over the dead man. Three rugged men in their twenties rush forward to overtake the killer. But Brett fires his revolver in the air as a warning, notices that the warning shot has stopped them in their tracks, and without any hesitation fires a bullet into his brain. The body topples at the foot of the altar while Naomi's screaming pierces through the congregation's rising protests of disbelief and outrage.

This premonition of tragedy, this foreboding of evil, this danger signal with its flashes of the future and its dire implications—all these responses to Brett's ominous remark shake Lisa's self-assurance, though only for a moment. Tough-minded and resolute, she quickly finds words that will calm Brett as they conclude their meeting in the glamorous surround of the Greenwich Country Club.

"Of course you will be the winner," she tells him. "That is why Naomi will choose you to be her husband. Naomi knows how to pick a winner. You are her Mister Wonderful."

Hearing this remark, Brett says nothing. Ominous stillness comes with its harnessed menace to watch him.

Brett orders another scotch. Right after that, a sneer pushes its way into the corner of his upper lip. Only after that does he reveal his dark thoughts.

"Naomi belongs to me. I'm not letting any other guy have her."

Lisa recognizes the dangerous implications of those words. Instantly, even while she continues to placate Brett, she plots her next move. She will draw Tate into this new scheme. With him, she intends to rescue all of them—Lisa, Jake, and Brett, as well as Tate and herself—from the tragedy that is waiting for them. Cautiously, with firm self-control and devious motives, she will alert her husband about the dangerous triangle that—like a trip wire or trap or land mine, even—may suddenly destroy them.

A few days later, when Tate returns from his business trip, Lisa broaches (as though it were an awareness altogether new) this matter of the triangle.

She chooses an after-dinner hour when, alone in his study, Tate is reviewing a legal brief.

"I need to talk with you," she begins.

She keeps her voice matter of fact, yet soft and understated.

Tate looks at her, surprised and displeased that she has entered his study when he is planning new strategies for his next-day's appearance in court.

"Can't it wait?" he asks her.

"I've already waited too long," she answers him. "We have a problem. I've tried to fix it, without any success."

"It must be a very serious problem to make you come up short. You are not a person who allows yourself to fail."

"It *is* serious, and I *have* failed—though Heaven knows how hard I've tried to resolve it."

"Tell me about it, then," Tate says as he puts aside the legal document that with keen-minded acumen he had been studying. "Tell me all of it."

Her words come quickly now. Her voice grows urgent and, at times, tremulous, because her heart is bitter and because her fear of oncoming tragedy looms closer and closer.

"Naomi's engagement to Brett is in trouble. Jake has crossed a line that was never his to cross. He's drawing Naomi away from Brett, the man who really loves her. Jake doesn't love Naomi. To him, she's merely a plaything—a spoiled, rich girl who doesn't know her own mind. He enjoys confusing her. He enjoys knowing that he can make her do anything he wants her to do. He has the edge in what has turned into an unpleasant triangle. Jake knows that he can use Naomi to speed his way to the top. He's trying to connive you, too, into believing that he is the right man for Naomi."

Abruptly, she pauses. Her quick words have left her breathless. She watches Tate watching her. She waits for him to impart some words or some gesture that will tell her whether, to unravel the complications of the Brett-Naomi-Jake triangle, they are going to join forces. Suddenly, as though this other fear is also rousing her attention, she wonders whether she and Tate will be on the same team.

When he speaks, Tate's words express neither regret nor pity that she has become too involved in a problem that belongs to Naomi. Nor does he allow her to imagine that he will join her in her foolish efforts to manipulate and control the romantic relationships of his daughter and her two suitors.

"You are entering private territory," he tells her. "Naomi's love life belongs to her and to the young men who are courting her. Don't be a trespasser," he says. "The world is filled with do-gooders who have a knack for messing up other people's lives."

"Naomi's in trouble," she tells him. "She's in real danger."

"Danger? Nonsense. You are imagining things."

"Please listen to me. Believe what I am telling you."

"Stay out of it. Their relationships shouldn't concern you."

"I'm telling you what I see so clearly. I'm telling you what you don't see because you are never around often enough to see how things are with them. Brett is a loose cannon. He's a trip wire ready to explode. I'm afraid of what he may do to Jake and to Naomi, too."

"Nonsense, I say! I know Brett better than you think I do. If what you say is true, he will still make all the right moves."

"You know him as a lawyer. You know him as a savvy participant in the world's maneuverings. But you don't know who he is when he is involved in a matter of the heart."

For an instant, Tate's eyes glare with secret awareness and with hatred that is so fierce, it surprises even himself.

"Do you?" he asks. "Do you know who Brett is when he is involved in a matter of the heart?"

At first, she does not speak, enclosed as she makes herself inside the ambiguous safety of silence.

Tate knows, she tells herself. He knows about Brett and me.

She rallies. She finds once more the hardened part of her nature. She seizes the moment.

"Of course not," she says. "Of course I don't know who he is when he is involved in a romantic relationship."

Tate throws out another challenging question.

"Then why are you so concerned about him?"

She parries his remark with nearly imperceptible tension.

"I'm concerned about the three of them. I'm worried that Brett will do something crazy. I believe that, if he's pushed to it, he will bring harm to Jake and maybe to Naomi and himself."

Self-satisfied because he has shaken her duplicity, Tate takes up his legal brief and, while poring over it, dismisses her with these callous words.

"You are overwrought and with no valid reasoning to back you. Frankly, Lisa, I'm disappointed. Rarely have you behaved in such a conventional way. You are thinking strictly as woman. Go on being a woman, by all means, but always think like a man."

She refuses to be dismissed. She pushes herself to tell him more. She uses a new tactic. She makes him feel that she has failed in her mission to uncover the anguish that is overtaking Brett. She allows him to believe that he, the reliable Tate Calhern, can accomplish the mission that has defeated her.

She pleads with him. Her words carry conviction. Her appeal comes forth as a sensible quest. He looks up from his legal brief and ponders her new spate of words.

"Maybe I've got it all wrong. Maybe I'm letting my emotions get the better of me. But I'll feel better if you speak to Brett. Try to figure him out. Find out what he is feeling about Naomi and himself. Ask him what he thinks about Jake and Naomi."

Perverse and malevolent, Tate still resists her.

"I'll do no such thing. If Brett is the gutsy man that I believe he is, he'll accept the way things are. He'll shrug his shoulders. He'll bear up. He'll get on with his life. He'll go forward."

Her appeal becomes more emotional.

"What happens if Brett finds out that Jake has won Naomi? What if he doesn't accept the situation? What if he becomes violent?"

Now Tate answers her with harsh and cold-hearted words.

"Then he's a fool, and I want no part of him."

Having delivered his opinion, Tate turns back to his legal brief. At the same time, with an imperious wave of his hand, he signals that he has concluded his discussion with her.

Intuitively, Lisa guesses what Tate plans to do. He wants to punish Brett and her because of their illicit relationship. He will never forgive them for their betrayal. Nor will he make any scenes or become trapped in the role of an aggrieved husband. Instead, he will push Jake into a marriage with Naomi. After that, he will push Brett out of his law firm's New York office. He will send him away to the firm's London office. He will send him away from Lisa.

So Lisa imagines, because Randall and Melanie have woven a magical spell that influences her thinking.

Frightened and disheartened, Lisa returns to her bedroom. Minutes later, lying in her bed while the light of the moon imbues the darkness with a lingering glow, she longs to free herself from her problems, from her husband, and from her rivalry with Naomi for the love of Brett. She feels trapped. New fearful awareness holds her in its chains. She is not going to save Brett from himself, after all. She is not going to prevent the tragedy that is hurrying toward them. Nor can she convince Tate that she has always remained faithful to him.

She tries to fall into sleep. She tosses and turns. Then, just as she takes the plunge, dropping down and down into the freefall of slumber, a nightmare rises before her. So dangerous and violent is this nightmare, so vivid are the killings that flare their violence before her and in their wake leave the blood-riddled corpses of Brett, Naomi, Jake, Tate, and her that—with a piercing scream—she pushes herself out of the nightmare.

Trembling, she flicks on the lamp that stands in the center of one of the tables that flanks her bed. She takes a cigarette from a gold case on that same table and lights it with the gold lighter that sits as its companion nearby. She almost enjoys the first drags on the cigarette. She finds a small pleasure in noticing the smoke from the cigarette wafting its way around and above her, carrying its vapors into the moonlit darkness beyond the bed and almost convincing her that the privacy of this room could ease her tensions and save her from the danger that she is expecting.

But this illusion of safety quickly vanishes, like the vaporous smoke that rises from her cigarette. There is no way out of her dilemma. Tough-minded and embittered, she compels herself to accept this moment. In the morning, though, she will devise a new plan. She won't give in. She won't give up. She will do everything that she can to save Brett, Naomi, and Jake from themselves. She tells herself that she will give up Brett. She won't stand in his way. He truly loves Naomi. They belong together. Perhaps, she can convince Naomi to move past her distrust of men. She will convince Jake that he, too, must not stand in Brett's way. He can have everything he wants without Naomi. He must not ruin her life or Brett's or his own.

"I've got to make all these things happen," she murmurs to herself. "For once in my life, I've got to do the right thing."

No sooner does she make this promise to herself, than a dazzling light rises around her. So dazzling is the light that it momentarily blurs her vision. After her startled eyes have adjusted to its radiance and after she becomes aware that she is entering an otherworldly scene, Melanie and Randall appear to her. In some way that is mysterious and yet familiar, she believes that she has met these two in other scenes that drew her into otherworldly realms. Now, in this latest meeting, she rises from her bed and stands before them, poised as she is between the here-and-now reality that she has always inhabited and the enchanted realm that, in her mind, is merely an extension of her earthbound home.

They, too, Melanie and Randall, live on two co-existent planes. So she tells herself, remembering that inside the reality that is most familiar to her, Melanie is an esteemed psychologist and Randall a respected attorney. The other world that they inhabit with so much ease and confidence is somewhat, though not altogether, new to her. It is a world of visions and spells and enchantments. It is a paranormal world, mystical and supernatural because it exists apart from ordinary explanation.

Standing before her, here in the privacy of her solitude, Melanie and Randall quickly tell her why—suddenly, when she has not been anticipating them, yet in some intuitive way has been calling to them, quite suddenly, while fatal chance and unforgiving violence are threatening her hopes for devising rescues—they are appearing to her in this grievous moment because fury and danger and death are about to ignite their powers.

Randall, in the black suit and robes of a stern judge, is the first to speak.

"Your plots are backfiring," he tells her. "You won't be able to stop Brett from killing all of you."

"All of us?"

"Naomi and Jake. You and Tate. And himself."

She holds herself very still. She refuses to give in to despair or panic or to believe that the fatal endings of which Randall speaks will happen.

"The killings won't happen," she tells him. "I'll make certain they don't happen. There's still time. I can stop them from happening."

Melanie, appearing lovelier and more radiant than ever in a white organdy dress, offers another warning.

"It's too late, Lisa," she says and says the words again while melancholy touches her voice and sorrow creases her brow. "It's too late. You can't stop the killings from happening. You can't undo the wrong that you have done. Your plots are unleashing all their powers. Death is carrying them forward. Death is coming to claim all of you."

"It's not true. You're just trying to frighten me. Besides, you don't know what is going to happen. You can't predict the future. Nobody can do that—at least, not with any certainty."

Randall comes into it again, sterner than ever and even more formidable.

"We can," he tells her. "We can predict the future whenever the First Spirit gives us that power."

"The First Spirit?"

Randall explains.

"The First Spirit made everything and everyone. He has created worlds that we humans here on Earth do not know and cannot see. It is He Who sent me here as a lawyer and Melanie as a psychologist. He wants us to save all of you if we can. He wanted us to save you from yourselves first of all, without enchantments or spells or magical visions. But, despite our counsel and the warnings that we have delivered, none of you has changed. Brett, Jake, and Tate remain arrogant and devious. Naomi continues to trap herself inside her uncertainty. You are faithless, narcissistic, and promiscuous."

Lisa protests, her vehemence pushing back her apprehension and her startlement at seeing Randall and Melanie as themselves and as supernatural beings, too.

"I live by my own codes! I live my life as Lisa Caulfield Calhern and nobody else. I'll be no makeshift Lisa. I'll not be your puppet or anyone else's. I tell you that I'll make things happen as I want them. I will! I will!"

Randall delivers a harsh verdict. He will not tolerate her lies or her schemes.

"Because of the things that you have already done—the wrongful actions and wily plots of your devising—consequences are already erupting. There will be shootings. There will be killings. There will be everlasting death for all of you—for Naomi with her weak will and suppressed hatred of her father, for Brett and Jake with their hoodlum hearts and rancid greed, for Tate with his ugly tyrannies, and for you with your need to manipulate people."

Once more, Lisa screams out her defiance.

"No! Oh, no! I tell you that those horrible things won't happen. I won't make them happen. I'll stop them."

With her innate sympathy and her capacity for pitying even wrongdoers, Melanie speaks words that make Lisa pause.

"Take a look, Lisa," she says. "Take a look at the future that is almost here."

No sooner does she speak these words, than a glamorous scene unfolds across a supernatural video that rises around the room. It does not presage horror and murder, yet somewhere in the back of her mind—somewhere way, way back—she senses that this scene she is experiencing in this very instant has lain hidden within her most secret memory. She has witnessed this scene before. She recognizes the lift and radiance of its exuberance. She suddenly recalls—as though it has lived as a vivid presence inside her darkest hidden memories—that the glamour and the exhilaration will soon turn to horror and mayhem and multiple killings.

The horror has not yet happened.

Glamour and artifice and celebration leaven the scene with joyous excitement and the promise of lasting happiness.

This future that is hurrying toward her belongs to a sun-misted day at the end of September. Once again, as in her sighting of this same scene in some visionary moment that, unexpectedly and all too suddenly, she is re-experiencing, a festive wedding celebration in the sumptuous ballroom of The Blue Ridge Country Club is bringing a more-than-ordinary elation to the faces of the hundred twenty-five guests that she and Tate have invited to Naomi's wedding to Jake Boldwood. Once more, as if the unfolding scene is part of an inevitable transaction, these favored guests include Wall Street executives and government officials, film stars and television celebrities, two seasoned astronauts and three Nobel Prize-winning scientists and their wives, and some of their most affluent Blue Ridge neighbors. Women young and older, with slender or full-bodied figures, have adorned themselves in pastel gowns and dresses. Brawny men and scrawny men with handsome or cragged features wear gray satin dinner jackets with black shawl lapels and black trousers, white shirts, and black bow ties. Some men wear two-piece medium blue suits with notched lapels, basted sleeves, flap pockets and two-button front. They also wear azure blue shirts and paisley jacquard silk ties.

One hundred twenty-five guests are having a good time. Many of these guests are sitting at the six long banquet tables that dominate the south corner of the ballroom. Everyone appears affable. Everyone looks privileged. Everyone seems carefree and articulate and even elated. These guests talk of many things, including their recent visits to the Bahamas or Hawaii or Palm Beach; their thrilling experiences water skiing, skydiving, and sailing; and their piloting their private planes—a Bombardier Challenger 350, a Cessna Citation Latitude, and a Boeing VIP Dreamliner. They speak of the recent merger of three global corporations. They mention top-performing stocks; controversial happenings in Washington, D.C.; the imminence of commercial flights into space; medical breakthroughs in the treatment of brain tumors and heart maladies; and the current season's most promising baseball teams. Young waiters, proficient and agile, have cleared away pristine chinaware and delicate crystal from the long, ornate tables where, two hours earlier, the guests partook of a five-course meal that included split peas soup with bacon, sorrel, and lettuce; puff pastry shells with salmon, asparagus, and lemon butter sauce; stuffed loin of veal with artichokes; orange sorbet; and a four-foot-tall, strawberry-filled wedding cake.

In the east corner of the ballroom, an orchestra is playing romantic ballads. A young blonde woman, glamorous in a chartreuse gown, is singing about the happiness and the adventure of love. In this specific moment that Lisa is observing from her place outside the wall video, couples young and older are giving themselves completely to the flowing movements of a waltz. Jake and Naomi lead the dance, the groom in a cobalt blue tuxedo and his bride in a white, appliquéd wedding gown that has lace over satin, a scoop neck, and half sleeves. They look as though they have stepped out of a fairy tale. They dominate the room, and they revel in this once-in-a-lifetime moment. Tate, tuxedoed in early autumn burgundy and genuinely ebullient, is dancing with a distinguished French ambassador's red-haired, fashionable wife who looks stunning in a pleated, emerald-green gown that is trimmed with ruffles and has a jacquard belt. Lisa—looking lovelier than ever in a pale-mint, lace gown—partners with a Wall Street broker, a stately white-haired charmer in a cobalt blue tuxedo. Hayden, handsome in a steel gray tuxedo, and Kayla—beautiful in a floral watercolor gown made of silk chiffon and enhanced by an A-line silhouette, a spread collar, three-quarter sleeves, a button front, a self-sash at the waist, and a floor-sweeping hem—are circling the dance floor with easy, rhythmical turnings. Randall, dashing in a navy tuxedo, and Melanie—exquisite in an azure blue gown that has a scoop neckline, pleated shoulders, long balloon sleeves, and beaded cuffs—sway and lean into the music with poise and precision.

Everything about the room seems sumptuous and pristine. Everything about this wedding imparts a festive atmosphere. The splendid scene has a fairy tale glow to it. So Lisa believes as she continues to peer at the video wall. Round and round the ballroom the apparently happy couples whirl. As though they are actors in a dazzling film that want to draw her notice, the essential persons in her life and the friends who have proved themselves loyal dance before her astonished seeing. She recognizes all of them. Yet the one person who is most essential to her happiness is missing. Why has Brett gone missing?

Surely, Tate would have insisted that he attend Naomi's wedding. Though he is not the groom, Brett is an important part of the Calhern law firm. In the spirit of *noblesse oblige* or good-natured camaraderie or disciplined sportsmanship, he should be here. What has kept him away—unbridled jealousy or hardhearted betrayal or trouble-haunted memories of the thrilling year he was engaged to Naomi? Lisa wonders. When Hayden and Kayla dance by her once again, she extends her right hand, imagining for an instant that she can enter the scene and halt their progress. She needs to speak to them. She needs to ask them why Brett has failed to attend the wedding. But, try as she does, she cannot enter the scene. She cannot halt Hayden and Kayla's dancing.

Now, remembering that Randall and Melanie are standing behind her and observing her responses, she turns away from the wall video. She notices at once that Randall looks even more official and more grim-faced than ever in the black robes of a judge. Melanie continues to add radiance to her white organdy dress. Turning quickly back to the wall video, she sees that Randall and Melanie are also inside the video, dancing. The time frame is different. It represents the future that might be. In that potential future, they appear exactly as she noticed them a few moments earlier, when she began watching the video. He is wearing a navy tuxedo, and she is dressed in an azure blue gown.

Once again, she turns away from the video wall and gazes upon Randall and Melanie. Then the questions that are goading her curiosity and her tension leap from her lips.

"Why isn't Brett at the wedding? Why hasn't he accepted the invitation that Tate and I sent to him?"

At first, Randall and Melanie stand silent before her. There is no happiness in their faces. Randall shadows his handsomeness with tightlipped contempt. Melanie brings a frown of disappointment and melancholy to her lovely face.

When Randall does speak, his voice is filled with brusque words that are accusatory and bitter. They are the echo of words that she has heard before.

"You want it all. Tate and his money aren't enough for you. You want your illicit affair with Brett, too. You want him at the wedding as a sign of his bond with you. You want to imagine that he is not only your lover. He is the man you regard as your real husband, even though he has never married you."

Lisa doesn't want to hear any more of his words. She flings her own harsh words at him.

"I love Brett! I'll never stop loving him. He belongs to me and to no other woman! But I'm willing to give him up. I don't want any harm to come to him. I don't want him to bring harm to anyone else."

Melanie comes into it.

"Oh, my dear, don't you know what you have done? Can't you see the wrong that you have plotted? Can't you imagine what is going to happen now that you've pushed Naomi into Jake's arms?"

"I'll persuade Naomi to go back to Brett. I'll make her see that Brett loves her more than Jake could ever love her."

"It's pretty to think that you might change her mind," Melanie tells her. "But it's only wishful thinking."

Randall, still grim-faced and insistent, has more to say.

"Turn back to the video wall. Look at the scenes that are rushing relentlessly toward you. You can't stop them. Nobody can. Your plan to keep Brett has loosed its powers, and Brett, Naomi, and Jake are caught in its undertow."

Lisa turns her gaze back to the video. The music has stopped. The musicians are taking a break. Merry voices and lighthearted laughter are influencing the atmosphere. The dancers have returned to their places at the banquet tables, or they have sauntered onto the terrace or wandered to the bar. Everything about this moment seems jubilant and life-affirming. Happiness has found a place here with all these guests and plans to stay with them even after they leave this wedding celebration.

Lisa wants to believe in such a scenario, despite Randall and Melanie's troubling prediction. As she looks at the wall video, she sees herself chatting amiably with Hayden and Kayla. A television celebrity and a Washington senator join them in quick-witted repartee about the best ballroom dancers, the most recent medical breakthroughs, and the fastest thoroughbreds. Jake and Naomi are holding court at the opposite end of the long table. Guests young and older are greeting them with genuine well-wishes and, at the same time, sharing with them the afternoon's *joie de vivre*. All the other guests are also giving themselves completely to camaraderie and exhilaration.

Suddenly yet inevitably, Brett has entered the wedding banquet. He is wearing a steel gray tuxedo that intensifies his handsomeness. His brown-haired crewcut, his broad-shouldered muscularity, and his straight-back posture give him the appearance of a well-trained Army captain or a battle-tested Air Force major. His brown, gleaming eyes show the weariness of sleepless nights and brooding anticipation. He searches the room with steadfast and accurate gaze. Many of his friends notice him and wave to him. Invariably, they call out to him. They would like him to join their tables. Though he waves back, he moves past them and, with athletic agility, continues to make the journey that some unkind Fates or his own conflicted nature have devised for him. He hurries toward Jake and Naomi. They are his chosen quarry. They are part of his fatal destiny. As he approaches them, he brings a smile to his lips. The Fate that cuts the fragile thread that measures each of their lives is making the final cuts. He is the instrument. He is the messenger of death—their deaths and his own.

Peering at him from her place outside the video wall, Lisa knows his thoughts. Somewhere in her nightmares or in the spells that Randall and Melanie have cast upon her, she has already watched this scene. Once again, she watches Brett as he takes the fatal steps that will bring him before Naomi and Jake. Once again, though this time with a more anguished awareness of the horror that is about to unfold, she perceives Brett's bitterness and his murderous hatred. She wants to warn him against his self-destructive intentions. She wants to save him from his violence and his wretchedness. She wants to save Naomi and Jake, as well.

Vaguely, she remembers that in her previous sighting of this supernatural moment she called out to him.

She calls out to him now. She screams her warning.

"Don't do it, Brett! Don't do it! You will ruin everything for them and for yourself! You will never come back! Never! Never!"

Brett doesn't hear her cries. How can he? He is locked inside a future that has not yet unraveled the intricacies of these happenings that Lisa is now watching. He arrives at the table where Jake and Naomi, the dashing groom and his lovely bride, are holding hands as they converse with their friends. As soon as they and their six friends notice him, a hush falls around them. His being here in this specific moment astonishes all of them. Though the three young men give him a good-natured military salute and their girlfriends offer him a cordial smile, nobody speaks. Jake stares at him, guarded and tense. Only Naomi nudges the silence away. Only she speaks the words that are meant to ease the tension that suddenly has come to watch them, here at their festive wedding table.

"How good it is to see you, Brett," she says. "I'm glad that you are here to wish us well."

Brett stands before her and Jake, the smile never leaving his lips. He finds the ironic words that will serve as a preface to his wrongdoing.

"I've brought you a present," he says. "It's a special present that you and Jake and I can share. Each of us deserves it."

As he speaks, he opens his jacket, removes a Ruger Super Redhawk revolver from a leather chest holster, and swiftly fires .44 magnum rounds into Jake's and Naomi's brain and heart. Then, he turns to Tate and to her—Lisa Caulfield Calhern, whom he had once loved so passionately. His bullets pummel Tate's chest and forehead with their power, and they pierce her heart, instantly killing her. Only after he watches the dark red blood and the brain cells and the jagged pieces of flesh and hair spilling out of their heads and their hearts and spilling, too, across their startled faces—only then does he point his revolver inside his mouth and fire. His head explodes with blood. His left eye spills out of his head. His face becomes warped and distorted. His rugged body drops down upon its knees and stays kneeling for a few eerie moments. Then, swaying uncertainly, it leans forward and slowly falls upon the gleaming hardwood floor.

"He's killed me!" Lisa cries out, as she stands outside the wall video. "He's killed all of us!"

Randall and Melanie stand there with her outside the wall video and inside it, too.

"You couldn't stop him," Randall tells her, rigorous and unemotional in his appraisal of the scene. "Nobody could."

"You least of all," Melanie says, "even though your deceptions ignited Brett's fury."

To these remarks, Lisa says nothing. Instead, she looks back at the wall video and at the consequences of her plotting.

The six guests inside the wall video who have witnessed closeup these cold-hearted murders draw back, horrified and speechless. Two of the young women begin screaming and wailing. One of the men, an intern at Blue Ridge Medical Center, quickly attends the bodies of Naomi and Jake and of Tate and herself that have slumped inertly against the back of their chairs. Randall and Hayden assist him. Melanie, sorrow-laden but holding back her tears, kneels by Brett's body. She notices the Ruger semi-automatic revolver with its brushed stainless patina, its redwood grips, and its length of approximately thirteen inches. The revolver lies inches away from Brett's right hand. She whispers a prayer that asks The First Spirit for His mercy upon this tormented man, this lost soul, this crazed sinner. At the same time, the entire ballroom is seized with terror and amazement. There is a rushing toward exits. There is a crescendo of fear-ridden and screaming voices. There is the genuine sobbing of women and the tight-lipped sorrow of men who have witnessed death intruding upon a wedding celebration and scattering its happiness into a fathomless darkness.

Outside the wall video, Lisa is screaming a new protest.

"It won't end this way! It will be different. I'll make it so."

Randall and Melanie, no longer observing themselves in the video that instantly fades away, turn their attention to Lisa.

Melanie is the first to speak.

"You tried to change things and failed," she tells Lisa. "You failed to become a different person."

"I will change, I tell you," Lisa says. "I will. That's a promise."

Randall has more to say.

"You don't have the willpower to change. You have lost your soul," he tells her, stern and judgmental.

In the black robes of a judge, he seems to be passing sentence upon her.

"You no longer have the capacity to change for the better. You have lost the Spirit power that enables you to be the best human being that you can be. You lost your soul not all at once. You lost it gradually. You began to lose it when you made avarice and infidelity your intimate friends. Finding your soul again will be a rigorous test for you. The journey of a soul-seeker is always hard and sometimes terrifying. Only time will tell whether you can make that journey successfully. Only time will show whether you rediscover the Spirit power that can influence you to follow the right path. You won't discover it alone. You will need our help, Melanie's and mine. Most of all, you will need the help of the First Spirit."

"Why should you or the First Spirit care what happens to me or to the others? We are all fallible human beings. We've made plenty of mistakes."

Melanie, with her forgiving nature, answers her question.

"The First Spirit wants to save all of you, because he knows that this second chance that he is giving you will change all of you for the better. In special and important ways, all of you will make the world a better place."

Randall tells more.

"Left to your fallible devices, all of you are headed for destruction. Brett will kill you, Tate, Jake, Naomi, and himself. Your bad end is inevitable. Each of you is your worst enemy. All of you are enemies to each other. Knowing this truth, the First Spirit has allowed us to cast magical spells and enchantments to change all of you for the better."

Lisa ponders this information—these paranormal communications, these supernatural messages, these otherworldly dispatches—that Randall and Melanie are bringing to her. Her self-reliance rears its protest. Her arrogance reveals her reluctance to accept their offer of assistance or to imagine that the First Spirit has noticed her travails or the danger that is stalking the four persons who may influence her future happiness and her grief.

"You mean well," she tells them. "You want to help me, and for that I am grateful. But I want to resolve my own problems. I want to chart my own journeys. I need to make my own decisions about my life and the ways that my life may influence others."

Randall listens to her every word. She senses that, despite his negative judgment of her, he respects her need to remain self-determining. Nevertheless, her tough-mindedness and her resilience are pushing her toward a precipice from which she will plunge to eternal destruction—the forever death of her body and of her Spirit.

His next words suggest his patience and offer an explanation that carries with it what Lisa recognizes to be a final pronouncement, a Heaven-sent edict, an austere decree, and an urgent directive.

"Sometimes, only enchantments can prevent fatalities," he tells her. "Sometimes, only magical spells can rescue us from the evil of others and from our own evil."

Melanie says more.

"Believe us when we tell you that the First Spirit knows that all of you are worth saving."

"What do you want me to do?"

"You must accept our enchantments. Usually, you do not have any say in the matter. The First Spirit allows us to cast our enchantments upon you without your anticipation or your permission. But this time is different. This time you must choose to save yourself or to accept your imminent ending. This time you must accept the spells that we cast upon you. You must accept them while knowing that they come with unexpected perils, with dangerous chances, and with soul-saving sacrifices."

Lisa ponders these words that sound like a challenge as well as a call to endure painful ordeals, the severest tests, and soul-awakening episodes.

While she reflects upon the conditions that Randall has explained, Melanie tells her something that is equally important.

"You will confront new problems. You will face difficult tests. You will have to change things for the better."

"If you fail," Randall tells her, "there will be no other chances for you or for the others."

Lisa's realistic sense tells her that there are no better options. Her current life has been sending her many danger signals. Not even her toughminded resilience can guarantee her victory over those dangers. No longer does she hesitate. She perceives at last the path she must follow, the journey she must make.

"I do accept," she tells them. "I accept the danger that lives in the enchantments. I accept the sacrifices they may demand of me. I accept the mystery of becoming new."

"Good," Randall says. "That's settled. Now let's get to work."

CHAPTER TEN
SOULFINDERS

LISA AND TATE

It is always the same dream now—an enchantment in the form of a dream that some guardian Spirit or ambiguous Fate or ghostly Randall and Melanie may have sent to her. Lisa sees herself as the epitome of artifice and glamour. She is splendidly gowned in bright red as she cavorts and dances with three wily partners—Brett and Jake and Tate. They are in the center of the ballroom within the Blue Ridge Country Club. In the distance, accomplished musicians are playing romantic ballads that intensify the sensuality and the ambivalence of the dancing. Two of her partners, Jake and Brett, move with sensual abandon as they take their turn circling and swaying, bending and twisting about her. The movements of Tate, her third partner, are unlike the movements of Jake and Brett. His movements lack the younger men's sensuality. They are detached. They are robotic. They are lock-step simulations of sensuality. Yet they are more aggressive and more calculating. They are proprietary and domineering. There is neither romance nor love in his movements.

Each of these men is dressed in black, their long-sleeve, open-collar shirts and form-fitting trousers allowing them to move with athletic assurance and precise timing. Their strong arms are reaching out to take hold of her, possessing the woman who has already taken possession of their senses, their yearnings, and their plotting.

Before they can take hold of her, though, she moves out of their reach. Graceful movements of her upraised arms signal her playful eluding of their attempts to possess her. Her lithe body dips and sways and darts away from them. Yet she does not altogether resist their overtures. Only for a few moments does she dance away from them, pirouetting with ballet knowledge as her delicate body spins on her right foot and as her raised left foot touches the supporting leg. She spins and gyrates and twirls with merry abandon. She holds her back straight and bends her knees, achieving the delicacy of a smooth *plié*. Exhilarated now, she gleefully jumps from one foot to the other—a perfect *jeté*. Only after that supremely graceful motion and after another succession of spins does she allow Brett and Jake and Tate to move near her. Only then, as they stand swaying behind her, does she allow each of them (Brett first, then Jake, and finally Tate) to enfold her body within their muscular embrace. Jake and Brett bring their warm bodies to the embrace. Tate's touch is cold and disturbing. Right after he has embraced her while standing behind her, he steps away and vanishes inside the darkness.

Brett and Jake stay with her. They become mirror images of one another. They are twins, and they are rivals. Each of them auditions for her acceptance. Each one kisses the back of her neck. Alone with her, each one sways in sensual possession of her.

Now, in cadet-like unison, they step back and allow her to turn so that she can once again see their handsome faces. But her sight of them draws from her a cry of horror. The instant that she looks upon them, some black magic or evil enchantment tears away the flesh from their faces. This same black magic—this diabolical enchantment—rips the flesh from their entire bodies. Their handsome faces and their athletic bodies instantly become skeletons. Their eyeless skulls, nasal bones and collar bones and sternum, as well as their pelvis, thigh bones, knee pans, and phalanges of toes glow with after-horror eeriness.

A shriek rises out of Lisa. The sight of Brett and Jake as rotted cadavers leaves her confused and terrified. She goes on screaming, her cries despairing and bitter. Only the sight of Tate's skeleton, sprawled on the polished floor in the center of the ballroom, halts her screaming. Tate, also, has become an eyeless, grinning cadaver. This ghastly sight of his corpse has a strange and unnatural effect upon her. She begins laughing hysterically. If anyone were there in the ballroom to ask her why she was laughing at the sight of Tate's corpse, she would have offered an honest answer. The sight of his corpse was one of the few times that she noticed him grinning.

Her uncontrollable shrieking and her odd laughter break the spell that is binding her. She bolts away from this nightmarish apparition. With a blink of her eyes and tight-lipped resolution, she escapes from the phantom terror that has left her breathless and conflicted. Willful and rebellious, she resists the message that the dance of death has sent her. She hurls away all thoughts of these wraiths and specters. She is not afraid to face the truth about herself. With vivid clarity, she remembers her adulterous relationships with Brett and Jake. With them, she reveled in her promiscuity. She flouted all the rules that would otherwise bind her to society's rigid conventions and to the worn-down rules about marriage.

She remembers, too, the early days of her career and her promiscuity with many other partners who happened to be high-powered attorneys and corporate leaders that pushed her forward to the top. Earning the right law school credentials helped her. Keeping calm under pressure helped, too. Knowing how to make sharp-witted decisions and how to compete with the big boys on her law team made her success plausible. The power links in her life made the highest levels of that success inevitable.

She reaches for a cigarette from the gold case that lies upon the night table beside her bed. She takes hold of the gold lighter and quickly ignites the cigarette. She enjoys a long drag and, now alert and self-protective once again, she watches the smoky vapor rising from the cigarette and partly concealing her as she leans against the softness of her pillows and contemplates the next step that is needed if she is to save herself from herself and save the four persons against whom she has plotted.

"Saving them will not be easy," she hears Randall saying.

Though he is in her bedroom, he is not yet visible to her seeing. He is a disembodied voice. He is an interpreter sent by the implacable Fates or, more probably, by the stern First Spirit. He, Captain Randall Johnson, is a rugged soul who brings to her many fierce challenges and more than a few harsh truths.

"Even if you do the right things," he tells her, "you may not be able to save all four of the persons against whom you have plotted. The path to salvation is not an easy one to tread. You may lead them to the path, but you cannot make the journey for them."

Exactly at that moment, Randall stands before her, full-bodied and commanding. He is wearing the same bomber pilot's uniform that he wore during the aerial battles he fought in the Second World War.

His wife, Melanie, stands with him. She is wearing a navy tailored suit, not unlike the one she wore on that day in 1943 when she received word that Randall had been killed during a bombing mission over Nazi Berlin.

Temperate and helpful, she offers this advice.

"Keep in mind that you are making your own journey. You need to discover the better self that you have lost. You need to find the soul that you have abandoned."

Randall echoes her concern.

"Doing the right thing can be a dangerous experiment. It becomes dangerous for you when you make the wrong choices. It turns dangerous for others when you steer them in the wrong direction."

This talk of the danger of her choices gives her pause. She has come to believe that danger also flares within Randall's commands and Melanie's expectations. Way back in the back of her mind, there lives a memory of other night-time visits that have brought Randall and Melanie into the privacies of her pensive vigils here inside the artifice and glamour of her bedroom. Burdened by insomnia and by the guilt that all too frequently weighs upon her every action, she has often listened to their urgent calls to action.

They want to help her. They want her to help herself.

Now, during this latest visit, Lisa draws upon unsentimental words to indicate her self-awareness and her new-found goal.

"Making the wrong choices and misusing other people have been my specialties," she tells them. "I'm ready to reclaim the soul that I lost a long time ago."

Melanie asks her a probing question.

"How will you do that?"

"I'll begin with my husband," she answers her. "I'll tell Tate that I want to make our marriage work. I'll tell him that we should stop lying to each other. I'll tell him that I'll try to fall in love with him. I'll tell him that he has to learn to love me more than he loves his dead first wife."

She lives through two conflicted days and two restless nights before she confronts Tate about the problem that belongs to both of them. She needs all those hours to reflect upon the artificial construct that, together, they have devised—the fake marriage, the simulated union, the loveless partnership. Facing the harsh facts of their relationship, she once again admits to herself without flinching that she has consented to their marriage because of the financial and social powers that Tate represents. Her background and breeding have afforded her many luxuries, and her ambivalent parents, a favorite aunt, and a protective uncle have established in her name generous trust funds that assure her of a life of continued wealth and privilege. But always she has wanted more wealth. She has wanted more than wealth. She has been pleased to be partnered with Tate's immense fortune. More than that, she has craved to be entwined within the tremendous influence that he wields across the globe. That she has not loved Tate has never before caused her any pangs of conscience. Her keen awareness of his coldhearted regard of her as a prize he has easily won had never, until these recent days and nights, dismayed her. Nor had she much cared that their marriage had always included three persons—Tate; his first wife—Amelia; and herself.

After her days and nights of soul-searching, though, she now admits that she and Tate have made a mockery of marriage. Anguished misgiving and genuine remorse weigh heavily upon her awareness. Whether it is some magical spell or subtle enchantment that inspires her new perception of her situation, she cannot say. She can only tell herself that the time has come for her to live in a different and authentic way.

"We have to talk about our marriage," she tells Tate after she approaches him in his study.

It is midnight on a Wednesday evening. Abiding by his rigid schedule, he is at his desk, seated before his computer as he pores over a legal brief that, she imagines, relates to a hedge fund fraud case that has made international headlines.

Tate looks away from the legal brief with a spark of interest. That she so suddenly and even willfully intends to discuss their marriage at midnight intrigues him. Never before has she made a remark or posed a question about this artificial and loveless union that has connected them. Their being together has everything to do with power. Their marriage is a wily exchange of power. He expresses his power in many ways, not only through his immense wealth and his influence as a toughminded lawyer, but also through his having connected to *her* power—the power of her glamorous presence at his side. She is a badge that he can proudly wear. She is a coveted prize that he has won, leaving in the dust the many eligible suitors who had been pursuing her. Their being together has nothing to do with romantic love. Theirs is a marriage of shrewd bargaining and safe accommodation. He is keenly aware of what they represent to each other and to the society that watches them.

What can Lisa tell him about their marriage that he does not already know?

Her wanting to speak of their marriage in this quiet hour of midnight quickens his curiosity.

Cynical and even contemptuous, he prods her to explain herself.

"Why do you want to talk about our marriage?" he asks her. "Is there some new revelation at hand—some new clue to its meaning and its implications?"

"Don't you know? Can't you guess?' she asks him, her tone more emotional than she expected it to be and tinged with regret and melancholy. "There *is* a clue, and it is not a new one. Our marriage is a sham. It's no marriage at all. It's a business arrangement. There's not an honest emotion in it, except our consenting to its duplicity. We've been fooling the public. We've been living a lie. I'm weary of the lie. I want us to change things. I want a real marriage with you or none at all."

At first, Tate says nothing. Instead, he glares at her. Very carefully, he studies her face. He parses the meaning of her words and the rhythms of her speech. Only after he guesses at her motives for speaking to him in this somber way does he respond to her complaint.

"Who is he?" he asks her. "Who's the guy?"

"What do you mean?"

"There has to be a guy—the stud who has convinced you that he can make you very happy, especially if you marry him. He's convinced you that being especially rich and married to an aging powerbroker isn't enough. You need a young man who really loves you."

She resists the sting of his words. Her next words flash both anger and discontent.

"I don't need a young man to tell me that. Our marriage tells me all that I need to know. It isn't going to work anymore if you allow a ghost to come between us."

Tate bristles.

"Ghost?"

"Amelia."

His face turns fierce and pale. For an instant, his eyes stare at her, wild and resentful. His lips and his jaw tighten. He clenches his fist. For a moment, he has an impulse to slap her face. But the moment passes. He steadies himself, invoking well-learned disciplines. He keeps his voice even-tempered yet commanding.

"I don't want to hear this, nor have you a right to mention her name."

Lisa hurries forward with a new protest.

"I have every right. Amelia is dead. She is no longer your wife. I am your wife. I am alive, and I am asking you to treat me as a wife."

Tate turns away. He begins to scan once again the legal brief that seems more important to him than this heated conversation. While he busies himself with this simulated attention to the brief, he throws out new words.

"I've given you everything that a wife needs or desires."

Lisa pauses, disheartened by his turning away from her. Quickly, she finds softer words that are no less effective because of their poignancy. She moves closer to him, and she places her hand on his shoulder.

"You've given me everything except yourself. I want you to fall in love with me. I want you to make our marriage honest and real."

He covers her soft hand with the roughness of his larger hand. Then, because he wants to distance himself from her, he pulls his hand away and rises from his chair. He takes a cigarette from a gold case and, with his thumb pressed down on the spark-wheel of a gold lighter, brings a flame to the tip of the cigarette. Only after he has separated himself from her by walking away from his desk does he express his own thoughts about making their marriage honest and real. His words are matter of fact. His manner is brusque and accusatory.

"You and I made a bargain. We've always known where we stand with one another. I've been on the level in everything I've told you. Can you say the same?"

Once again, his words sting at her. She winces. She stays calm. She remains tough-skinned. She is determined to admit her failings. At an intuitive level, she is aware that the same enchantment that has been influencing her transformation is in this very moment working its powers upon her.

Her words become a confession.

"No. I haven't always been honest. I haven't always been on the level."

Tate lashes out at her.

"I know you haven't been on the level. I'm no fool. Every day of our marriage I've watched you. I've even set detectives to watch you. I know about Brett and Jake. I know that all of you have two-timed me. As a wife, you have seldom been honest."

Lisa tries to defend herself, without denying her guilt.

"Honesty isn't enough," she says. "A marriage isn't worth anything if there isn't any love in it."

Tate ignores the hard truth of her remark. He hurries forward with new, lacerating words. His manner is that of a prosecuting attorney.

"It was first of all Brett, wasn't it? He's the young stud that you took to your bed. He was your lover."

"That's finished," Lisa quickly answers him. "That belongs to the past. Now he's your business associate and Naomi's fiancé. He means nothing more to me than that."

Tate presses on, still hostile and accusatory.

"What about Jake? He's been your lover more than a few times. I imagine that he will be your lover again."

"Not if you become my real husband."

Hearing these words, Tate falls silent. Their blunt honesty pushes away the fury and resentment that he had untypically allowed himself to reveal. When he does find new words to explain himself, his voice is softer, and it is bitter.

"I can't love you. I might be able to forgive you your promiscuity. But I can't allow you to replace Amelia. She was pure. She was faithful. She was devoted to me. She is the only woman I can ever love."

Lisa wants to make their marriage work. The magical spell that is helping her to find her soul induces her to beseech Tate to begin a new journey with her.

"What if I tried to make you love me? What if I became faithful and devoted to you?"

Tate hears her words. He ponders their meaning. He sifts their implications. He recognizes in them a heartfelt petition and a promise of steadfastness. Adamant, he turns away from their hope and from their reformation.

"It wouldn't matter," he tells Lisa. "You are not Amelia."

Still Lisa pleads with him.

"What if *you* tried to fall in love with me?"

Made even more tense by her suggestion, Tate frowns. His first marriage still lives within his everyday awareness. It is an always-present memory. It is a haunting reality that he does not want to escape.

"I can't," he tells Lisa. "I can't fall in love with you or with any other woman. I can't betray Amelia."

"Then we are finished" Lisa says. "Our marriage is over. We have nothing more to say to each other."

JAKE

Suddenly Jake awakes from a deep sleep. October sunlight is washing his bedroom with its luminous reveal. Every object in the room appears to be perfect in its symmetry. His gray cashmere King-size bed with its nail-head trim and button-tufted headboard gleams with beams of sunlight. Flanking his bed, the matching three-drawer night tables, with their inlaid walnut veneer, clean-line nickel pulls, and tapered legs, also catch the glow of this new day that to his quickened perception seems the beginning of something extraordinary—some special chapter or more-than-ordinary occurrence. The instant he leaves his bed, intent upon hurrying to the panoramic window so that he can experience the exhilaration of watching the new day rising before him, he notices with equal surprise the plush Florentine rug that covers the area around his bed. Never before has its blue and burgundy and gold colors married themselves to a vibrant and otherworldly blaze of light. So, too, does the crystal pendant glisten, as does its hand-carved hunting images and the gold silken fabric cord from which the lighting fixture is suspended.

He feels reborn. He feels disconnected from the Jake Boldwood that for so many of his thirty-two years has existed as a cynical and troubled man. For the first time in his awareness, he believes that he is being given a chance to reinvent himself. A conviction is seizing him that he can become a morally-centered human being. His intuition tells him that Randall and Melanie are influencing this change in him. A memory, hazy yet reliable, allows him to recall their visit to him right after midnight when, after a challenging courtroom day as Tate's ambitious assistant, he had quickly fallen into a deep sleep.

In this very moment that he is hurrying to meet this most unusual day, he relives the midnight hour when Randall and Melanie suddenly and mysteriously called him awake.

Suddenly and mysteriously and wondrously, Randall—with husky and impatient voice—is once again calling him awake.

"It's time," Randall is telling him. "You need to wake up. You need to see the world with inspired eyes."

Melanie—with her genteel manner and compassionate words—is also urging him forward.

"You can do it, Jake. You can become new and inspired. You are capable of drawing upon the divine and supernatural impulses that lay dormant within you. You can waken your soul. You can become a first-rate human being."

He remembers scoffing at first at this idea of regeneration. There is self-contempt in that scoffing and a tinge of melancholy.

"It's too late," he tells her. "I've journeyed far away from any impulses that will bring my soul to life."

"It's not too late," Randall says. "You still have time to discover and claim your soul."

"I tell you that it won't happen. I've done so many wrong things. I can never find my way back to goodness and integrity and honor."

Randall has more to say.

"Melanie and I know about your past. We know all about your hedge fund scandals. We know that you were brought low because of your links with New York racketeers. Six years ago and more, you were one of the most successful hedge fund managers on Wall Street. But your greed overtook your quick-witted awareness of the punishing way the world works. Your wily disposition failed you in crucial episodes that called for keen-sighted planning and fail-safe chicanery. Overconfident, you stole millions from your clients and left them stranded when hedge funds bottomed out. Your four years in prison—harsh though they were to mind, body, and spirit—reinforced your plan to steal from the world again and this time to run scot free with the plunder. Your prison sentence might have been longer. But, with your lawyerly connections and your payback of ten million dollars, you secured your early release after you had completed four years of imprisonment.

"We know that you have gone a few rounds with Lisa. We are also aware of the plot you devised with her to steal Naomi away from Brett. With Lisa's help, you have made a friend of Tate. You have primed yourself to move forward, away from the luxury car front that satisfied your parole officer and away from the escort service that turned you into a male prostitute. Now, as a lawyer in Tate's firm, you are ready to win the equivalent of high-yielding blue-chip stocks or of a grand, once-in-a-lifetime lottery. You want to marry Naomi, even though you do not love her."

Randall pauses. He takes a moment to study the effect of his words upon Jake. Melanie moves closer to him. Together, they wait to hear what Jake has to say.

A flush of shame covers his face. He tightens his lips, and his mouth grimaces. Never does he turn his eyes away from them. He has listened to them. He has received Randall's words as though they are a courtroom sentence that condemns him because he is a man who has lost his soul and lost, too, his honorable place in the world.

"Everything you have said is true. I'm guilty on all counts."

Melanie comes back into it.

"Are you willing to change? Do you want to make a special effort? Can you believe that, if you really try, you can become a good man?"

Jake reflects upon her questions. He wants to be honest with himself and with them.

"If you had asked me those questions yesterday, I would have said that I didn't care to change. With Naomi as my wife and with her father as my mentor, I have it made. I'm winning the pot of gold and the fair maiden. I even have a chance to win a kingdom."

His honesty pleases both Melanie and Randall.

"You believed that yesterday," Randall says. "What do you believe today?"

"I'm weary of being lost," Jake admits. "Why, so suddenly and unexpectedly, I feel this way, I cannot really explain. I only know that a change has overtaken me. I want to be a good man. I don't recall having ever thought about being good until this past week. Every morning when I waken from a deep sleep, I feel as if some magic spell or enchantment is altering for the better all my wiliness and my selfish inclinations."

Melanie tells him what in his heart he already knows, though he has not yet discovered the intricacies of its meaning.

"Enchantments *are* influencing you. Call them magic spells or supernatural messages. Randall and I are sending them to you. During this past week, because of our influence upon you, you have grown weary of your wrongdoing. By accepting the spells that we have placed upon you, you have shown us that you are ready to receive the enchantments. Now, at last, you are willing to use them."

"What must I do to win back my soul?"

"You must find your way to forsake Naomi and to move away from Tate's hold upon you."

"That will be hard for me to do," Jake says. "I may lose my best opportunities. I may slide back to failure and poverty."

"Not if you consent to become a better person," Randall tells him. "If you really want to change for the better, you must accept the enchantments that we create for your benefit."

"What if I don't accept them? What if I don't care to take the risk of becoming a moral person?"

Melanie answers his questions.

"Then you will be forever lost. Remember, wealth and prestige are fleeting. But the good works of the soul last through all eternity."

Not given to sentimental remarks, Jake responds with matter-of-fact bluntness.

"I'll try to change," he says. "Some Spirit power inside me is compelling me to try. I'm going to try very hard. I'm going to give it my best shot."

During the next week, Jake applies for and wins a top spot in the estimable Templeton Law Firm. Located in Virginia, the firm will connect him to the powerbrokers in Washington, D.C. It will disconnect him from Tate and Naomi. Low-key and straightforward, he takes his leave from Tate's firm and from his romantic friendship with Naomi.

"I need a change," he tells Tate. "I need to be around new people, and I need new challenges."

He is not surprised that Tate accepts his resignation. Tate is no fool. Thanks to the detective that he placed on his trail, Tate knows about his ongoing affair with Lisa. He also knows that he has been courting Naomi without really loving her. He—Jake Boldwood, the streetwise careerist—has been in the game for big money and for the legal assignments that will win him political favors and an entire squadron of ambitious followers.

"You're doing the right thing," Tate tells him. "You know when it's time to move forward to a different challenge. You know how to move toward the top."

Having said so, Tate turns back to the legal brief he has been studying, but not before waving him away. The waving of his hands might be a salute to his enterprise and his ambition. That same waving might signal Tate's coldhearted dismissal of him. Their time together is finished. There is no more to build on together. The father-son relationship that each of them affected has completed its run. Now they can admit (to themselves in silence and not to anyone else) that it was always fraudulent.

"Goodbye, Tate," Jake says, still low-key and straightforward. "Thanks for the ride."

To Naomi, he offers a heartfelt goodbye. He has begun to love her, and he does not want to hurt her.

"I'm not the right man for you," he tells her on a crisp October afternoon when they are sauntering at the edge of the lake behind the Georgian-style Calhern home in the upscale district of Blue Ridge. "You need someone without a dark past. You need a man who loves you more than he loves his dreams of advancement."

His words surprise Naomi. Their honesty surprises her.

"You are a charmer," she tells him. "A fantastic charmer. You know how to keep a woman surprised. You must never underrate that talent."

"Do I really surprise you?"

"Your honesty surprises me. That your love has always been skin-deep has never surprised me. We've been playing a game. I've enjoyed it. It's allowed me to be freewheeling. It's allowed me to keep Brett guessing."

"He's a better man than I am."

"Maybe. Maybe not."

"Believe what I say. He is the better man."

"He could be a better man," she says, "if he makes the right choices."

"I think he will."

"Let's see what happens."

Hearing her say so, Jake plants a brotherly kiss upon her forehead. In silence now, they turn from the path along the side of the lake and walk back to the house. Each of them experiences a finished feeling. Whether an enchantment has weaved its spell upon them or whether it is their ingrained realistic sense that makes them understand that the time has come for them to go their separate ways—whether it is one of those things or their combination, neither Naomi nor Jake can with certainty explain. Their mutual consent to this leave-taking softens whatever regret lives in the deepest parts of their souls.

Jake's farewell meeting with Lisa is a different matter.

A few days after his meetings with Tate and with Naomi, Jake meets Lisa for lunch at an upscale restaurant in Manhattan. By this time, Jake has left Blue Ridge and will be flying to Virginia the following morning. Lisa has also left Blue Ridge behind her. She has resigned from her place in Tate's law firm and plans to spend some free time in New York. She will be staying at the penthouse on Sutton Place that she and Tate shared while they appeared to be happily married.

"Tate won't be there with me," she says. "He agrees that I should have some time to get my bearings, to find out where I want to be, and what I want to do with my life without him."

Jake is excited to be with Lisa on this evening when almost everything else in his life seems finished. They go back a few years, yet their passion for each other has not diminished. He wonders whether they too will separate forever and whether the Fates have something else planned for them.

He swallows his scotch and picks at his steak dinner. She sips a Champagne cocktail and shows little interest in her soufflé.

He is interested, though, in finding out where she plans to make her more permanent home.

"Do you have any place in mind," he prods her to tell him, "or is it too early to ask that question?"

She offers him a gleaming smile and looks more beautiful than ever. His interest in her future pleases her.

"You may ask the question, but I do not yet have any clear-cut answers. I can tell you that I may settle right here in New York. I've always loved this city, and I've already had a couple of promising offers from law firms here that believe I can be an asset to them."

"So you're moving on, too—away from Blue Ridge."

"Yes. We are both moving forward."

All about them there is the quickened movement of waiters and the exquisite aromas of French cuisine. From the distance, a pianist is playing softened love ballads from the long-ago Thirties, Forties, and Fifties—the lilting notes and the melancholic implications of Cole Porter and George Gershwin.

The music stirs his memory of his romantic time with Lisa. Suddenly, he longs to be with her through all the days and nights of his lifetime. He cannot imagine that he will ever want to let her go. Is it Randall and Melanie's enchantment that stirs his need of her? Is it the stirring of the soul that he is slowly discovering? Without answering his silent questions, he prods her with an idea that may influence her future.

"Do you think that you may eventually head to Virginia?"

She reflects upon the question with pursed lips and with bright blue-eyed gaze.

"It could happen," she tells him before asking him a similar question. "What about you? Do you think that you could ever make New York the scene of your new conquests?"

Without hesitation, he answers her.

"It could happen."

Now, her eyes become even more elated as she playfully offers him other pleasing words.

"Let's see what happens."

BRETT AND NAOMI

It was as though a young, lovely woman was hurrying out of his happier dreams and, without the hesitation that sends even a happy dream scattering and vanishing from his quickened awareness, she was standing here before him— suddenly and predominantly and romantically. Her blue eyes were flashing *their* happiness at seeing him as he lay in his hospital bed, newly conscious only in these latest days, three weeks after an assassin's random bullet had nearly killed him.

When, suddenly and wonderfully and against grievous odds, Brett awakened from his coma, he could not at first remember who he was. Neither his gifted surgeon, nor three caring nurses could prod his remembrance. Nor could the arrival of visitors whom he later recognized as his weeping mother and the sudden and equally unrecognized appearances of pensive Lisa, sober Tate, and tight-lipped Jake stir his memory.

Then, an hour afterward and just as suddenly and as wonderfully as his awakening, a lovely young woman was hurrying toward him while he lay here in his hospital bed. As she moved closer, he saw that she was Naomi Calhern and that she was essential to his happiness. He remembered that, before a crazed assassin's random bullet blasted into his chest, he and Naomi were drinking champagne in the VIP lounge of a New York airport and talking of their happy future together while they waited for their flight to take off and bring them to Hawaii. Whether it was her witty repartee that quickened his heartbeat or her sunny disposition or her softened, love-filled glance or whether it was her smoky voice that most intrigued him—whether it was just one of these things or all of these things that deepened and refined his feelings for her, he could not with certainty say. Whatever it was, he was certain of a profound change within his mind and his soul. He was amazed that his feelings toward her were now honest and open. He was learning in ways that always surprised him that he was truly in love with her.

For days after his awakening from the deep sleep that had imprisoned him, he kept thinking of all the wonderful occasions that had brought them together. He remembered their skydiving exhilaration in Connecticut. He recalled their exciting kayaking over the furious white waters of the Kennebec River in Maine. He mused upon the adrenalin rush of their copiloting a Gulfstream G550 across a turbulent sky that overlooked Narragansett Bay. He enjoyed most of all his memory of their dancing cheek-to-cheek in the center of a grand ballroom within New York's

Café Carlyle and in the company of twenty loyal friends right after they —Brett and Naomi together —announced their engagement. It was not just any Brett who spoke the words that connected his destiny to hers. It was *he* himself— Brett Robinson, who felt completely reborn and truly alive. Nor was it just any Naomi who joined him as they announced their engagement. That special Naomi was Naomi Calhern and no other. She promised that her love for him would last forever.

In these present days, when he is once more reborn, he reflects upon all these happy occasions. He has made a friend of good fortune.

Sometimes, he allows himself to recall the shooting that nearly stole his life away. He is not acquainted with the assailant. Nor did any of the other victims know him. A tall, muscular thirty-year-old Caucasian and a heroic veteran of the war in Afghanistan, the shooter is—a team of medical specialists reported—suffering from post-traumatic stress. Nobody died in the random shooting, but all six victims of the shooting were grievously wounded. Despite that violent hour, he still believes that he is a fortunate man.

He remembers the punch of the bullet as it invaded his chest. He remembers the jagged pain and the raging fire that was exploding inside his chest and his back and engulfing his consciousness. At the last moment, before the swirls and gusts and twists of the fire inside him swept him deep within its churning vortex, he was wondering whether his throwing himself in front of Naomi might save her.

Now, suddenly and wonderfully on this fourth day after his gradual release from his deep sleep, he notices her and wakens completely—fully alive and absolutely awed by her presence.

"You *are* here," he tells her, his heart beating faster and his slow words creating their own special elation. "You are alive, after all. I have not lost you."

Naomi beams with love for him and with the happiness that has so suddenly and mysteriously touched their lives.

"You will never lose me," she says while she sits by his bed after planting a kiss upon his forehead and while she holds the warmth of his hand in her own. She is as elated and surprised as he is by the grand luck or blessed chance that has favored them. "If you ever have to get lost again, let's get lost together."

"That's a promise," he tells her and tells her once more, the echoing words pleasing him as much as they please her. "That's a promise easy to keep."

For days afterward, when he is alone in his hospital room in those quieter hours after his astute surgeon and three dedicated nurses and a well-trained physical therapist have attended him, he ponders and even meditates upon the tremendous love that he feels for Naomi. He searches for a clue to the unanticipated cause or extraordinary occasion that quickened his love for her, even as it displaced his cynical regard of her and of the shallow codes of the society whose approval they carefully pursued. The clue that he finds is no ordinary explanation of the tremendous love he feels for Naomi. Soulful and life-altering, the clue has its source in the supernatural, the paranormal, the otherworldly, and the transcendent.

The clue reveals itself through Randall and Melanie's ghostly visits to him, always here in his hospital room and always at night. Fully embodied at first, they draw him away from his reveries. Their so suddenly being *here* in the privacy of his room compels his attention. Without opening the door to his room and without being announced by a nurse, they are *too* suddenly standing by his hospital bed and whispering his name over and over until he hears their calls that sound like a mystical refrain. Wakened from a deep sleep and leaning into a galaxy of comfortable pillows, he peers at them, startled and uneasy. The surprise and strangeness of their presence compel his attention. But no sooner does he acclimate himself to their being so suddenly and so strangely *here* as Randall and Melanie Johnson, no sooner than the moment he has recovered the ease of his responses to them, than they surprise him once more. Their bodies begin to fade, dissolve, and vanish while before his astonished eyes the room lists and tilts, leans and tips and somersaults.

Over and over the room somersaults until it comes to rest in the glow of the moon that arrives as a familiar presence through and beyond the panoramic surround of the window to solace his hospital loneliness and to apprehend with him the magical transformations of Randall and Melanie, who—suddenly and wonderfully and eerily—reappear at first as their full-bodied selves. Only for an instant do they claim their bodily forms—*he*, the tall, conscientious lawyer with dark hair, handsome careworn face, brown-eyed penetrating gaze, athletic build, and steel-true disposition, and *she*, the dedicated psychologist—a lovely, blonde-haired, blue-eyed woman with willowy figure and that rare, pristine gift, empathy— the ability to relate to another person's pain vicariously as though she herself had experienced the anguish.

Only for an instant does Brett once again come face-to-face with Randall's and Melanie's embodied forms. His startlement at seeing them right *here* in his hospital room quickly gives way to greater astonishment. Once more, as in recent nocturnal visits that he can only vaguely recall, full-bodied Randall and Melanie are pressing the second finger of their right hand to their lips as though they are pledging him to silence. Then, right after making that gesture, they begin vanishing away by degrees and returning just as quickly and as mysteriously inside the nebulous and ghostly forms of Specters. Sometimes, he thinks of them as Phantoms, as Shadows, and as Apparitions. Whatever he privately calls them, they are always ghostly, elusive, and visionary.

Always, when they appear to him as these supernatural forms, they hover about him with eyes that glow with radiant, spectral powers as they carefully observe him. Always, they probe his mind with unanticipated questions. Always, they test his awareness of the blemished self that he has left behind and the new-born individual that he has become.

During one of their paranormal appearances, Randall begins the questioning and the testing with a more probing intensity.

"What caused you to change?" he asks him. "What experience urged you to reassess your goals and your ambitions?"

Before he answers him, Brett reflects upon the words in the question. He deciphers their emphases. He parses their implications. Confident now, he proceeds to explain himself. He understands that whatever force bonds itself with the words that he chooses must represent the accuracy and honesty of his perceiving.

"I fell in love with Naomi," he says. "I saw that she needed me as much as I needed her. When I believed that I was going to lose her to Jake Boldwood, I felt lost. I felt fragmented, broken apart without the capacity to become whole again. I have only a vague memory of the previous nights that you and Melanie appeared to me. The words that passed between us on those nights have become dim echoes that I hear only once in a while. But their influences stay with me. How else can I explain the changes that have made my life so different?"

He pauses, not yet satisfied with what he has said and groping for the exact words that can explain who he is to Randall and Melanie, as well as to himself.

Randall nudges him forward. He wants him to say more.

"Are you telling Melanie and me that we are responsible for the change that has overtaken your life?"

"You *are* responsible for the change, though not completely."

Now Melanie comes into it.

"In what ways are we responsible?"

"As otherworldly guardian Spirits, you advise me to be honest with myself. You suggest that I keep looking with new eyes upon Naomi. You tell me to find out the always-new ways that she is essential to my happiness and to the fulfilled human being I want to become."

His reply pleases Melanie.

"You *do* recall the advice that Randall and I offer you."

"In our meetings, I recall everything very clearly. But when I live through each new day, I have only a vague recollection of our meetings."

"That is all we want you to remember. The changes that you make must spring from your will, at least in part. Your life choices must belong to you, even though our words and our supernatural presence may point you in the right direction."

"The First Spirit wouldn't have it any other way," Randall says. "He wants you to accept the responsibilities and the decision-making that identify the level of humanity you achieve."

"Every day I am more certain of who I am and of my love for Naomi. Whether we are sailing on the lake behind her father's house or reading aloud a chapter from one of her novels or dancing together at the Blue Ridge Country Club or conferring with an architect about the house in which we plan to live after we marry—whether it is just one of those things that help me to love her more profoundly or all of those things, I cannot rightly say. But I do know one thing for certain. Naomi and I complete each other. Without her, I am incomplete. I am a body without a soul. I am a searcher who asks the wrong questions and never discovers the correct answers. All my ambitions seem like shallow goals. All my quests for recognition and every scheme I devise to become wealthy and influential seem like makeshift compromises and false suppositions."

Melanie has more to say.

"What wonderful news you are bringing to us!" she exclaims. "Your love for Naomi has helped you to find your soul."

"It *is* wonderful news," Brett agrees. "I have found my soul because of my love for her. I am in love not only with her body. I also love the mind and Spirit that make her the woman she is. Because of her, I have discovered the Spirit that lives within me. That Spirit gives life to my body and my mind. I feel like a man enchanted. I feel reborn."

Randall wants to know more.

"What about the love that you once felt for Lisa?"

Once again, Brett pauses. A frown creases his brow. The question confuses him. He cannot connect it to any emotion that he has felt for Lisa. Randall and Melanie understand his confusion. They are waiting for him to recognize that confusion and to go past it.

"I have always admired Lisa for many reasons. She is a beautiful woman. She is an excellent lawyer. She has sometimes been a helpful stepmother to Naomi. But I have never really been in love with her. Ours was a temporary affair. It is over. It is finished."

Randall has more to say.

"One day, you will not remember your affair with Lisa. All that happened before you found your soul. You *have* been reborn. You are creating a better version of Brett Robinson. Nothing comes easy. Every day will be a test for you. Every day will bring new challenges and temptations. More Spirit-driven now than you have ever been, you will stand a better chance of maintaining the health of your soul. You are learning how you can keep it as a sacred friend and as a powerful advocate."

Before she and Randall leave him, Melanie advises him further.

"You won't remember your affair with Lisa," she says. "Nor will you remember many of the words that have passed between us this evening. Perhaps, a word spoken by a casual friend or a loving glance from Naomi or a homily delivered by a devoted priest will remind you of some of the words that we have spoken tonight. Some of those words will stir your soul. Some of them will serve as a warning. Even powerful souls need to be safely guarded."

Having spoken those words, Melanie moves closer to Randall. In the next instant, the two of them become Apparitions with whirlwind capacities and quick-changing aptitudes of swift motion beyond the orbit of his seeing.

Brett remains leaning into his pillows, reflecting upon his nebulous meeting with them. In the morning, he will remember almost none of the details that made the meeting extraordinary. When he awakens, he will be aware that something more has changed in his perception of his life and of the life around him. Without verbalizing it with specific words, he will *feel* the change and move more briskly forward to the challenges and obligations of the life he regards as quite splendid.

RANDALL AND MELANIE

When they are once more alone together as fully embodied human beings in Randall's study, Randall and Melanie greet Robert Steerforth with congenial words. They find Robert seated at Randall's desk, looking comfortable and precise in the swivel chair that Randall has come to favor.

"We have completed our mission," Randall tells him. "It was more complicated that we expected."

"Ah," Robert says, "that is the way with complications. They are always unexpected."

Melanie has more to say.

"We have tried our best to change things for the better," she says. "We nudged and coaxed and prodded the five people we were sent to save. They kept resisting our influence. Finally, we had to rely upon magic spells and similar enchantments."

"We gave the mission our best efforts," Randall tells Robert. "I think you would have accomplished more than we did and without the uses of enchantments."

"Maybe. Maybe not," Robert answers him. "You and Melanie were dealing with hard cases. Everyone of these five people kept clinging to wily plots and devious maneuvering and self-defeating fears. They had lost their souls. Your presence and Melanie's, as well as the enchantments, helped them to find their souls. You helped to save four of them. Without the enchantments, even they would have been lost."

"You are so right," Melanie tells him. "We needed the magic. We needed to draw these lost persons inside our enchantments. The enchantments were their saving grace. They were a blessing. They meant salvation for every one of those persons who were really struggling to change for the better."

Robert wants to know more.

"What have you learned from this mission?"

Randall and Melanie ponder this question. They search their minds and hearts and souls for honest and accurate answers.

Melanie is the first to answer Robert's question.

"I learned that willful and recalcitrant persons condemn themselves to be lost eternally. Not even enchantments or the First Spirit's promise of the happiness that lasts forever can save men like Tate Calhern. Their self-hatred and their hatred of others are diseases that have overtaken them. Their duplicity, their arrogance, and their hardheartedness have destroyed their humanity and disarranged their souls. I pity Tate Calhern and all the other human beings like him. I shall keep praying for Tate and for all the wrongdoers like him. I shall pray that they find their souls because I know in my heart that, if they do not change, their hardheartedness will condemn them to eternal disappearance."

Robert is pleased to hear her appraisal of her mission.

"You have learned well, Melanie. Your belief in the goodness of most human beings does you credit. Your influence over them is remarkable and its own reward. But knowing that you cannot save every person that you help will keep you aware of the earthbound reality that weighs heavily upon every human being. Sometimes—in fact, often—only enchantments and blessed chances and guardian Spirits can save human beings from their fallible natures."

His remarks please Melanie. She understands that Robert is the spokesman for the First Spirit.

"I shall keep believing in the human capacity to change for the better," Melanie says. "I shall go on believing that human beings are an extraordinary species."

"Of course, you will," Robert says. "That is your special gift. If the Earth did not have people like you to influence the goodness that lies dormant within men and women, what would happen to faith and regeneration?"

Now Robert pauses while with Spirit-gleaming eyes he observes Randall. Only after he studies this formidable and militant leader does he ask him another probing question.

"What have you learned from this mission, Randall? What new insight have you taken from the conflicted human beings that you have recently observed?"

Without hesitation, Randall answers him.

"I have learned that even the most fallible people need a chance to redeem themselves. They *will* redeem themselves if they accept the beneficent influences of good people and the powerful effects of Spirit-sent enchantments. I have also learned that bitterness and arrogance dry up the soul. I shall try not to be bitter about my war experiences. I shall try to believe in the goodness of most people. Of course, persons like Tate Calhern are different problems. They are their own worst enemies, not only during their Earthbound time, but for all Eternity. They do not understand the sacredness of Creation. They rarely free themselves from their blindness and from their self-made prisons."

"That's the clue to everything," Robert says as he concludes his meeting with Randall and Melanie, who—

full-bodied and inspired—will continue to bring their influences upon other troubled human beings. "While we live on Earth, each of us needs to experience the whole meaning behind Creation. Each of us needs to help the people around us. Each of us needs to protect the Earth on which we live. To do these worthy things, each of us needs to cast out our blemished self. Each of us needs to become a soul. That is the great magic. That is a true enchantment."